FORCE
OF FIRE

ALSO BY SAYANTANI DASGUPTA

KIRANAMALA AND THE KINGDOM BEYOND

Book One
The Serpent's Secret

Book Two
Game of Stars

Book Three
The Chaos Curse

THE FIRE QUEEN

Book One
Force of Fire

Book Two
Crown of Flames

FORCE OF FIRE

THE FIRE QUEEN: BOOK ONE

SAYANTANI DASGUPTA

Illustrations by

VIVIENNE TO

SCHOLASTIC INC.

Text copyright © 2021 by Sayantani DasGupta
Illustrations copyright © 2021 by Vivienne To

This book was originally published in hardcover by Scholastic Press in 2021.

ISBN 978-1-338-63665-9

10 9 8 7 6 5 4 3 2 1   22 23 24 25 26

Printed in the U.S.A.   40
This edition first printing 2022

Book design by Abby Dening

For Mago, Tata, and Thamma

And all the revolutionary ancestors

Table of Contents

CHAPTER 1

Why None of What Happened Is My Fault at All

The day I lost control of my rakkhosh power, fire-vomited in front of half the school, and then basically started a kingdom-wide revolution was absolutely not my fault.

All right, whatever, maybe it was a wee bit my fault, but there were *reasons*. Good reasons. Serious. Extenuating. Circumstances.

We were in one of the outdoor classrooms at Ghatatkach Academy of Murder and Mayhem, with long benches organized around a circle of banyan trees—their thick trunks, branches, and roots so long and strong that each tree seemed like a dozen. The sun was merciless, the crows were screeching, the tree frogs were burping, and the open sewers were belching out their nauseating, gaseous vapors. In other words, a picture-perfect day.

I was in Demonic Combat, the class taught by our head-mistress, Surpanakha. The class I was, let me just come out and own it, in serious danger of failing. And since failing Combat class would not just tank my GPA but humiliate me in front of the entire school, I was already feeling like an about-to-explode pressure cooker.

The problem I had with Combat class wasn't all the violence, pain, and destruction. I was fine with violence, pain, and destruction, at least theoretically. But that said, rakkhosh, like any other sort of being, aren't all the same. Sure, we have fangs, horns, tusks, and occasional issues with drooling. Yes, our skin does sometimes tend to the warty, and we are, on the whole, strong and fast. But that doesn't mean we don't enjoy poetry, or elemental physics, or calligraphy. We contain, as they say, multitudes. My problem with Combat class was the practical doing-it part, the "teamwork" and "cooperation" involved in sparring, that seriously gave me hives. (I mean, I couldn't even say words like *teamwork* and *cooperation* without putting them in air quotes.)

The truth is, since the first day I'd arrived at school, I'd been forced to be a solitary diva-loner type. It wasn't my fault. It's not like I didn't want friends, at least at first. But I'd had to get very good, very fast at pretending the other rakkhosh kids' mean comments about my family history or my being on full scholarship didn't bother me. I quickly learned to ignore their snickers at my patched-up school sari and lack of pocket money. I got used to eating lunch alone, usually in the library, an expert at pushing down all my angry feelings so deep into myself I was like a walking volcano, always ready to blow. Or maybe a volcano isn't the right analogy. Maybe I was more like a bomb. All I needed was one spark of fire to explode. Which is kind of what happened that unfortunate day.

The odds were so not in my favor. For starters, one

of the students I was assigned to spar with that day was Kumi, the water-clan rakkhoshi who also happened to be my roommate. She had just tried to pelt me in the face with a fire-hose stream of water, but since we'd lived together so long, I knew all her tells. The moment she scrunched up her nose like she was about to blow out a big fart, I guessed she was actually about to shoot a water cannon out of her crocodile tail, so I jumped out of the way in time.

"Good defense, Pinki, but let's see some better offense!" shouted our noseless headmistress, Surpanakha, clapping her hands together. She was wearing a silver whistle like a necklace over her multicolor sari, as well as a hideous vinyl sun visor. "You can't keep running away from your opponents, or yourself!"

I wasn't sure what the headmistress meant by that last comment but didn't want to think too much about it. I could feel the eyes of all my watching classmates like so many tiny fires on my skin. But even with my hearts hammering like trapped birds in my chest, I tucked the end of my sari anchal more tightly around my waist and made my voice as bored as possible.

"Is that really all you've got for me, Kumi?" I squinted at her, a shadow against the harsh sunlight. "Or are you just all wet?"

"Is that supposed to be a water-clan joke?" My roommate circled me like some kind of predator looking for a soft place to take a bite.

"Ooo, you got me," I deadpanned. Kumi was so easy to bait—all brawn and shockingly little sense of humor. "It was super complicated, but somehow you put the word *wet* together with *water*. How did you do it? I am in awe."

I heard some snickers from the crowd and couldn't help but smile myself. It was so much easier to spar with words than with bodies. But then I had to get my head back in the game quick, because with a roar, Kumi somersaulted at me, spitting a wave of ocean water in my direction. As she flipped all the way around, her sopping hair slapped against her furious green face.

To avoid her seaweed-stinky wave, I dived behind Aakash, the good-looking but not-too-bright air rakkhosh who was also a part of our sparring trio that afternoon.

"Hey! Don't mess with the hair! Uncool, man!" Aakash lifted off the ground just in time to avoid both Kumi's wave and the smoke bomb I had half-heartedly thrown at his head. The air-clan boy re-fluffed his hair over his curved gray horns, then adjusted the tight white school kurta he wore over his muscular chest.

"Relax, flyboy." Kumi spun around, shooting out sharp

water barbs through the gaps in her teeth. "No one wants to touch that bird's nest you call a hairdo."

My roommate's words gave me a brilliant idea. There was a whole field of magic based on rakkhosh hair, nails, and teeth—I'd been reading about it in a book of old spells I kept by my bed. Tearing off a few strands of my own long hair, I threw them at the water rakkhoshi while muttering a brief enchantment. The moment the handful of my curly black locks hit her, my roommate froze in place, a grimace on her water-sopped face, then dropped like a stone to the ground.

My triumph was cut short by Surpanakha's whistle sounding, shrill and long. "Illegal maneuver, Pinki!" The teacher magically woke Kumi back up with a wave of her hands. "The assignment was to only use powers specific to your clan! You can't avoid using your flames forever!"

There was a tittering from someone behind me. Ugh. Among all the different kinds of sneaky laughers, titterers are the absolute worst.

"Who was that?" I felt my cheeks warm and spun around in a circle. "Show your face, coward!"

Another sharp whistle from Surpanakha. "Never turn your back on an opponent, Pinki! You've got to keep your eyes on them to anticipate their next move!"

I kept my eyes on Kumi but felt myself seething inside. I knew everyone was just *waiting* for me to fail. You see, to make up for being excluded and alone all the time at school, I'd always thrown myself into my classes. From Rodent Disemboweling to Enemy Brain Dissection, from Erupting Effusive Boils to Inflicting Intestinal Ailments, from Causing Cannibalistic Chaos to Tormenting Tiny Tots with Terrors, I'd aced them all. My only real academic weakness was the fact that I kind of couldn't control my fire. I mean, yes, I'd possibly exploded those beakers in Putrid Poisons class when some of my classmates were whispering about my parents, and sure, I'd mistakenly singed off my Torture teacher's left eyebrow after she unfairly took off a point on that one pop quiz, and fine, there were the number of times I'd set Kumi's entire wardrobe on fire, but nothing to get your talons in a twist about. Not until that day in Combat class, that is.

"Drown, weirdo, drown!" Kumi vomited out an even more powerful wave at me. It smelled of salty fish and anger. She was obviously miffed about the magic hair trick, which meant she'd probably try to kill me in my sleep again once we were back in our dorm room. But what else was new.

The millisecond before Kumi's stinky wave hit me, I took in a big, shaking breath and did the thing I hated the most. I produced a mouthful of flames. I prayed to all that was evil in the multiverse that Kumi's water would douse any out-of-control fire I might produce. And by some miracle, it actually worked. The water and fire basically canceled each other out and fell to the ground in a harmless puff of steam. I'd done it! I'd actually done it! Well, I hadn't exactly controlled my flames, but at least I hadn't destroyed anything. I felt downright giddy with relief.

"What else have you got?" I slithered my long tongue at Kumi and Aakash, blowing them each some belchy fire-sparks. Suddenly, I was feeling much more in control. And control was something I liked. A lot. "You two are a joke! This time next year, I'm not voting for either of you as Demon King or Queen!"

"I won't need your vote, there are plenty of others who'll elect me king!" Aakash flexed a giant bicep midair. "As opposed to *some* rakkhosh, I actually have friends! Well, friends who aren't, like, books."

I heard a cheer from the air-clan bench. Aakash's pathetic friends were cheering on his pathetic comments. They were all so full of dung balls. So what if I preferred the company of books to other rakkhosh?

"Rude!" I snorted some white-hot embers into my fist

and threw them at the air-clan boy's fat head. He flew left just in time to miss them.

"No way! Bow down to your next Demon Queen right here!" Kumi whipped torrents of rain at me that left me spitting water. "Aakash may be more popular, but I'm definitely the most powerful rakkhosh in this school!"

"You wish!" I jumped awkwardly out of the way of the storm.

"What, you think you're more powerful than me? You may be better at taking tests, but raw power? I don't think so, loser! You're still scared to make an actual fire stream from your mouth," said Kumi, hitting me where it really hurt. "'Cause every time you do, you just lose control and destroy something!"

"You're, like, too scared of your power to figure out how to tame it." As Aakash spoke, he generated a wind gust with his flapping insect wings that almost knocked both Kumi and me over. "You're too freaked about crashing and burning—like, literally—to even try. Probably the same reason you're not running for Demon Queen!"

Out of the mouths of ding-dongs, as they say. Okay, so, yes, Aakash was in fact right. I wasn't running for Demon Queen because, well, I was too afraid of failing to even try. But I wasn't about to admit anything of the sort out loud.

"I'm not running for Demon Queen because it's basic and bo-ring!" I singsonged. All three of my hearts were racing now, and poofs of smoke were sneaking out of my ears and nose. "Just like you two!"

"Enough talking, more sparring!" shouted Surpanakha over the wind. "Moves and countermoves, folks! Moves and countermoves!"

The three of us circled each other, breathing hard.

"Yo yo yo, catch this action!" Aakash spun his arms and wings around his muscular body, creating a swirling dust tornado in the little banyan grove.

"Show-off!" I coughed. In a second, he'd raised so much dirt into the air, the hot afternoon had turned into a dark night.

The land-, fire-, water-, and air-clan students gathered on the benches around us began to choke as the air became filled with particles of dust and dry soil.

"Enough! Desist!" Surpanakha was blowing her whistle in between coughs. She took off her visor and waved it ineffectively in the air. "Sparring match over! Aakash, fix this mess!"

"Aw, bummer." Aakash slowed down his wingbeats, clearing out the dust. His air-clan fan club let out a cheer. Kumi created some sprinkles of rainwater to tamp down the earth. I sent up sparks to burn out the remaining dirt from the air. And in a matter of minutes, the sparring arena was once again put to rights.

"Sit down, you three!" Our noseless headmistress shook her sun visor at us in fury. "Do you demonic degenerates think this is a game? Sparring isn't a joke; it's battle training! And showy antics like that won't help in the coming revolution!"

"Here we go again," muttered Kumi as she squeezed the water out of her green hair. "My parents say she's hopelessly out of touch. I mean, the demonic stock market is doing fine, so whatever, right?"

"The glorious revolution: so yesterday's news!" Aakash flexed his wings. "Who even cares about all that goody-goody freedom and liberty stuff anymore?"

I wanted to say something too, but the topic of the rebellion against the snakes was way too close to home. So I quietly made my way to the fire-clan bench and pretended to occupy myself with organizing my class notes. My skin prickled as our headmistress started in yet again on the unfair rule of the Serpent Empire over the Kingdom Beyond Seven Oceans and Thirteen Rivers, and the need for us rakkhosh to rise up and overthrow our snakey overlords.

"There are rumors in the wind—about disappearing

human and khokkosh children, fairies sold into slavery. For years, we rakkhosh have ignored the fates of our fellow citizens in the Kingdom Beyond, but we can do so no longer. All our fates are intertwined!" The headmistress swept from bench to bench, her sari end flapping dramatically behind her in the still dusty breeze.

I seethed inside, trying to ignore all the students who were already whispering and pointing at me. Why would Surpanakha bring up the revolution now, of all times? Then again, of course the headmistress would say that the fate of rakkhosh-kind was tied to humans. I mean, everyone knew Surpanakha had lost her nose in an epic battle with a muscle-bound hero of old. Worse, she'd actually been in love with the guy who did the deed. Ever since I'd learned that, I'd lost all respect for her. What kind of rakkhoshi dims her power—sacrifices literally the nose in the middle of her face—for the love of a human being? I mean, humans were revolting—what with all that bathing and armpit washing and whatnot.

"There are even whispers about the vanishing moon." Surpanakha's eyes were half-glazed as if she were feverish. "They say the snakes have the Old Moon Mother in their custody, that they are siphoning off her strength! Already, the days grow longer, and the nights shorter! The day the sun stops setting on the Serpent Empire, the snakes will have gained a superweapon that will make them undefeatable!"

To be sure no one thought I could ever believe the kind of nonsense the headmistress was yammering about, I pretend-yawned. Loudly. A few fellow fire-clan gave me odd looks. I glanced away, wondering if I'd overdone it.

"We must stop the serpents, halt all their nefarious plans! But how?" A little spittle escaped around Surpanakha's long fangs as she pounded her fist down on a random land-clan boy's head. "It is blood alone that can pay the price of freedom. Give me blood and I will give you freedom!"

"Blood?" The word tumbled out before I could yank it back.

From over on the water-clan bench, Kumi made a gleeful "gimme" gesture with her hands as a seaweed-covered hulk next to her reluctantly gave her a stack of rupees. From the air-clan bench, Aakash chuckled as some of his winged buddies handed him fistfuls of cash. "I told you," I heard the flyboy mutter, "Pinki wouldn't last five minutes before she had to say something."

I felt the heat of embarrassment burn my face and body. Jumping jackfruits, they'd been *betting* on me? Unbidden, a low growl escaped from my throat. Some dorky land-clan kids snickered, putting their warty hands in front of their crooked-tusked mouths. Even the crows stopped their cawing, as if afraid to get caught up in whatever came next.

And unfortunately, what came next was the beginning of the end. Or the beginning of the beginning, however you want to look at it.

Regardless, it was so not cute.

CHAPTER 2

In Which I Lose It Big-Time (But It's Still Not My Fault)

Did you say something, fire-demoness?" Surpanakha peered over her glasses at me. How she kept the spectacles on that noseless face I'll never know. It was a miracle of physics.

"Why should we give you our blood?" I knew I shouldn't have, but I just kept going, letting all my humiliation burn on the flames of my words. "Why should we young demons sacrifice our lives? Why should we worry about some lost human kids, or flaky fairies, or a decrepit old moon granny who's so demented she's forgetting how to shine? You'd think we'd have learned from the last time!"

That got some approving snaps from my classmates. I tried not to look too pleased at their support.

Surpanakha took off her glasses as she gave me a chilling smile. "What do you know of sacrifice, you selfish girl?"

How could she ask me, of all rakkhosh, that question? The open sewers belched out some rotten gasses, like a warning. My gut started to churn with bile and heat. I remembered what Kumi and Aakash had said about the revolution being yesterday's news and the headmistress being out of touch.

"If the Empire of Serpent Overlords want to rule the Kingdom Beyond, so what?" I snapped, not sure I believed the words coming out of my own mouth. I felt my three hearts beating hard in my chest. Somewhere in the school honeycomb, my soul-bee was buzzing in angry, sympathetic fury. Flames of anger licked out of my nostrils.

"But those missing human children!" said a warty-faced land-clan girl named Harimati.

"And that moon-powered superweapon!" added a muscly guy named Gorgor.

"So what, some human kids ran away from school? So what, a few dopey khokkosh students and dingbat fairies disappeared? Who cares?" I was on a roll now. No matter what everyone thought, I was not cut from the same cloth as my delusional parents. I was not, like Surpanakha, still caught up in dreams of freedom and that kind of fluffy, idealistic stuff. "Plus, no way this nonsense about a super-weapon can be real! And even if it is, the snakes don't stop us rakkhosh from roaming and plundering and scheming! They allow us to torture and scare the humans, so why should we care if they want to do the boring work of ruling the Kingdom?"

There were murmurs of surprise from around the open classroom, like a rising swarm of angry soul-bees. "But how can you of all rakkhosh say that?" a water-clan rakkhosh started to say. "Didn't your family—"

"I know you don't want to finish that sentence!" I screeched, swirling around to stare him down with my most frightening face.

The boy backed off immediately, dripping scared water droplets from his fingers and toes. But behind me, Headmistress Nose-zilla cleared her throat.

"I would think you, more than anyone, would know that the legendary rakkhosh of old were never content to be 'allowed' to do anything." Surpanakha was speaking in a kind of scary whisper. "What a disappointment you must be to those who sacrificed so much. I suppose you think it's rebellious to be self-centered, only worry about number one? Have you never thirsted to be a part of something greater than yourself?"

My nostril flames were coming out in jets now, and smoke was streaming through my teeth and ears. I tried to get myself under control but felt myself spinning more and more out of it. If there was anything that got me hot under the horns, it was hypocrisy. How could this noseless, human-loving headmistress know what I'd sacrificed, or what I thirsted for?

"So I suppose that's why you're teaching here in this school?" I snapped. "Instead of joining the rakkhosh resistance, or buying the old lady of the moon some vitamins or something? Because you care so much about revolution and freedom?"

The entire class got funeral-pyre quiet at that, except for one tiny-winged air rakkhoshi who let out a shriek so sharp, she actually lifted several feet off her bench and practically hit the tree branch above her. Surpanakha narrowed her eyes but didn't say anything.

Maybe, just maybe, I should have stopped there. But I was never one to cut my losses, and I was blazing with anger by now, downright dizzy with my inner fire. In retrospect, I admit that this next part was maybe a *leetle* bit too far.

"If you're such a powerful rakkhoshi of legend, Headmistress," I said, jumping up from my bench, "why aren't *you* spilling your own blood to get rid of the serpents? Or is it that you're more comfortable letting others sacrifice themselves while you let your, ahem, crushes cut off your facial features?" I looked pointedly at her missing nose.

There was an excited murmur from my classmates, as if everyone was anticipating my imminent beheading. The twin jackals that Surpanakha always kept with her woke up from their naps and began to growl. As for the head-mistress, she grew to her full rakkhoshi height, her talons out, her eyes bright red and her neck long and goose-like above her now-towering body. I felt a surge of triumph. I'd made the headmistress lose control. The only problem was, I was about to lose my own.

"Get out of my sight, you little fart!" Surpanakha's words whipped across the clearing like a flying helicocroc's thorny tail. "Before I stew and eat your heart!"

Every student in the banyan grove gasped. We all knew about Empire of the Serpent Overlords Decree #1830, declaring that rakkhosh over the age of ten were not allowed, under pain of death, to speak in our rhyming dia-lect. True, Ghatatkach Academy had magical barriers all around it that theoretically protected us from serpent spies. But still, the fact that the headmistress was rhyming was clear evidence of how upset the she was with me. Maybe it was time to call it quits.

"Fine. Forget it. I'm out!" I picked up my books, jumped up from the bench, and tried to swirl out of the clearing in some sort of semi-graceful exit.

But because, in my experience, disaster usually breeds more disaster, just then, my totally incompetent baby cousins, Kanchkawla, Kaanmawla, and Deembo, bumbled into the banyan grove and straight across my path. The three land-clan siblings made me trip over their bat-like wings and warty feet. I wondered for the hundredth time why I'd promised my scrambled egg–brain aunt to look after them while they were at the lower school.

"Thorry, Didi! Don't lose your cwown!" lisped Kawla, using the word for "elder sister." The squat little rakkhoshi kept trying to hug me around the knees, thereby making the whole tripping situation even worse. "Leth turn that fwown upthide down!"

"Why did your teachers send you up? What did you do now, you fools?" I hissed, almost losing hold on my overfull inkwell. The eyes of the other students felt like mocking razors cutting into me.

"Yo! Yo! Cuz, let's go! Let's get you away from this horror show!" said Kanchkawla's twin, Kaanmawla. I knew the hairy-faced rakkhosh boy was trying to be helpful, taking the books, scrolls, charts, and pens out of my hands, but in doing so, he only made me stumble even more.

Kawla and Mawla's younger sister, Deembo, just grinned, offering me a boiled egg from the pocket of her dirty kurta. My worry at how long it had been since Deembo had last uttered a single word out loud only added to my already-out-of-control emotions.

"Enough, brat! You can't keep stealing boiled eggs from the dining canteen!" I snapped, throwing down the egg from Deembo's hand. It splattered over the ground, yellow yolk spilling like so much broken sunshine. Okay, maybe the egg hadn't been boiled after all. At the sight of the egg corpse on the ground, Deembo started to cry. Loudly. Students around me were laughing now. At me. They were laughing at me. I felt my vision narrow and my head begin to swim.

"You soft-boiled ding-a-lings!" I raged, not I sure if I was talking about my cousins or classmates.

And then I felt it rising up through my throat, a molten flame I couldn't control. It was fueled by my raging emotions and turned hotter by the mockery of my fellow students.

"Get out of my way, buffoons!" I shouted, trying to make it out of the clearing before the inferno escaped my mouth. But it was too late.

"Watch it! I think she's going to blow!" one of the land-clan boys yelled. He was right. Before I could stop it, a giant ball of flames erupted from my lips, lighting up the long bench before me. Students jumped left and right as the wood under them was incinerated to dust.

"Dude, you'd think she would have learned to control her fire by now," Aakash said.

"It's not something you can learn from a book," Kumi answered, her voice loud enough that everyone in the clearing could hear. "I guess we can't all fulfill our potential."

That made everyone laugh even more. To my utter humiliation, a few more flames tumbled out, hot and fast, out of my mouth.

Through the smoke, I saw some of the water-clan students belch up water and make it rain to stop the ancient banyan grove from burning to the ground. Kumi was among them, whipping water out of her scaly tail to reverse the damage I'd done.

The embarrassment of having to be cleaned up after made me feel even worse. At least Aakash had helped fix the mess he'd made before, but I didn't have the self-control to do so. I clamped my lips together, trying to rein in my emotions, but it was too late. The fire in me was burning too fierce for me to tamp down.

"Watch it!" somebody yelled. A whole chain of orange-red fireballs shot out through my left nostril, singeing a land-clan girl's spiky horns. She was so startled she made a little tremor under our feet, splitting the soil and making roots shoot up from underground. The smell of burned bone filled the clearing as some water-clan ran over to extinguish her head.

"Jerk-butt fire face!" the burning girl snarled.

I couldn't even apologize. It was so humiliating.

"Out of the way! No time to spare! Our cousin-lady needs some air!" My bumbling relations grabbed me by both arms and bustled me away.

I let Kanchkawla, Kaanmawla, and Deembo pull me along, my nose and mouth still burning with fire, my eyes burning with furious tears, my ears burning with embarrassment. On the way, I laid waste to another bench, a small tree, and even an official school sign pointing out the direction of the torture grove, disemboweling labs, and dormitories.

I ran out of the clearing, head ringing and the laughter of my classmates burning at my back.

Oh, I'd make them pay for this. I'd make them all pay.

CHAPTER 3

So It Turns Out Maybe Not All Humans Are Completely Gross (But Don't Quote Me on That)

I knew I wasn't supposed to take the little ones outside Ghatatkach Academy's magical protective barriers, but I was too upset right then to care about school rules. So after my cousins dragged me from the outdoor classroom and looked like they wanted to stop, I started dragging them. I dragged them along behind me beyond the rickets fields, then beyond the school gates, all the way until we reached the deepest darkest corner of the Thorny Woods. There, surrounded by the comforting smell of poisonous saplings, the bloody bites of mosquitoes, and the sounds of cacophonous frogs, I finally let myself relax.

The fire in my gut had gone out, but I was still huffing

streams of smoke from my singed nostrils. Struggling to control my firepower was like being locked in battle with another, fiercer version of me. She was a wild warrior who wore my face and was fighting to get out from inside me, threatening to burst through my skin. I didn't want to even imagine the mess if she finally did.

I rubbed my aching chest. Unfortunately, uncontrolled fire making also gave me serious heartburn. One more reason I preferred books to battles.

"Tho thorry, Didi, you lost it so quick," Kanchkawla lisped. A giant string of drool dangled from the side of her mouth as she spoke. She really did look like a cross between a bat and a demented rabbit. "Did you twy doing that meditation twick?"

"No, I didn't twy any meditation trick!" I burped delicately. "It all happened too fast!"

"Anyway, cuz, why were you in such a huff?" Kaanmawla's finger was knuckle-deep inside his drippy nose as he asked this question. "Is it because of our family and stuff?"

"Bup-bup-bup!" I rubbed at my chest again, feeling the fire still tickling my insides. "Don't you try to distract me from the real issue—what did you three nincompoops do to get you in trouble? Why did you get sent up to the banyan grove in the first place?"

At first, no one said anything, but then I fixed my eyes on Kawla. Carefully, I raised one arched eyebrow, a trick I had only just gotten down after hours of practice in the mirror. It took my cousin about three seconds to break. That eyebrow raise was powerful magic.

"Mawla might have picked a girl'sth nosthe!" Kawla blurted out, ducking behind me for cover as her brother growled and dived for her. "She scweamed and then they came to blowsth!"

"Mawla!" I grabbed the squat rakkhosh by the scruff of his neck, lifting him up so we were eye to eye. Kawla used the opportunity to get out of his reach. "How many times have we talked about this? You cannot pick other people's noses, at least not without their permission!"

Mawla squeezed his giant eyes shut and put his hands over his pointy ears, like he could make me disappear by blocking out my face and voice. I shook him a bit but was stopped from saying more by something I heard coming from the clearing ahead of us.

"Get down!" I hissed at my cousins, forcing them behind some thick bushes.

I suddenly remembered that I'd brought them outside school grounds without permission. Part of the reason the Academy's rules about not going off-grounds were being taken so seriously was Deembo's unfortunate incident. Six months ago, she'd wandered off for a few hours and come back with a gash on her neck, weirdly unable—or unwilling—to talk. The Academy doctor said she'd probably been attacked by a wild beast and she was suffering some sort of trauma and would talk when she was ready. But what if something like that happened again? I'd never forgive myself. Plus, my aunt would probably feast on my liver while I was still alive. For good measure, I pushed Kawla, Mawla, and Deembo's horned heads even lower behind the foliage.

The ground was dry and dusty under our hands. The rains hadn't come yet, and the long days and short nights caused by the weakening moon were cracking the very land beneath our feet. I saw Deembo about to sneeze from some of the dust but quickly squeezed her nose shut with my fingers. I'm not sure if it was the nose squeeze or the fierce look on my face, but she swallowed her sneeze with a gulp.

That's when I heard the sound again. Someone was singing. Not just someone, but a group of high-pitched someones. And what they were singing was the . . . Bengali alphabet song?

"Aw, Ah, Hrosho Eee, Dirgho Eee!" shouted the childish voices.

What in the demon-snot? With another warning look to my ridiculous relatives, I peeked up from our hiding place.

What I saw almost made me laugh. I was clearly a little too on edge. It was just a small patshala, an informal school set up by people from a nearby human village. I'd heard there were a lot of them these days, now that serpent budget cuts had made it almost impossible for regular human schools to keep open.

The teacher, though, didn't look like any ordinary village schoolmaster. He was pretty young, not much older than me. Even though he was wearing a patched kurta and dhoti, there was something about the way he held himself that made him seem almost royal. Yet he had no books and no classroom but the open forest. I saw that he had drawn the shoroborno in the dirt with a stick and was pointing to the twelve vowels of the Bangla alphabet as the village children sang.

"Bah! Darun! That was, um, wonderful!" the teacher said in a pained, unconvincing voice. I had to stifle a laugh. It was true, those kids had been *way* off-tune.

"It's very important you learn these letters and how to put them together. You see, students, our mother language is the source of our strength." The young teacher reached down and gathered a fistful of the dry red soil in his brown hand. "Our language runs in the veins of this land."

Next to me, Deembo gurgled, letting some dirt run through her fingers just like the teacher had. As I pushed Deembo back down behind the foliage, I studied the boy. I'd never had many dealings with humans, certainly not humans my own age. I'd been sure they were all weak-limbed and pathetic. But this teacher didn't seem like that at all. Okay, he didn't have any horns popping up through his thick hair, or fangs hanging from his mouth, but still he looked strong and smart—for a person, anyway. He was actually handsome enough that I started to under-stand how Surpanakha had gone all gooey for her human warrior.

"It's an undergwound school I sthink!" Kawla hissed, right at my shoulder. "They're so poor they usth dirt for ink!"

I put my hand over her mouth, shushing her and scowl-ing. I wasn't ready to reveal ourselves just yet. Despite being easy on the eyes, there was something that didn't sit right with me about this teacher dude.

"Why don't the snakes want us to speak Bangla, Shurjo-da?" one of the human schoolchildren was asking.

The teacher they called Brother Shurjo smiled, poured some soil into the boy's hand, and then closed the child's small fist tight with his own. "I know this might be hard to understand, but the thing is, destroying a people's language, not letting children learn the ways of those who came before them, is the surest way to kill a culture."

I noticed Kawla, Mawla, and Deembo all copying the gesture now, running dirt through their hands and making it swirl around a few inches off the ground with their small magic.

"So we could get in trouble for speaking our language? Even with our families?" a worried-looking boy with cracked eyeglasses asked the teacher.

"Should we ssstop? Ssspeak more like them?" asked a dirty-faced little one, drawing out her *s*'s like the snakes did.

"I heard they took some kids away from another patshala and made them go live at a snake retraining school!" said a third child with the thinnest arms and legs I'd ever seen. "Is that why we have to keep our school a secret?"

I started at this piece of information about the snake boarding school and wondered if it had something to do with the missing human kids Surpanakha had been talking about.

"You can adapt; you can learn new things." The teacher was talking to the little girl who had been speaking like the snakes. A beam of sunlight shooting through the leafy canopy illuminated his features as he spoke. "You can even leave behind some beliefs of your parents that don't serve you well. But you can never forget who you are or where you come from. That is your strength. That is the source of your real power."

Then the teacher led the kids in singing again, this time with a song about walking alone when no one heeds your call. Despite how annoyingly noble the guy was, I found myself getting caught up in his musical voice, "Jodi tor daak shune keu na ashe, tobe ekla cholo re."

Without realizing it, I found myself humming along under my breath. That is, until I caught my cousins' expressions.

"Didi, it's been a while," whispered Kawla, her voice filled with awe. "But is dat on your face a smwile?"

"What? Ridiculous! Why would I be smiling?" I immediately fixed my expression, putting back on my normal, scowling face. "I'm not smiling! Where did you get that idea? I just have a little indigestion!"

Mawla snickered, and Deembo wiggled her eyebrows at me.

"Stop that!" I hissed through clenched teeth, pushing their heads even lower behind the bushes. "Be quiet already!"

The young schoolmaster was looking around at his students, repeating the last words of the song they had sung, "If there is no light, if the path before you rages with dark, then light your own heart on fire. Be the beacon. Be the spark."

Even as the teacher's words made the human children ooh and aah, turning their fangless mouths into soft, rasagolla-like circles, I rolled my eyes. Hard. And made sure my cousins saw me do it.

"Humans are so earnest and sappy!" I said in a low, extra-disgusted voice. "Makes me want to gag!"

"Then should we scare them? Can we, please?" Mawla whispered. "I'd like to go and bite their knees!"

Deembo, for her part, held out some eggs in her dirty fingers, like she wanted to share them with the thin, scabby human children.

Then, for no obvious reason, my three hearts sped up, and I broke out in a sweat. I had the most uncomfortable feeling that something—or someone—was coming. I heard it in the way the overhead birds stopped singing. I sensed it in the way the forest creatures suddenly all grew still. I felt it the same way the teacher boy seemed to feel it too. His posture went rigid, his head upright. At his change in behavior, his young students also all stood up, like a pack of frightened rabbits readying to flee from a fox.

I honestly can't tell you why I did what I did next. I

plead temporary insanity. Or maybe that human boy put some kind of a spell on me—someone should look into that. Because without really thinking about it, I leaped out of my hiding space, fangs popping and talons reaching.

"Run away, you human meat!" I screeched, my eyes red and mouth wide. "Run, before your toes we eat!"

I didn't even mean to rhyme, but somehow it felt right in the moment.

At my fearsome yell, the students did the expected, foolish, human thing. They began running and shrieking and making all sorts of undignified ruckus. People were so pathetically predictable.

"Rakkhosh!" they screamed. "Run! Rakkhosh!" This made Kawla, Mawla, and Deembo get into the act, snarling, chasing, and growling at the already-frightened students.

Their teacher, on the other hand, didn't seem really scared—certainly not as scared as he should have been. Instead, he locked eyes with me. I'd never met him before in my life, but I felt like this ragged human *knew* me. Something in his expression really got under my skin— like a killer hornet. Honestly, it made me want to smack him. But just as quickly as it had come, the moment was over. The teacher boy quickly rubbed out the letters he had drawn in the dirt. Then he scooped up the smallest of his students under his strong arms and began to run out of the Thorny Woods.

"Don't!" I grabbed Kawla and Mawla each by the scruff, stopping them from chasing the humans very far. "We've got to get out of here too! And school is the other way!"

"Aw! We were just starting to have fun!" whined Mawla. "You can't make us stop because they run!"

"We've been outside the Academy grounds too long." There was something about the woods that was giving me the serious creeps. "It's way past time to go back!"

We would have turned around and made it to safety too if it hadn't been for that nincompoop Deembo. Of course, instead of listening to me, she had to get distracted by a shiny bird on the ground at the edge of the clearing. It was a fake bird—the kind that was a whistle you make sing by filling it with water. It had obviously been left there to tempt one of the human children, because the little bird was attached to a completely obvious wire.

"Deembo, you deviled egg!" I snapped when I saw what she was reaching for. "Don't touch that bird!"

But Deembo, queen of the ding-dongs, didn't listen to me. Instead, she went ahead and tripped the crudely

placed trip wire. Before any of us could react, Kawla, Mawla, Deembo, and I were each lassoed with vine ropes that had been hidden under the leafy forest floor, and found ourselves hanging upside down from the tree line by our feet!

CHAPTER 4

In Which I Meet Another Cute Boy (Cute but Homicidal)

Yaaaaaaaagh!" yelled Deembo, articulate as always.

"Didi, get usth down! Upside down, my sthmile's a fwown!" screeched Kanchkawla.

My books, scrolls, pens, and inkwell all tumbled out of my shoulder bag—the inkwell exploding beneath us in a small river of red ink. Then a hot breeze came by and blew half my notes into the dark reaches of the forest. Oh, that was just perfect. A new inkwell would cost more rupees than I had, and those class notes had taken me weeks!

"Deembo, you cracked omelet!" I snapped as we all hung uncomfortably by our ankles, swinging slowly like pendulums. I felt the sweat trickling from my cheeks and into the corners of my eyes. "As soon as I get down from here, we are seriously going to have to discuss the five signs of a trap again! I mean, I made you that Venn diagram! This is not the first time you've landed us all upside down, young lady!"

"Cousin, please, use your fire!" yelled Kaanmawla. Off the ground, any small powers my land-clan cousins might have had before were useless. "My ankles hurt something dire!"

But the truth was, I couldn't use flames to burn the ropes that held us. Not without risking burning all our legs off too. Oh, *why* hadn't I learned to master my power better yet? More importantly, who had placed these traps in the first place—and when would those hunters come to get their prey?

It didn't take too long, unfortunately, for my questions to be answered, because just then, the forest air was filled with an ominous, trumpetlike hissing. The ground beneath our dangling heads started moving. It was covered with skittering dung beetles who pulled, of all things, a long red carpet in their wake. Then I couldn't help but yelp in surprise when, from the thorny trees above us, at least a few dozen snakes in official heraldic uniforms unfurled themselves. Their wiggling bodies made a sort of wall on either side of the red carpet.

I realized the hissing had been coming from them.

My stomach flip-flopped with anxiety. Kawla and Mawla started mewling and crying to the sides of me. Deembo, for her part, just dangled quietly, her saucerlike eyes wide with terror, her black tongue sticking out a little between her crooked teeth. Oh, this was bad. This was really bad.

But even as I felt fear begin to gnaw at me, I pushed it down, hardening myself the same way I'd had to my whole life. There was no point in being afraid. Afraid was for losers. Afraid would get us killed. I gulped hard, calling on my fire to warm my heart with bravery. Okay, yes, we were in a not-ideal situation. We were hanging from ankle ropes in the middle of the forest in a trap that had obviously been set by the Serpent Overlords. And I was essentially alone, since my three bumbling cousins didn't count as any help. But what was new? I'd been alone and in trouble more times than I could count, and I'd always managed. So this was no time to panic.

As I thought all this, a green-and-black boa constrictor wearing a ridiculous number of medals along his lapels slithered down the red carpet, yelling, "Hear ye! Hear ye! All you loyal subjectsss of the crown do now rissse for Princcce Sssesha, honorable ssson of the Sssserpentine Governor-General!"

Rise? I looked around the forest from my upside-down

perch. There was no one else but us here, and we clearly could not rise. Or move. Or do anything but hang there like fools.

Seeming to realize his mistake, the boa changed into a more humanlike form, at least one with arms and legs. Then he pulled out some hard tea biscuits and crumpets from his jacket pocket and started pelting us with them as he added, "Or jussst continue dangling inelegantly there in our trapsss. Regardlesss, ye common folk ssscum, join usss posssthassste for a resounding chorusss of 'God Sssave the Sssnake'!"

Oh, farting frog butts, what was I supposed to do now? Kawla and Mawla were shooting me frightened looks as they munched on some of the crumpets they'd managed to catch out of the air. Deembo was crying around a cardboard-like biscuit, snot and tears and crumbs all mixing together and rolling down from her face in rivulets to the ground. My mind was racing at top speed, but short of risking a full-blown incinerating firebomb, there was no way to free us all.

There was nothing else we could do but hang there, singing along to the Serpentine national anthem, mouthing the confusing words when we didn't know the lyrics. The problem was the song was so blasted long, with different stanzas about the glory of sloughing skin, killing victims with poison, and other favorite snaky activities.

"Snake save our glorious snakes! Snake bless our noble snakes! Snake save the snakes!" I sang as I dangled, trying to keep my sari down and tucked in between my legs so I wouldn't flash my petticoat at these strange serpents and humiliate myself any more.

And then he was here, walking down the red carpet beneath us, hands in his pockets as if out for an afternoon stroll among the poisonous thornbushes. I'd seen him on too many posters and in too many newspaper articles not to recognize his handsome, if slimy, face. It was Sesha, son of the Serpentine Governor-General: a kid so rich and pompous, he actually insisted everyone call him Prince Sesha.

Prince Sesha was young like me, but he was dressed head to toe in green velvet finery. Even though the material was way too warm for the weather, he looked as cool as a sloth's underbelly. He even had a cape that swished on the red carpet when he walked, seemingly making a white swirl of sea foam rise behind him. When I looked carefully, I realized that the white stuff wasn't foam at all but an army of squirming maggots who traveled with him, holding up the end of his cape. I have to say, I was impressed. I mean, I'd never met someone with their own maggoty cape holders before.

I felt a little breathless but then wondered if that was just all the blood rushing into my head. I knew it was important to speak first, to establish the fact that despite being trapped upside down like a hapless chicken, I wasn't some passive victim. And since we couldn't exactly fight him, outnumbered as we were, I'd have to get us out with some verbal sparring. I felt my fire bloom in my veins, steadying me. I could do this. I would do this. And I would do it with swagger.

Clearing my throat, I called out to the snake prince, lacing my voice with as much boredom as I could manage: "What's up, colonizer?"

That got Prince Sesha's attention. He turned up his face to look at me.

"What'sss up?" he drawled in an upper-crusty voice that sent shivers down my spine. "Apparently you are, my not-so-loyal sssubjectsss!"

The snake boy paused, like he was expecting us to laugh. When we didn't, he went on, dropping his snaky accent. "All jokes aside, you're certainly not who I was expecting to drop by today. You rakkhosh haven't seen any human villagers around, have you?"

"Um, no?" I said in what I hoped was a believable voice, adding in a growl for good measure. "If we had, we would have eaten them anyway!"

Sesha gazed at the clearing occupied until only recently by the students and their teacher, as if he could smell their shadows. Then, in a gesture almost identical to the one that Shurjo had made, he picked up some dry red dirt in his fist and let it run slowly through his fingers. For a moment, I held my breath, hoping that the human teacher boy had successfully erased all the letters he had drawn on the ground. But then I mentally kicked myself. If I hadn't acted on my ridiculous, off-brand impulse to help them, it would be the human and his students, not me and my cousins, here in this humiliating trap.

Sesha sighed, brushing off the remains of the dirt from his hands. "Cut the rakkhosh down, minions!" he shouted.

When the aforementioned minions took too long to do it, he raised his long, multiringed fingers. "Oh, forget it. I'll do it myself," he said, shooting out the most perfectly formed bolt of green lightning toward the ropes that bound my ankles.

I fell lumpishly to the ground like an overripe mango but got myself together in time to see the snake boy repeat the trick three more times—cutting down Kawla, Mawla, and Deembo in turn. Each time, his lightning was precise and targeted, no more and no less than he needed. Each time, his power was utterly and completely in his control.

I felt flames of jealousy start to burn hot in my chest. Oh, what I wouldn't have given to control my power like that. Then I could have burned the ropes myself instead of hanging there waiting for rescue. How did he do it? How did he learn to control his power so well?

Just then, drat him, the snake boy caught me looking at him. He smiled, his expression full of smug self-confidence. He knew I was admiring him. And he liked it way too much. So I did what I'd learned in Surpanakha's sparring lesson. At least kind of. I was feeling defensive, so I went on the offensive.

"What you need is a theme song," I said in as haughty a voice as I could manage. I stretched my cramped limbs and smoothed out the folds of my sari.

Sesha didn't miss a beat. He raised one of those wicked eyebrows and drawled, "I'm fairly sure I just heard you singing about the glory of snake-dom? Or was that not you?"

"An anthem that applies to the entire Empire isn't the same thing as an evil villain's personal theme song." I returned my own raised eyebrow to his raised eyebrow. "Don't you think?"

Sesha grinned. "Well, you clearly think so, and that's what counts."

Something inside me flipped, and I did my best to hide my own smile. Words really were the best kind of weapon.

In the meantime, Kawla and Mawla, fools that they were, ran around in frightened circles, trying to take cover behind too-narrow trees, too-small rocks, and then finally my legs. Deembo, for whatever reason, seemed terror-frozen to the spot at the sight of the snakes. I grabbed her by the shoulders and shoved her behind me too. I wished yet again I'd left these frittata heads back in the safety of the school grounds.

"Bow down, you multilimbed losssersss!" boomed the boa constrictor who had spoken before. "Bow down to our young Princcce Sssesha!"

I didn't want to of course, but I had no choice. So I gave a small bow, as graceful as I could make it but also as quick as I could manage without appearing insolent.

"Ssstate your namesss!" shouted the boa, and when I did, Sesha's green eyes lit up, making my stomach do a loop-the-loop.

"Pinki! Why, just my luck!" Sesha drawled. "My human trap has caught me the rakkhoshi I've been looking for all my life!"

"All your life?" I ran my slightly shaking talons through my luscious dark locks. "How is it possible you've been looking for little ole me?"

"Oh, it's true!" Sesha was tossing something in his hand that at first looked like a piece of fire but that I soon realized was a perfect bloodred ruby. I watched, mesmerized, as he tossed the jewel up, then caught it every time as it came down, flickering in the forest-dappled light. "You're that fire demoness who is already a legend at Ghatatkach Academy."

Fear bubbled again in the pit of my stomach. But with that fear, something else heady and intoxicating. I was kind of enjoying this game that the snake boy and I were playing, even though I wasn't sure I knew the rules. I felt grown-up all of a sudden, and dizzy with the power of it.

"You've heard about me?" Then, before I let myself get too flattered, my suspicious nature kicked in. This was the son of the Serpentine Governor-General. He didn't know about me because of my excellent grades and stellar rat-dissection skills. If he knew who I was, it was because he knew about my family. And if he knew about my family, we were all in some serious trouble.

"I'm not in the resistance, you know," I blurted out in a puff of acrid smoke. "Unlike some other people I'm related to, I don't even believe in rakkhosh liberation."

Above our heads, a jay screeched as if in warning.

"She's weally not a webel bwighter!" Kawla volunteered from behind my thighs, her speech even more garbled than usual due to the large amount of crumpet stuffed into her cheeks. "She's too sewfish to be a fweedom fightah!"

"Oh, I know that." Sesha flashed a set of perfect, sharp teeth. The sunlight angling through the trees cut him across the face, leaving half his features illuminated and half in shadows. "I would have had my snakes throw you in irons already if I'd thought you were following in the footsteps of your rebel-scum parents."

I gulped, trying to play it cool. I fiddled with the glass bangles on my arm, pushing them up to my elbow and letting them fall again with a clatter.

I'm not sure if he noticed my expression, but Sesha went on, "Believe me, you're the last rakkhoshi I'd suspect of being a collaborator. You've seen firsthand what happens to rebels."

I had. He was right. But I couldn't bring myself to say anything.

"So, you're sure you didn't see any human beings?" Sesha asked, abruptly changing the subject. "Maybe a young schoolteacher, a bit out of place in his dirty clothes?"

"No, no one like that." I tried to keep my voice even. Sesha was, of course, perfectly describing the teacher, Shurjo. I felt Kawla and Mawla draw in breaths of surprise, but I gestured behind my back to shush them. "Why?"

"No reason." Sesha waved a hand in the air, trying to sound casual while appearing anything but. "Just that there's a dangerous revolutionary who's been disguising himself as a village schoolteacher, is all."

"I told you, we didn't see any humans, rebel or otherwise," I insisted. I myself didn't see the point in risking my neck for the revolution, but that didn't mean I was ready to squeal on those who did. Just because I'm a demoness doesn't make me a rat fink. "If you set all these traps for just one guy, you must really want to get him, huh?"

"Oh yes," Sesha said, biting a greenish lip. "He's a special thorn in my side. But those traps were actually for the schoolchildren."

"The schoolchildren! What do you want human kids for?" Then I lowered my voice as a thought occurred to me. "Don't tell me you snakes have started to *eat* them?"

"Not to eat!" Sesha made a broad, magnanimous sort of gesture. "To educate! We want to enroll all human children in a free snake retraining school. To teach them how to speak, and dress, and bathe properly! How to brush their teeth and clean their little bottoms! To help them move into the future with confidence!"

So it was true, the whole boarding-school thing. But

what Sesha was describing didn't sound so bad. These human patshalas had no funding, no books, no classrooms even. Wasn't it better to give the kids better opportunities at snake-run academies?

And yet, it didn't all add up. I tried to phrase my next question tactfully, but I'm not sure I entirely succeeded. "No offense, but if your snake schools are so great, why do you need to trap new students with ropes around their ankles?"

Deembo made a small noise, continuing to cower behind me. She tried to hide by pulling the end of my red-and-orange fire-clan sari over her face. Which left her round bat belly and hairy-toed feet totally visible.

"Sometimes, humans don't know what's best for them." Sesha gave me a thousand-watt grin. "Same goes for other species. Even rakkhosh."

I narrowed my eyes at the snake boy, wondering what he was getting at. Behind me, Deembo was shaking so hard, she was making me seriously nervous. Maybe it was time to stop playing games and start finding out what these snakes were up to.

"So what is it that you want from us?" I summoned the biggest flame I could, turning it over and over inside me, ready use it against Sesha if I had to. I wasn't exactly sure we wouldn't all burn up from its power, but that was a risk I'd have to take if the snakes wanted something from me that I didn't want to give.

But I never had to see if my self-control was good enough. Because what Sesha said next wasn't scary at all. Actually, it was kind of intriguing. And definitely not boring.

"Pinki, listen," he said. "I'm glad you got caught up in those human traps. In fact, it's like a sign from the multiverse."

"Why?" I sensed the attention of all his snake minions on us. Even the birds in the trees and small animals in the undergrowth seemed to be listening for Sesha's answer.

"The thing is," Sesha finally said, "I need your help."

"My help?" Unbidden, a weird, smoky laugh bubbled from my throat. "What kind of help could you possibly need from me?"

Sesha smiled. "I'll assume you don't have any problems with some petty larceny?"

"I am a despicable rakkhoshi, aren't I?" I tossed my hair and did the one-eyebrow-raising trick again. "*Larceny* is my middle name!"

"Oh?" smirked Sesha. "I thought your middle name was Dimple?"

I tried to hide my surprise. I'd hated that name so much

I'd even left it off all my official school documents. "What do you need me to steal?"

Sesha gave me a long appraising look before his face drew into a broad grin. "Oh, nothing big. Just the last remaining strands of moonbeam in the kingdom."

Say what?

I can tell you that wasn't what I'd been expecting to hear.

CHAPTER 5

Okay, I Know, I Probably Should Not Have Agreed to Do the Thing

Y ou need me to steal moonbeams?" I repeated. "Like beams, from the moon?"

"That's usually how it works," Sesha agreed.

"Why do want me to steal moonbeams?" My head was spinning, and I tried to remember what Surpanakha had said in class about the snakes and the moon. "It's not something to do with a"—I waved my fingers, making air quotes—"'superweapon' or anything, is it?"

Sesha had a funny, frozen expression on his face. I felt Kawla and Mawla shuffling around behind me, as if trying to warn me against saying more. Deembo, for her part, was still clutching at the back of my sari and trembling.

When the serpent boy spoke, it was in a strange, flat

voice. "Absolutely, that is exactly it. We are building a moon-powered superweapon."

I saw all his snaky minions swing around to look at him in surprise.

"Should you be admitting that to me so easily?" I squinted at Sesha. He'd clearly not taken a class like I had in Strategic Communication for Villains. "Do you really want to be revealing serpent plans to everyone—especially plans about a secret superweapon?"

Sesha slapped at a mosquito on his cheek, flicking away the bloody body. He looked strangely uncomfortable. "You would think so, in normal situations, but I really feel like I can trust you, Pinki."

Behind me, Mawla gave a loud laugh. I swatted at him without turning around. My brain was whirring, trying to figure out what the serpent boy was telling me.

"So this weapon must be a big deal, huh?" I asked in a conspiratorial voice. "Powerful enough to destroy galaxies and stuff?"

"Yes, that's why I want you to steal the moonbeams!" Sesha said quickly. "So that we can build our moon-powered superweapon and so that the power and glory of our Empire will never fade! So that the serpents can rule without ever worrying about rebels or revolution again!" The snake boy made a little flourish with his arms in the air as he finished talking.

I stared. That was the worst evil-villain speech I'd ever heard. Had this guy seriously never learned about not broadcasting your plans, and keeping your dastardly moves to yourself?

"I still don't get it." I pointed through the treetops at the still-bright sky. "You seem to have control over the moon anyway, right? She barely rises, and it's hardly dark these days, even at night. What do you need a few extra moonbeams for?"

"If only the Old Moon Mother were the problem," Sesha muttered, fiddling with the collar of his green velvet sherwani.

"What's that?" I leaned toward him, cupping a hand to my ear.

"It doesn't matter. What matters is, will you steal those moonbeams? Will you help me?" Sesha seemed so desperate it was really kind of pathetic.

"Why should I? Because if I do, then dear old daddy will finally looooooove you?" As soon as the words were out of my mouth, I regretted them. I mean, this guy was the son of the Governor-General, the ruler of the entire

Empire. He could probably have me arrested for my insolence or killed and stuffed with crumpets or something. But luckily, he didn't get angry. My words seemed to have struck a chord.

"No, that's not it. It's not about getting my father's approval," Sesha shot back. "Well, not totally."

I tried really hard not to roll my eyes, but ugh. Yawnsville. Another dude with an "I have to please my evil father" complex. So predictable. Why couldn't everyone just be their own individuals, not try to live up to what their parents had done before?

"If I decide to help you, what's in it for me?" I picked at my long talons, trying to paint the ultimate picture of "I seriously don't care, do you?" chill. "Why should I agree to steal these moonbeams?"

Sesha ground a clod of dirt beneath his boot, then looked up, giving me an appraising look. "What's in it for you is the one thing you desire the most."

There was a rush above us as a flock of small starlings took off, and then a chilling screech as the kite they were fleeing swooped in pursuit, its dark wings wide.

I made a little scoffing sound in the back of my throat and peered at Sesha over my raised nails. "What I desire the most? What's that?"

Sesha's mouth twitched in a half smile. "Control over your power."

I stopped pretending to care about my manicure. "Say what again?"

Kawla and Mawla squawked in excitement, flapping their ridiculously large hands and running around me in a tight circle. Even Deembo peeked out from behind my legs, as if the magic of Sesha's promise was too powerful for her to ignore.

"You can't control it yet, can you?" Sesha held up the ruby he had been tossing and now looked at me through its prism. "Otherwise you would have burned those ropes right off your ankles and been long gone before I came by."

I felt the balance of power shifting between us. Just seconds ago, I'd been thinking I could see Sesha's innermost desires, his need to suck up to his father. Now I was pretty sure he could see right through to mine. Could he be telling the truth? Could he really be able to help me control my power? I could still hear the mockery of my Combat class ringing in my ears. Oh, what I wouldn't give to make them all eat that laughter.

I tried very hard not to show my eagerness. "All right, say I am having some difficulties, um, harnessing my great power. How can you help teach me what all my professors can't?"

"Let's just say that control over our power is the heart of the Empire's strength." Sesha's voice lowered a little, like he was telling me a secret. "It would please the Serpent Overlords to see you, the most powerful young rakkhoshi of your age, learn how to control your fire."

If I'd been some kind of simpering heroine, I might have swooned right into his arms at these words. After all, they were the ones I'd been longing to hear for so long. But I wasn't some kind of gullible maiden—the ones who talk to forest animals and flying horses, the ones who sing their way through housecleaning, the ones who believe every good-looking stranger who saunters into their lives, promising to fulfill their deepest wishes. I was the kind of girl who ate gullible maidens like that for breakfast.

"And naturally, the Serpent Overlords would be happy to have a rakkhoshi like me on their side?" I picked up a fallen stick from the forest floor and started tracing letters in the dirt. "Particularly someone with my rebellious family history?"

"Indeed." Sesha's grin widened as he caught sight of the letters I'd written. I quickly erased them with my foot. "So what can I do to convince you?"

"I want to see proof." I threw away the stick and brushed the dirt off my hands. "You say you can help me harness my fire. How do I know you really can?"

Somewhere, deep in the forest undergrowth, a small animal skittered away for cover.

"Come here." Sesha led me away from his minions, farther into the trees, and Kawla, Mawla, and Deembo followed. When Sesha's snakes made a motion as if to come along too, he waved them away.

Then the serpent prince wrapped his hands around both of mine in an uncomfortable grip. At my alarmed expression, his shook his head. "Relax, I'm not going to hurt you."

"As if," I said under my breath, but Sesha's eyes sparkled like he had heard.

"Now, go ahead and blast something," he said. "Say, that tree stump over there."

"But I usually don't . . ." I hesitated, eyeing the dying old stump. "My fire usually doesn't come out of my fingers . . ."

"So where does it come out of?" Sesha asked all innocently.

I scowled. "My mouth. I usually make my fire with my mouth."

"Ah." The snake boy's grin grew broader. "Okay, no problem." He changed his position so that he was now standing behind me, his hands resting on either side of my lips.

"What are you doing?" I protested, trying to shake him off. I could smell his poison cologne, feel his scaly skin, hear his breath in my ear. Just the nearness of him, and my own embarrassment, made the fire in my stomach roil up to a high burn.

"I'm helping you focus your fire," he said in a too-soft voice. "Trust me."

I hesitated, feeling the flames filling me, tickling at my insides, wanting to come out. And then I felt a tiny tug on my sari. When I looked down, I saw Kawla and Mawla peeking out from behind my legs, their faces full of awe and wonder.

"Do it, Didi! We know you can!" said Kawla. "You're the sthrongest rakkhosh in the land!"

But even as her words filled me with confidence, I caught sight of Deembo's worried expression. The little rakkhoshi shook her head no, like I shouldn't do it.

"What are you trying to tell me?" I muttered. "Just speak! I know you can!"

Deembo just drew her gaze from Sesha to me and back again. She looked terrified, her eyes round like full moons. But she didn't say a word.

I sighed. Well, two-thirds of my family behind me was better than none.

"All right, then, let's go for it." Sesha still had his hands on my face, and they were making my cheeks, and my entire face, far too warm for comfort. "What do I do?"

"Let your fire fly," Sesha said.

"But . . ." I protested, eyeing the miles of trees in front of me, trees made of very flammable wood.

"Don't be scared; you're not alone," said the voice in my ear. "I'm here with you."

It was, of course, pathetic and ridiculous. I didn't need anyone. I was used to walking alone, being the spark in the dark, etc., etc. But for whatever reason, Sesha's words left me raw, remembering a long-ago time when I was small, and scared, and alone, desperate to hear someone say they were there with me. I started to burn even hotter, the flames rising now in hot spurts from my gut to my mouth.

"I really don't know if I can control it," I muttered. The heat of my inner fire was almost overwhelming with its intensity now.

"You don't have to," said Sesha. "I'll help you."

"But . . ." I breathed, fear gnawing at my insides. What if I couldn't?

"Go!" shouted Sesha. "Burn it all down!"

"Burn, Didi, burn!" shouted my goofball cousins, at least the ones who could speak. "It's now your turn!"

I opened my mouth, not knowing what to expect, and my fire exploded out. As always, the feeling was energizing and terrifying at the same time. Could I control it, or would I swirl into an inferno of raw power, as usual?

But my worst fears didn't come true. I didn't whirl out of control. I didn't burn down the entire forest. I could have. I might have. But I didn't. Because Sesha was there.

The moment I opened my mouth to let my fire fly, I felt his cool force guiding my power. He created a green barrier on either side of my flames, a wall of sorts that hemmed my strength in, limiting my destructive reach and focusing me. I was shocked when I hit the tree stump I was aiming at and incinerated it but nothing else. So shocked, I shut my mouth, dousing my flames almost right away.

"See?" Sesha said, removing his hands from my face.

"Cousin-sister, don't you fwown!" lisped Kawla. "You didn't burn the fowest down!"

Mawla linked arms with Deembo and did a happy jig.

"Can you teach me to do that by myself? I mean, without your help?" I demanded.

"Sure. If you find the Moon Mother's stolen moonbeams and bring them to this spot in one week's time." Sesha gave a dramatic swirl of his cape, as if to sweep away.

"Wait." I grabbed the edge of his velvet robes. "Where's

the Moon Mother? Do you have her in custody or something?"

"Custody?" Sesha scoffed, twitching the cloth of his cape out of my hands. "Why would we have her in custody? We owe her everything!"

"But . . ." I tried to make sense of the snake boy's words, recalling what the headmistress had just said earlier that day. "You're siphoning off her power! She grows weaker every day! She must be your prisoner!"

"She's old, that's all," Sesha said with a bored-sounding yawn. "But she's the one who first allowed us snakes to move from our underwater kingdom up here! She controls the tides and the water, so she's the one who made us passages connecting the undersea realm to the land. Without her, we never could have taken over the Kingdom Beyond."

Wait. What? I blinked my eyes. It was the Moon Mother who had first allowed the snakes to colonize the Kingdom Beyond Seven Oceans and Thirteen Rivers? Why wasn't this common knowledge?

"But what about the moon-powered superweapon?" Something was smelling seriously past its due date here.

"Oh, right." That brought Sesha's attention back to me

quickly. "Well, the thing is, we can't build the superweapon without every single last moonbeam in the kingdom."

I narrowed my eyes. "If she's such a friend of yours, can't you just ask the Moon Mother where her missing beams went?"

"She doesn't know." Sesha shook his head, looking increasingly desperate. "But we know for a fact that a significant stash of beams were stolen from her a while ago and are somewhere nearby, just hidden away."

"So how am I supposed to find them?"

Deembo rubbed her furry head into my hand. I absent-mindedly scratched behind her ears, her fur both rough and soft in my hands.

"If I knew that, I would have gotten them myself, wouldn't I?" shot back Sesha, suddenly irritated. "But with your rakkhosh connections, your family history, you should be able to find some simple stolen moonbeams. Everyone you ask will assume you're doing it for the resistance. To stop us from building our, uh, moon-powered gizmo."

I felt hot and cold as all sorts of conflicting emotions whizzed through me like so many comets flying through a dark night sky. "But how do you know I'm not going to double-cross you? Join the resistance anyway?"

To my humiliation, he out-and-out laughed at this.

"Oh, come on, yaar, you're not going to give up learning how to control your power," Sesha said. "Besides, I have it on good authority you're too selfish to be a rebel fighter."

The snake boy tweaked Kawla's crooked nose, and my annoying baby cousin actually giggled. At this, Deembo gave a squeal of alarm, grabbing for her sister's arm. Sesha raised an eyebrow, as if shocked by Deembo's boldness.

"Relax, Deembo, it's fine." I don't know why, but the whole interaction made me queasy. I grabbed both sisters none too gently by the shoulders and shoved them behind me.

"Look, I really don't have the time to stand around arguing with you about this." Sesha looked pointedly at his bejeweled wristwatch. "If it doesn't appeal to you, don't accept the mission. I'm sure I'll find another rakkhosh willing to help."

"No!" Even though something felt off about this whole thing, it was my chance to learn control over my power, and I wasn't ready to give that up. "Fine. I'll do it. I just wanted to know all the facts."

"The facts are these: I have something you want, and I'll give it to you if you get me the thing I want," Sesha said in a too-patient voice. "But I don't have time for hand-holding."

"Hand-holding!" I practically squawked. "Don't get any ideas, Mr. Big Shot, I have no interest in holding your hand!"

"Oh, really? Not what it seemed like before." Sesha grinned and then, unexpectedly, touched the side of my mouth again. I shivered and felt myself grow warm with embarrassment as I saw his grin widen. "I'll see you here in one week, with the moonbeams. Then we'll have another lesson."

What was it about this guy? He made me both want to punch him in the self-confident nose and . . . what? I couldn't even let myself imagine what that other feeling coursing through me was. "Fine," I gritted out, "in one week."

"Use whatever force you need to keep those moonbeams safe." Sesha lowered his voice into an intense whisper. "Don't let anyone, and I mean not a snake, human, rakkhosh, or anyone else, hurt those moonbeams. Get it? Keep them safe, or I will make you regret the day you met me!"

I must have looked shocked. What the heck was he blathering about? How could anyone hurt a moonbeam, anyway? But without another word, Sesha swept out of the forest with his snake and insect minions in tow.

The snake boy wasn't boring, I had to give him that. But how in the dimensions was I going to find those dratted moonbeams?

CHAPTER 6

Spying Behind Doors Is for Punks and Losers

As luck would have it, my first class the next day was Honors Thievery with Professor Ravan. Elder brother to our headmistress, he had made his mark on rakkhosh history with the kidnapping of an important queen in a flying chariot, an incident that caused a full-out human-rakkhosh war that he was usually blamed for. Never mind that he was actually just getting revenge for the way that the humans in question had treated Surpanakha, his sister. But now that he was retired from supervillainy and warmongering, Ravan was an excellent teacher. He was low-key cool, a little scary but seriously inspiring. I'd already learned a lot this semester. So far, we'd finished chapters on petty larceny; distraction-based theft; disguises; and, my favorite, snatch-and-run stealing.

After staying up most of the night unsuccessfully researching moonbeams in the library, I knew I had to ask Ravan. I got to the classroom early, a first for me, and went straight up to the teacher's desk. Instead of the banyan grove, Ravan preferred to teach in one of our indoor classrooms. He said it was his allergies, but I had a suspicion all that open space made him nervous.

"Um, Professor?" I ventured, clearing my throat as I entered the room.

It was a bit ramshackle, as were all our rooms at the Academy, with peeling paint and a dusty ceiling fan. Half the chairs were wobbly and broken, most not even big enough to fit some of the larger rakkhosh students, and we never had enough textbooks to go around. The school budget cuts were the sort of thing that revolutionaries got furious about, but I'd never thought too much about it. After all, I'd never had much money, so everything at the school looked pretty fancy to me. But now, after meeting both the rebel teacher boy and the serpent prince in the woods, I was beginning to notice all sorts of things I never had.

"Yes? Who are you again?" Ravan was wearing an immaculate homespun panjabi and dhoti and peered over his smudged reading glasses at me.

"I'm Pinki? From your first-period class?" I tried not

to let my nervousness show. My professor's gray hair, bad memory, and failing eyesight didn't change the fact that his chest was the size of a tree trunk and his shiny teeth were huge and sharp in his mouth.

"Of course, Pinki." The professor shut his book, one on famous kidnappers in history. The illustration on the tattered front cover featured a young Ravan himself, decked out in his war armor, flying away in his magical chariot with the captive queen as she threw her jewelry to the ground so her husband would know she'd been taken. "I'm sorry, my dear, I was engrossed in the past. What can I do for you?"

"Sir." I didn't meet his eyes but stared at his one earring dangling from a thick lobe. "I was wondering, is it possible to steal *anything*—say, the stars from the sky?"

"Well, the right thief can steal anything." Professor Ravan reached out and waved his hand by my hair. When he opened his fist, I saw that one of my hair clips was in it. Wordlessly, he handed the clip back to me. "But I would discourage you from any star stealing at this point in your career. Try starting smaller. Planets, small satellites perhaps."

"Satellites, do you mean like orbiting moons?" I asked a little too eagerly as I put the clip back in my hair.

Ravan took off his glasses and peered at me with sharp eyes. "What's this about, young fire demoness?"

I rubbed my cheek, remembering the spot where Sesha had touched it. "I heard that there might be some stolen moonbeams out on the market . . ." My voice trailed off.

Ravan's nostrils flared, like he'd smelled some tasty prey. "What did you say?" He looked around and then got up quickly to close the classroom door.

"Moonbeams, I heard that maybe the Old Moon Mother had some beams stolen from her? But maybe that's just a rumor," I mumbled.

Had I already said too much? I longed to ask him if he knew about the Moon Mother helping the serpents invade the Kingdom, but there was no way I could explain where I'd heard that. He probably already suspected I was working with the Empire of Serpent Overlords.

"Where did you hear this rumor about the moonbeams?" The professor's face had somehow sharpened, his entire posture going from vague scholar to hunter on alert.

"Just around," I said vaguely, trying to achieve a casual posture by leaning on his dusty desk. In the meantime, my palms were starting to sweat.

"Smart, very smart." Ravan lowered his gravelly voice, nodding. "Yes, don't tell me, it's safer that way. We don't know if the snakes are listening."

My nervousness gave way to confusion. Did Ravan

guess that I had gotten the information about the moon-beams from Sesha? But if he did, why was he looking at me all approvingly, like I was the best thing since fried shingaras?

"So do you know who I should talk to . . . who could help me find them?" I walked around the desk, closer to where he was standing, and lowered my own voice to match his cautious tone. "The moonbeams?"

"Shhh!" Ravan slammed his book onto an already-tottering stack on his desk. "Better not to say that word again. Call them the . . . thingamajigs!"

"Okay." I looked around the empty classroom too, feeling his paranoia rubbing off on me. "Do you know where I should start looking for the . . . thingamajigs?"

But Professor Ravan seemed not to be listening. Instead he was pacing in front of the classroom's bookcase full of thievery aids—lockpicks, sleeping drafts, black ski masks, and the like—with a bemused expression on this face. "A chip off the old rakkhosh, aren't you?"

"Sir?" All of a sudden, I remembered that he had gone to Ghatatkach Academy with my father.

"The revolution has been asleep for too long. Too many have paid a terrible price. That's why so few of us believed in this story about a moon-powered superweapon. It seemed too over-the-top, too outlandish. Out of a science fiction story. A trap, maybe." Ravan was still pacing. "But if this is true, it may be the unifying sign we've been hoping for." He turned to me, his thick moustache quivering with excitement. "Pinki, you may be the spark that ignites the dormant fires of revolution!"

"Th-the spark . . ." I stuttered, smoke coming out of my nose. This was going down just like Sesha had predicted.

"Yes!" My professor's laugh was hushed but excited. "I'm so proud of you. I know that my sister has been hard on you, my dear, but I told her that deep underneath all that bluster, the antisocial behavior, and, of course, the ridiculous selfish attitude was a brave heart! She didn't believe me, told me you were a hopeless loser, but I told her there was more to you than meets the eye!"

"Um, thank you?" I wasn't sure whether to be pleased or offended.

"Of course! I knew you couldn't let down your revolutionary lineage!" Ravan rambled on, twirling his already-stiff moustache into sharp points. "This is wonderful! The best news I've heard in weeks!"

Just like Sesha had predicted, Professor Ravan was assuming that I was looking for these moonbeams as a way to *stop* the Serpent Empire, not help them. What would he and the headmistress do if they realized that I was actually on the serpents' side?

"So, Professor, about where I should begin to look . . ." I started again, but Ravan hushed me with another vigorous wave of his hands. His face turned sharply away from me.

Then, with two giant steps, Ravan reached the classroom door and yanked it open, making the two rakkhosh who had been listening to our conversation tumble into the room. Ravan grabbed them each by the ear and dragged them over.

"Ouch, sir! Let go!" whined Aakash, his giant insect wings beating.

"Professor, please!" said my roommate, Kumi, her already-liquidy eyes filled with water.

"Listening at the door, were you?" hissed Ravan, twisting their ears even harder in his giant hands. "How much did you hear?" With a heave, he pushed them both into the room, then slammed the door behind them.

"Nothing!" insisted Kumi, rubbing her reddening ear. "We heard nothing at all!"

"Just some stuff about some stolen moonbeams and a mission to stop the snakes from making their superweapon and then ignite a revolution!" added Aakash, his face twisted in pain. "Nothing else!"

"Airhead!" Kumi snapped. "You just can't keep your mouth shut, can you?"

"What?" Aakash fluttered his wings and fixed his way-too-complicated hair style around his horns. "What did I say?"

Kumi looked like she wanted to strangle him. Kind of like how she usually looked at me.

"Well, you have obviously heard too much." Ravan's facial hair quivered in rage. "In which case, Pinki and I have two options." He gave me a warm look, and I felt a serious twinge of guilt shoot through me. "First option, we assume you're serpent spies and rip out your tongues right here and now."

Aakash clapped his hand over his mouth, and Kumi's eyes widened in fear. "What's option two?" she asked quickly. "Seriously, we're not spies!"

"We will see about that!" Professor Ravan was already pulling a small bottle out of his khaddar panjabi pocket. Like a flash, he grabbed Kumi's mouth and poured a few drops of the liquid into it. Then he did the same to Aakash. Both rakkhosh students spluttered.

"Hey, that tasted disgusting!" protested Aakash. "Like strawberries and chocolate! Ick!"

"Truth serum, my own recipe," Ravan said with a smile. "The nasty taste is purposeful! It only lasts a few seconds, but it'll get the information we need." He turned to Aakash

and Kumi, and demanded, "Are you working with the serpents? Are you spies?"

"No!" they both said earnestly. My hearts were pounding as I wondered what would happen if the professor used that serum on me. But he didn't. Instead, he just nodded at Kumi and Aakash and put the bottle away.

"Option two is that both of you accompany Pinki on her mission," Ravan said, waving two fingers in their faces. "And protect her with your lives."

"What?" they both yelled in unison.

"That's really not necessary," I added.

"I don't want to hear one word from either of you," the huge professor snarled. He turned to me, his voice softening a bit. "And you, Pinki, you can't take this entire thing on your shoulders. Think about what happened . . ." He let his voice trail off.

I didn't want to think about what had happened. I'd been living under the shadow of *what happened* my entire life. "It's just a rumor that these . . . thingamajigs are even out there," I said in a rush. "What if it's not even true?"

"But what if it is?" Ravan demanded, his eyes shining with something that looked like hope. "We're talking about finally kicking the Serpent Overlords out of the Kingdom and back to their undersea lairs. We're talking about being successful this time in getting our freedom! We have to at least try."

My mind whirred. This whole thing was bringing up way too many feelings for me about my past. A past I'd come to Ghatatkach Academy to forget. But there was no way to go except forward, if I wanted Sesha's help in controlling my power.

"Now, as for you two!" Ravan turned away from me again, his voice a low snarl. Aakash and Kumi both gulped, visibly terrified. "You have isolated Pinki, made fun of her for her successes, teased her, and called her names, but this classmate of yours has more courage in her little talon than any of you have in your entire bodies!"

Aakash and Kumi looked, as they say, gobsmacked.

I tried to arrange my features into what I hoped was a humble expression. Like "yes, it's true, you have under-estimated me all along, I'm actually this awesome." But I couldn't help but feel a bit oogly at all the praise Ravan was pouring on me.

"It's really nothing . . ." I started, but Ravan waved me quiet.

"While the rest of you are worrying about being elected Demon King or Queen, Pinki here has been upholding the honor of her family lineage and quietly working for all our liberation." The professor snapped his thick fingers in front of Aakash's and Kumi's faces. "Not many students would think of such an ingenious way to undermine the serpents at their own game."

"No way Pinki's all that . . ." Aakash said faintly, but Ravan cut him off. "Way.

"Now, let me think about your next step." Ravan plunked his glasses back on his nose and started digging through one of the many piles of moth-eaten books on his desk, knocking over a bunch in the process.

With our professor busy, Kumi just gawked at me. I couldn't resist getting in a dig. "Rui! Katla! Eeleesh! Close your yap, roomie; you look like a *feesh*!"

Both Aakash and Kumi gasped at my rhyming. But I grinned, remembering that goody-two-shoes teacher boy in the woods talking about how someone's language and culture are the sources of their strength.

"You're no freedom fighter," my roommate hissed in such a low voice, the professor couldn't hear it. "No matter who you're the daughter of. You're up to something, and you better believe I'm going to find out what."

"Yeah, find out what," repeated Aakash, throwing a casual arm around Kumi's shoulders.

"Put your arm around me like that again, flyer, and I'll sauté up your gallbladder and feed it to my hench-crocs!" snarled Kumi, spitting rain.

I swallowed a laugh. My roommate got on my last nerve, but she was no wimp.

Aakash immediately removed his arm from Kumi's shoulders, stretching it out, along with his wings, like that had been his plan all along. "Cool. Cool. Cool," he mumbled. "Sure thing, sure thing. Very cool."

I doubled down on my scowl as I turned on my roommate. "I don't know why you're such a suspicious little slug, or is it just that hard for you to imagine that I might be as much of a legendary villainess as I've always seemed?"

"The revolution is dead," growled Kumi. "Even if it wasn't, you're no legend in the making. You're too selfish."

I felt my fire simmering inside me as I stared her down. "Well, we'll just see about that, won't we?"

"Yes, we will." Kumi made that "I'm watching you" gesture where she pointed at her own eyes and then at me.

Aakash tried to copy her gesture, only he poked himself in the eye a little as he tried. "Ouch! That hurt!"

Kumi and I both snorted, a rare moment of togetherness.

Ravan finally looked up from his books. "I think your best bet to locate these stolen . . . whoziwhatsits, is asking Chhaya Devi, the Merchant of Shadows. She has her finger on the pulse of both the human and rakkhosh black markets."

"You mean the weird shadow seller with the stall at the edge of the bazaar?" I asked.

"That same one." The professor eyed the classroom door, through which more students would be coming in any second now. "And not one word to anyone else about this."

He glared at all three of us, his gaze softening a bit when he landed on me. "Aakash and Kumi, you will protect Pinki on this mission, is that understood? If you can find these . . . whatchamacallits . . . it will be a huge blow to the Serpent Empire. It may give the revolution the spark it needs to burst into flame!"

And then the door opened and dozens more students streamed noisily into the room. I glanced at the sundial. It was almost time for class to begin.

Professor Ravan pointed us to our seats, but not before issuing one more threat to Kumi and Aakash. "Remember what I said. Protect Pinki and her mission at all costs!"

Kumi gave me an evil grin, flicking her pointy tongue out a little. "Oh, don't worry, Professor, I won't let her out of my sight!"

"Yeah, not out of our sight!" Aakash tried that pointing-at-his-eyes-and-then-at-me thing again, looking ridiculously proud when he managed it without hurting himself.

"Mind that you do!" snarled Ravan as the other students settled into the room. "I'll have you for an after-dinner snack otherwise!"

I slunk to my seat, feeling nauseated. How was I supposed to find these stolen moonbeams and get them to Sesha with Kumi and Aakash breathing down my neck?

CHAPTER 7

In Which I Am Not Shopping for Butt-Powder No Matter What Anyone Says

I wasn't looking forward to the flight down to the bazaar, but it was too far to go any other way. Flying was unfortunately one of the things my stomach had clearly not been built for. It made me nauseous, gassy, and, honestly, a little nervous.

To make matters worse, because of Professor Ravan, I had the undynamic duo of Aakash and Kumi with me. The air-clan boy flew himself, his entire murder of hench-crows flying alongside him. My roommate and I flew on the backs of two of the school's borrowable helicocrocs. Part crocodile and part eagle, the flying creatures spat poison, stank, and were uncomfortably scaly, sharp toothed, and seriously

dangerous. I would have probably loved them if not for the whole part where they lifted me off the ground and took away my control over my own body.

Kumi had her tiny hench-crocs with her, and I had my whole bumbling family with me. I hadn't wanted to bring my cousins beyond the school barriers yet again, but after our little adventure in the woods, Deembo had experienced another one of her emotional freak-outs and was now totally refusing to be separated from me. At the first mention of being left behind while I went to the market, the little rakkhoshi had screamed and clamped herself onto my leg like a barnacle.

It was just after dinner, the meal the whole school ate on banana leaves on the long Academy veranda. Deembo's emotions had been so intense, they'd caused a little dirt storm to sweep up from the ground, making soil rain on the banana-leaf plates of students who were still eating.

"Hey, cut that out!" they protested, glaring at me.

"Like it's my fault!" I shook my leg, trying to pry her off, but Deembo just hung on tighter and kept wailing. Snot, tears, and whirling minitornadoes of magicked dirt flew everywhere.

"If she keeps that up, the headmistress isn't going to let you go to the market at all," Kumi had drawled, grinning. "Too bad. I guess your little pseudorevolutionary mission might fail before it even gets started!"

"Yeah." Aakash bent to pat Deembo on the head. "Go ahead, land kiddo, cry all you want!"

"Quiet! Quiet!" I'd hissed at my crying cousin. But her shrieks made her siblings start sobbing too, and now I had three blubbering kids on my hands. I could feel the eyes of the other students on us and hear their guffaws of laughter. Humiliation flamed in my chest.

"Fine! I'll take you all with me!" I'd snapped, grateful there were no teachers around. "Just stop crying already!"

Like a faucet, all the tears suddenly stopped. The dirt they'd conjured up to the balcony blew away too, and all three grinned up at me with infuriatingly innocent faces. And so I'd been forced to bring along my three cousins on our ride into the mosquito-filled evening.

I was trying to keep my terror from showing on my face, besides trying to keep my dinner down, when I saw something strange hanging midair right in my flight path. My helicocroc angled its body so as not to hit the thing— a sign with writing on it—and it was all I could do not to scream at the change in altitude. The sign itself was seriously bizarre:

**Empire of the Serpent Overlords Decree #1858
All Monster* and Human Flight Is Hereby
Prohibited
Unless for the Purposes of Commerce, Dental
Extraction, or Dancing the Cha-Cha
on Punishment of a Painful Death by Order of
the Serpentine Governor-General.
Have a Good Day.
#ComplianceOverDefiance
*Rakkhosh, Khokkosh, Bhoot, Petni, Doito,
Danav, etc., etc.**

"What's commerce?" Aakash shouted over the flapping of his crows. I couldn't help but seethe that the air-demon boy could afford such cool hench-creatures.

"*Commerce* means 'buying or selling stuff,'" I said, trying to keep my voice steady and not nauseated-sounding. "Which is what we're doing—flying to the market—so stop stressing."

"Capitalism for the win," said Kumi, but I couldn't figure out if she was being serious or sarcastic. Her hench-creatures, two little man-eating crocodiles, sat on her shoulders like twin dragons. They made her look so cool that I could spit.

The next midair sign was even more alarming.

Empire of the Serpent Overlords Decree #1947
No Monster* and Human will Hang Out, Interact,
Convene, or Cohabitate
Unless for the Purposes of Commerce, Dental
Extraction, or Dancing the Cha-Cha
on Punishment of a Painful Death by Order of
the Serpentine Governor-General.
Have a Good Day.
#ComplianceOverDefiance
*Rakkhosh, Khokkosh, Bhoot, Petni, Doito,
Danav, etc., etc.

"Again with this cha-cha business," wondered Kumi out loud.

"It's an awesome option if you're into the ballroom scene, and as social dances go, it's, like a killer workout," said Aakash as he and his crows banked a hard right toward the bazaar. "But why any self-respecting monster would wanna to dance with a human as a partner, I couldn't tell you. They're super bad with their footwork. Always offbeat."

"Oh, shut up, both of you." I felt acid rising in my throat. I wondered when all these new laws had been enacted. "So no interactions between humans and rakkhosh are allowed at all if we aren't buying and selling, getting our molars pulled, or dancing? What about human-hunting season? What about the Pan-Human Torture Olympics? What about just scaring them for fun?"

"All illegal I guess." Kumi shrugged.

The last sign we saw before landing at the edge of the bazaar was the most alarming of all. Besides the number being wack out of order.

Empire of the Serpent Overlords Decree #1492
No Monster* or Human Over the Age of Ten
Will Write Sappy Poetry or Dream in Their
Native Language

NO EXCEPTIONS EVEN CHA-CHA RELATED
on Punishment of a Painful Death by Order of
the Serpentine Governor-General.
Have a Good Day.
#ComplianceOverDefiance
*Rakkhosh, Khokkosh, Bhoot, Petni, Doito,
Danav, etc., etc.

"We already can't speak our own dialects on fear of death, but now we can't dream in them?" I whispered to myself. "How will they enforce that?"

"Cuz, this law is the absolute worst!" shouted Mawla from behind me. "I love writing rakkhosh verse!"

"Well, you're not over ten, are you?" I snapped. "So it doesn't apply to you!"

Mawla seemed happy enough at this, but I felt my stomach flip-flopping. This law was obviously a stepping-up of the old anti-rhyming one. If the serpents were banning poetry and dreams, what in the multiverse would they think to ban next?

I had to put aside my worries then, because we had finally arrived at the outskirts of the bazaar. I let out a big sigh as I dismounted my helicocroc, grateful to feel the solid ground under my feet and my stomach out of my throat.

The bazaar that housed the Merchant of Shadows's small stall sat between the mostly human and mostly rakkhosh areas of the Kingdom Beyond Seven Oceans and Thirteen Rivers. It was a lonely part of the market, a place with little foot traffic except the occasional rikshaw puller cutting through to get their client somewhere more appealing. It was the part of the bazaar where the roadsides were piled with garbage, where streetlights rarely shone, and where stray dogs and cattle roamed. It was the place where nefarious human-rakkhosh dealings took place, where illegal goods were bartered and sold. In other words, my favorite part of the bazaar.

"Let me go alone; it'll be too suspicious if we all crowd around her," I muttered to Kumi and Aakash as we neared the merchant's shop.

My roommate looked like she wanted to protest, but Aakash was eyeing a lizard-roll stall across the way. "We can keep an eye on Pinks the Jinx from over there. No harm in getting some grub while we're on this top secret mission, right?"

"Looking to buy something precious and secret, then?" The woman turned her beetle-sharp eyes in my direction as soon as I split off from Kumi and Aakash and approached her stall with my cousins in tow. "You better be, because I can't be seen fraternizing with a demoness like you if you're not here to buy something."

"A good evening to you too, Auntie," I said in as sweet a voice as I could manage.

Chhaya Devi's little shop smelled like musty magic and overripe shadows, a kind of green and cloying scent that reminded me of the bottom of the murky river running by school. It was lit only by a small kerosene lantern, a dull flame flickering inside dirty glass.

"What is it that you desire?" Chhaya Devi's long-fingered hands never stopped moving even as she spoke to me. They polished small bubbling vials, rearranged smoking stoppered bottles, and ineffectively dusted the cracked display case housing all her goods. "Something to help sharpen your rakkhosh magic? A tonic to disintegrate your enemy's toes?" She held up a tiny bottle shaped like a foot. "Or maybe a little potion to grow hair on an ex–love interest's tongue?" This time she held up a red vial shaped like, yup, a human tongue.

I told myself not to get distracted from my goal. Yet even though I didn't have any love interests—either ex or current—that toe-disintegration tonic seemed too good a deal to pass up. But when I heard how much it cost, I remembered that I still needed to buy a new inkwell and had to sadly give up buying it.

"You shouldn't take those demon-lings out of the school grounds," the Merchant of Shadows said with a look at my three cousins. The flickering kerosene lamp made her face seem shadowy and strange. "Not safe for little ones of any species these days."

"Are you talking about the disappearances?" I asked. "I heard those kids were being given the chance to go to a better school, with more opportunities."

"If you call being taken from your people, brainwashed by the snakes, and forced to forget who you are an opportunity." The shadow seller made a dubious sound in the back of her throat. "Anyway, young rakkhoshi, I know you didn't come here to discuss elementary education. What is it that you really want?"

"Now that you mention it, I was wondering about one other thing." I took a quick glance over my shoulder onto the empty market by-lane.

I could still see Aakash and Kumi across the dusty path. They were standing at the stall for lizard rolls and were taking their time placing their orders. Kumi was glaring at me every five seconds and scowling in a super-unsubtle way. Aakash was even worse and kept mouthing, "Hurry up!" in my direction.

I turned back around quickly to meet Chhaya Devi's all-knowing eyes. "Yes, I'm looking for something special." There didn't seem to be any point in beating around the bush. "It's just a rumor, but I thought you might have heard about where these precious items might be."

I paused, wondering how I could imply that I was looking for the stolen moonbeams without actually having to come out and say the word *moonbeams*. I was nervous to begin with, and all the new Empire of the Serpent Overlords Decrees had made me even more jumpy.

After a few minutes of no one saying anything, Kawla blurted out, "We don't mean to poke, we don't mean to pwy, but have you any stolen light from the night sky?"

I tried to shush her, but then Mawla piped up to add, "The thing for which our cousin dreams, rhymes it does with *prune creams*!"

Deembo, who was feeding some stray dogs boiled eggs from her pocket, smiled and rubbed her stomach. The dogs wagged their tails, and one gave a sharp, happy bark as it licked the little rakkhoshi's egg-covered face and hands.

I was so distracted by Deembo and her new pets that I

didn't notice the Merchant of Shadows frown. I practically jumped when she started shouting, in an unnaturally loud voice, "No, I do not carry that brand of butt powder, young demoness! You'll have to take your tuchus problems somewhere else!" As she spoke, the merchant grabbed Kawla, Mawla, and Deembo each in turn and yanked them behind her counter.

"Butt powder? I'm not looking for butt powder!" I whirled around to see where she was looking and realized there was a squadron of snake dragoons slithering through the road behind us. The serpent soldiers snickered as they overheard Chhaya Devi's words, making farting noises and other crude gestures at me as they passed.

"Maybe you should stop shooting flames out of your bottom! That might help!" Chhaya Devi shouted.

"Will you stop that?" I hissed even as I ducked, trying to hide my face behind my hand. I could hear Aakash and Kumi laughing from clear across the road. The snake squadron was in absolute stitches, guffawing and snorting and making all sorts of gross comments.

After an excruciating few minutes, the serpent soldiers had finally all passed by. Chhaya Devi lifted her counter and shooed my cousins back out again.

"Haven't you heard about the new serpentine decrees?

It's not safe for us to be fraternizing, just like it's not safe for these little ones to be out and about either! Now, hurry up and get out of here before the snakes come back," the merchant harrumphed, then flung the end of her sari—heavy and clinking with a giant ring of keys—over her shoulder.

My eyes followed the heavy key chain hungrily. I wondered if one of those keys was locking away the moonbeams I needed.

The woman caught my gaze. She shook the gochha of keys noisily at me. "I'm not keeping what you seek here. Locked or unlocked."

I dropped my sweet act, irritation flooding my voice. "I could just threaten you—chew off a limb or something—until you told me."

"You could," the merchant agreed, capping some vials on her counters that were frothing with purple mist. "But I don't think you will."

"How do you know that?" I was genuinely surprised.

"You may be a rakkhoshi, and I may be a human," the merchant said, "but we're not that different, you and I."

"Humans and rakkhosh are sworn enemies." I gave a loud snort. "Always have been, always will be."

"That's what the serpents want us to believe." Chhaya Devi shrugged. "It might behoove you to wonder why, and why they're so nervous about us joining forces. In fact, in a different life, and if it weren't illegal, I bet you and I could even be friends."

"I don't need any friends." I don't know why, but there was something in Chhaya Devi's words that struck at me, somewhere deep inside. And I didn't like how they made me feel.

The woman didn't seem bothered by my attitude but kept fiddling with her misting vials. "We all need friends. Even if they're different than we are."

"Enough with the philosophizing! You haven't told me anything about the"—I lowered my voice until I was barely whispering—"moonbeams."

Now it was Chhaya Devi's turn to change her mood. "Who said I knew anything about anything like that?" she snapped. But her left eye was twitching, and her hands were fiddling, so I knew she must be lying. Humans were so bad at hiding things.

"There must be something you want—something I could give you in exchange for some information about the . . . thing I'm looking for?" I wheedled.

The woman took in a breath and then let it out slowly. "This is for the resistance?" she whispered. Her breath smelled like cardamom, cloves, and strong black tea.

I tried to keep my voice pitched as low as hers and not pause at all when I lied. I also maintained eye contact the whole time. "Of course! It's for the resistance."

Hah! I hadn't gotten an A+ last year in Prevarication class for nothing!

Chhaya Devi studied me, as if considering whether to believe me. She shook her head, muttering, and I wondered if the voices in her brain were arguing with each other. Finally, she gave a scratch at her salt-and-pepper bun and sighed.

"Well, if you can get me an item that I have been searching for," the merchant said, "then maybe—just *maybe*—I can give you information about what you seek."

"What item? What is it?" I thumped my palm on her glass display case, leaving a handprint in the dust. "Anything, I'll get it for you."

The woman distractedly jingled the keys on the end of her sari yet again. "Shonar kathi–rupor kathi," she said.

My hearts—all three of them—twisted in my chest. I knew exactly what she was talking about, of course, but I didn't want to believe it. Instead, I stuck a finger in my ear and rooted around, as if it was waxy and I couldn't hear too well. "I'm sorry, what did you say?"

"She wants the golden and silver sticks!" Mawla shouted,

practically exploding my eardrums. "Those ones that do the magic tricks!"

Deembo's eyes shone as she and Kawla embraced each other and jumped around. Of course they *would* be excited at the mention of those dratted sticks.

I stopped pretending I hadn't heard her. "How do you know I can get them?" I hoped that Chhaya Devi didn't know the current owner of those magical sticks.

"If you can't get them, who can?" the Merchant of Shadows drawled, winking at me. "Now, if you can get me those magic kathis, then maybe I can tell you where you might find the . . . object . . . you seek."

"What if the owner doesn't want to give the golden and silver sticks to me?" I tried my best to keep the desperation out of my voice. "What if I don't want to ask the owner to give them to me?"

"Well, then, I guess I won't be helping you." The Merchant of Shadows started putting her vials and bottles away in some cushioned cases, already packing up for the night.

"Isn't there another way?" My voice took on a pleading note.

"We're done here, young demoness." Chhaya Devi's voice snapped with the same intensity with which she slammed shut her cases.

"Stop. Wait!" I begged, but the woman had already pulled out a long metal rod with which she was pulling down the corrugated metal that covered her stall's opening.

I backed up to stop myself getting beaned in the head by the rolling steel.

"I told you what you needed to bring me if you want my help." The Merchant of Shadows bit off each word as it left her mouth. "Now, stop dithering and go get it!" With that she pulled down the metal shutter in front of her store and disappeared.

I stood in the dusty market lane, staring at the closed shop shutter. Finally, with a sigh, I gestured to Kawla, Mawla, and Deembo that it was time to go.

"So who has those golden and silver sticks she was talking about?" Kumi asked as we made our way back to the helicocrocs.

"It's not good." I swatted at my gleefully prancing little relations. "It's not good at all."

"Not good like running-out-of-your-favorite-moisturizer not good?" asked Aakash.

Kumi rolled her eyes. "Shut up, flyboy."

"You do you, girl. But seriously, you should think about taking better care of that dry skin," said Akash. The boy's crows were flying in circles by his horned head, like some kind of makeshift crown. At the sight, Kumi's crocodiles snapped their jaws.

"Well, then?" prompted Kumi, ignoring the flyboy. "Who has those sticks?"

"It's someone terrible," I groaned, pushing my palms into the sides of my head. "Someone awful."

Kawla, Mawla, and Deembo, who obviously had other feelings about what lay before us, continued whooping and dancing.

"Who is it?" asked Kumi and Aakash together.

I gave them a scathing look, meant to curdle the very milk of their souls. "Oh, just my completely bonkers mother!"

CHAPTER 8

I'm Not Proud About Fooling My Mom, but It Had to Be Done, Okay?

I know you're supposed to give a lot of leeway to legends. Especially legends who have nobly suffered for an even nobler cause. But it's hard when that legend is your own mother. It's doubly hard when that legend is as straight up wacko as Ai-Ma.

"Oh, Ai-Ma! Ai-Ma!" I called out as soon as I'd gotten through the magic barrier the government had placed permanently around my mother's cave complex. "It's your daughter, Pinki, come home to have some of your, uh, delicious cooking! And I've brought your nieces and nephew too!"

Somehow, I'd been able to convince Professor Ravan to let me travel home without my watch-rakkhosh the next morning, and this time I'd even gotten proper permission to bring my cousins. When we'd gotten back to school from seeing Chhaya Devi, I'd told him that having Kumi and Aakash with me would just make it harder to convince Ai-Ma to give me the magic golden and silver sticks. I'd painted a picture of an unreasonable and angry mother broken by the violences of the past—a rakkhoshi of sharp teeth and raging emotions who had to be tiptoed around in the manner that one might approach a rabid hippopotamus.

"Pinkoo! Arré, Pinki shona! Oh, my stinky, shutki fish chop! I wasn't expecting you this weekend!" When she heard my voice, my mother galumphed out to meet me at full speed. Because I was expecting it, she didn't entirely knock me over, but almost. Her arms and legs were beanpole long, her lips rubbery and dry, her salt-and-pepper hair thinning, and her rheumy eyes overflowing with delight.

"Careful, Ai-Ma!" I pointed at the glowing green wall flickering at the cave entrance. "Don't get near the barrier or you'll get zapped!"

"Oh, don't you worry about me, my dear golden beetle dum-dum! I've been living with that silly barrier for long enough to know its tricks!" Ai-Ma picked me up in her firehose arms and cradled me to her bony chest. "Oh, my sweet

pixie fart-bomb lollipop! What brings you home to your lonely, old Ai-Ma?"

As my mother squashed and gushed over me, I gritted my teeth and mumbled, "Oh, I just missed you!" I tried not to puke as she covered me with slobbery kisses, squeezing me so hard I was practically suffocating.

Okay, yes, clearly, I'd been not entirely truthful to Professor Ravan about my mother's mental state. Even though Ai-Ma had been scarred by her years in serpent prison, it wasn't in the way that most of rakkhosh-kind thought. The big, embarrassing secret I'd been successfully keeping from all the Kingdom was that my revolutionary, freedom-fighting mother had become totally unhinged by her time in snake jail. Whether it was whatever she endured as a prisoner, or the fact that my father had also been arrested and died in custody, something had scrambled in Ai-Ma's brain during those terrible years. Instead of making her scary and revengeful, though, it had made her extra loopy and wildly loving. Which was ridiculously embarrassing when you were supposed to be a fierce rakkhoshi.

I could never have kept it all secret, of course, if not for the Empire of Serpent Overlords putting Ai-Ma under permanent cave arrest. While it might seem odd that I went off to school and left my mother all alone in such a state, nobody worried all that much about me when I was just a little demon-ling left alone while my rebel parents were in snake prison. My aunt had been in school herself, too young to take care of me, and I'd been left to the care of a circulating bunch of my parents' revolutionary friends—none of whom really wanted to babysit a teeny, grumpy rakkhoshi. I was scared, and small, and alone. For years. It's all great and glorious to fight for your nation's freedom, I guess, but not that great when you're the kid left behind and forgotten.

"What are they feeding you at that school?" Ai-Ma set

me down, only to poke a long finger into my ribs, like she was testing to see if I was cooked through. "Not enough I see! Well, let me get some khichuri on the stove! Your favorite—with the crunchy earthworms on top?"

I stepped over some rotting animal carcasses in the middle of the cave floor and nodded with fake enthusiasm. "Sounds delicious."

"And what about you three?" Ai-Ma bent down now to scoop Kawla, Mawla, and Deembo into her warty embrace. As she nuzzled them, her long chin hairs tickled their bat ears, and they giggled like idiots. "Are you ready for some nice home-cooked food?"

"Oh yeth, Ai-Ma, pleasth!" cooed Kawla. "You're cooking'th the bee's knees!"

Of course my cousins thought Ai-Ma's cooking was delicious. News flash: It wasn't. I caught grumpy Mawla placing a wet kiss on Ai-Ma's withered cheek. And Deembo—ugh, that egg-brain rakkhoshi was practically melting in Ai-Ma's embrace, whining and licking and wiggling her furry body in delight. It made something burn in my chest to see them getting the love I never got at their age. When I was that young, I was putting myself to sleep hungry and lonely most nights, not sure if I'd ever see my parents again.

While Kawla, Mawla, Deembo, and Ai-Ma cooed over

each other, I looked around Ai-Ma's cave complex. It was a disastrous mess, of course, which was as it should have been. Ai-Ma was unhinged, but she wasn't so out of touch with reality as to spend her time cleaning. I saw evidence of her recent meals—rotting vegetable peelings and animals who had either wandered in or been magically lured by Ai-Ma through the serpent's barrier—a wall that only she couldn't cross. I didn't, however, see anything else suspicious. Except . . . What was that? I picked up the soft object from the floor and turned it over: a raven-black feather the size of my forearm.

"Ai-Ma, you aren't still keeping human pets, are you?" I asked in what I hoped was a casual tone, my eyes on the delicate feather. I was sure it was from a pakkhiraj horse, a favorite steed of princely humans. "It's such a bad habit, especially if they're not for eating. I mean, there's that new Serpentine Decree Number 1947, not to mention gossip from the neighbors."

Ai-Ma straightened up to give me a drooly mouthed glare. Kawla, Mawla, and Deembo tumbled from her arms and landed with soft thuds at her feet.

"Pets? Who said anything about pets?" she asked innocently. Then she turned to Kawla, Mawla, and Deembo, handing them a fistful of animal bones and the eyeball of an unidentifiable creature. "Go play some jacks, my sweetie num-nums, my evil little monsters."

My mother and I stepped away from the kids and kept talking in lowered voices.

"Ai-Ma, don't lie." I waggled the feather at her and started looking around the cave even more. "Did you lure in a human who rode a black pakkhiraj horse? Where are they? Do you know what kind of trouble you're going to get into if the serpents find them here?"

It was another one of Ai-Ma's embarrassing quirks. After I left for school, Ai-Ma got lonely. She couldn't leave her cave because of the serpent's cave-arrest barrier, so she decided to lure in not just food but pets. Only, instead of normal species of pets, like tarantulas or crocodiles or jackals, that old nutjob of a mother of mine decided to keep human pets—lost storytellers and runaway merchants' daughters and whatever other unsuspecting humans she magically lured through the barrier. Unlike any normal rakkhosh, Ai-Ma didn't keep these pets to eat; she kept them to dote on, cuddle, and adore. Even worse, she always let them go after some period of time, with gifts and clothes and open invitations to visit.

"Why are you so curious about my pets, Daughter?" Ai-Ma gave me a hurt look. Then she sniffed long and wet, a booger trembling at one nostril like a physical manifestation of her hurt feelings. "Are you spying for the snakes? Have they gotten to you? Asked you to spy on your poor old mother?"

My hearts froze. How could half-off-her-gourd Ai-Ma see what my teachers couldn't? "What are you talking about?" I asked in what I hoped was a not-guilty-at-all voice. "I'm the daughter of rakkhosh-kind's most famous freedom fighters! Why would the serpents hire me as a spy?"

Ai-Ma squinted at me, pulling absentmindedly at her booger. Then she abruptly turned around and went to get something from a dingy corner of her cave. "For years, they left me alone. But they've been paying a lot of unplanned visits lately, threatening to rough me up. And now see what they've sent me! Without you home, I can't even understand what they say!"

A knife-edge of guilt shot through me. The snakes had been threatening Ai-Ma? Before I could ask more about it, she dumped a bunch of papers into my lap, multipage citations filled with tiny printed writing. They were all stamped with an official Empire of the Serpent Overlords seal and covered in scary phrases like *private domicile* and *past inappropriate contact* and *future human-rakkhosh relations* on them.

"The snakes know you've been keeping human pets?" I finally asked, looking up at my mother. "This is really serious, Ai-Ma! The punishment for breaking that decree is death!"

"Oh, don't act innocently worried about me! They never caught me with any humans here!" Ai-Ma's eyes and nose were pouring out her sadness now in thick rivers onto the dusty cave floor. "The one comfort an old woman had, and the dratted snakes make it illegal! And now my own daughter is spying for them! For shame!"

"I'm not . . . um, spying for anyone!" I protested, sidestepping a muddy stream created by Ai-Ma's bodily fluids.

"Ho-ho!" With one giant step of her spindly legs, Ai-Ma was on me. "I know you too well for you to lie to me! You *are* spying for them! That's why you've come, isn't it? Not to eat my khichuri but to see if I'm still keeping human pets! Well, tell your serpentine masters I'm not! I'm not, I'm not, I'm not, all right?"

Now, if Ai-Ma knew me too well for me to lie to her, the same was true in the reverse. All of Ai-Ma's denials felt a little too much—a little too high-pitched, a little too forced.

"Ai-Ma, this is serious." I dropped my voice low. "If you've still got someone here, you've got to get rid of them.

Now! These snakes aren't kidding around with this decree stuff!"

"Oh, don't act like you're so worried about me, dumpling butt!" Ai-Ma pointed a giant finger in my face. Then she grabbed some of the citations and threw them in the air. "Go tell your snaky friends to stop bothering an old woman!"

I swatted at the papers that were falling all around me now like so much bureaucratic rain. How was I going to convince Ai-Ma I wasn't working with the snakes? Even though I, well, was? Obviously, the best thing to do was tell her some version of the truth. Another excellent lesson I'd learned in Prevarication class last year.

"Look, I went to see Chhaya Devi last night, the Merchant of Shadows. Because I heard she might know about some"—I lowered my voice to a whisper—"stolen moonbeams."

Ai-Ma lifted her head, her three long chin hairs quivering with agitation. "You're not saying what I think you're saying, my poo-poo dung drop?"

I had to say it. I had to own it. Or else I'd never get Ai-Ma to stop suspecting me. "Working with the resistance? Trying to beat the serpents by finding the stolen moonbeams and stopping them from building their superweapon?" I nodded, making an effort not to break eye contact. "Yeah, I am. A freedom fighter dedicated to rakkhosh liberation, that's me."

"Oh, my golden fart-bomb baby girl!" sniffed Ai-Ma, that same long booger flailing around as she grabbed me and squeezed me against her. "You're carrying on our family tradition! Your father would be so proud!"

"How could you think I wouldn't follow in your and Babu's footsteps!" I squirmed out of her embrace, shaking out my hair over my shoulders. "You all taught me how important it was to work with the resistance! Why, my entire childhood was shaped by it!"

This whole lie about being a rebel freedom fighter was sounding so believable on my lips, I was almost starting to buy it myself. Really, I deserved that A+ I'd gotten in Prevarication.

In the meantime, Ai-Ma sat down heavily beside me and began to cry. I awkwardly patted her back. "Are you crying because you're thinking about Babu?"

"No, because I don't want to give up my scrawny human babies! Ai-Ma wants to cuddle and coo with her sweetie-pie pets!" And then my mother placed her giant head on my shoulder and began to boo-hoo in earnest, making embarrassing squawking and burbling noises. Leaving her

siblings to play with some dubious-looking animal skel-
etons, Deembo crawled over and cuddled in my weeping
mother's lap. As usual, the little rakkhoshi was sucking on
an egg for comfort, and her fingers were tracing the edges
of her raised neck scar.

Ai-Ma kept crying as I just sat there making incoher-
ent comforting noises. Kawla and Mawla came over too.
They looked up at me, waiting for me to fix the situation
as they scratched and picked at various orifices.

"Tell me the truth, Ai-Ma." I kept my voice low and
calm. If she had a hidden human being here, then I knew
exactly where the shonar kathi–rupor kathi were too. "Have
you really gotten rid of all of your pets?"

"Well, maybe not all." Ai-Ma lifted her wet face, finally
snorting in that dangling booger, then wiped her eyes and
nose with the end of her sari. "But she actually came to me
on her own! So pretty please can I keep her?"

"You know you can't," I said sternly. "What if the serpents were to come check again and find a human being
here? What would happen to you?"

"Oh, pfft!" Ai-Ma made a rude buzzing noise with her
lips, scatting spittle everywhere. Deembo, who was still in
her lap and caught most of the shower, giggled. "I don't care
about any of that."

"Well, you should, because after they take you away, you know who they'll come for next?" I pointed at myself.

"No, they won't! Those snaky poopers!" Ai-Ma's voice was thick with shock.

"Of course they will! And then I'd be really following in your footsteps—right to jail!" I made my voice tremble. I knew I was playing dirty, but she hadn't left me with any choice.

"All right, stinky beetle bum, I'll take you to her," Ai-Ma said quietly. She lifted Deembo down from her lap and stood up.

I didn't like to see her looking so defeated, so I took up her giant hand in mine on impulse. "You're doing the right thing!"

Ai-Ma looked sadly down at our joined hands. "Promise me you'll keep my human pet safe with you until you find her family. I think it might not be safe for her out there."

I sighed, knowing that rakkhosh promises were near impossible to break. "Sure, Ai-Ma," I muttered. "I promise."

At the time, I figured, how hard could it be to find one silly human girl's family? If only I'd known then what I know now.

Leaving the cousins to chase some kitchen cockroaches,

I followed my mother through a hidden trapdoor and down the stone steps to the cave complex's basement chambers. As I walked, I tried to make sense of all my darn *feelings*. It didn't feel good to have to fool Ai-Ma, but on the other hand, I really wanted to learn how to control my power. And for that, I needed to play along with Sesha. I needed to get the shonar kathi–rupor kathi to Chhaya Devi, get the Moon Mother's stolen moonbeams to the snake boy, and finally get the lessons I so desperately needed. And what Ai-Ma didn't know wouldn't hurt her, I supposed. I had to keep my eyes on the prize. I needed to learn how to control my power. And that was all that mattered.

At the bottom of the stone staircase was the misty underground River of Dreams that was Ai-Ma's water supply while she was under cave arrest. At the edge of the shore was a whole line of clay pots of various sizes that made me pause a little—why did Ai-Ma need so many? And then I saw what else stood beside the pots—a powerful black pakkhi-raj horse. When it saw us, the animal snorted, then flexed its wings, as if guarding something precious that lay before it. In the dim silvery light, I could make out what it was—a wispy slip of a girl, fast asleep on a wide couch covered in delicate webbing and embroidered silver bedding. She was

dressed in a gossamer silver sari, along with tinkly earrings and delicate silver bangles and ankle bells. Her breathing was quiet, her hands folded daintily over her chest, and her dark hair spread around like in a fairy tale. I hated her right away.

But as my eyes focused away from the sleeping girl and her watchful horse, my hearts started to race. There they were—the keys to finding the moonbeams! At the girl's feet was a long, shining silver stick, and at her head, a glowing golden one. It was the force field created between the two swordlike sticks that kept her in her enchanted sleep. Of course, I'd known this all along. The shonar kathi–rupor kathi were what Ai-Ma used to keep her pets from waking when she wasn't with them. My hands itched to steal them and run, but I knew I couldn't.

"She's such a dumpling, dear; I hate to wake her." Ai-Ma looked like she was going to start crying again.

"You have to get her out of here," I reminded my mother, trying to keep my voice stern.

"What if the snake patrols catch you, Daughter?" Ai-Ma wrung her long fingers in worry.

"Look at my face, Ai-Ma, and please believe me when I say I'm not afraid."

Ai-Ma took out her dirty reading glasses and peered through the one uncracked lens at my face. She focused on my chin, my left fang, and my right nostril before putting the glasses down with a nod. "You've always been so brave. I'm so proud of you, my beautiful fart flower."

Again, I felt that pang of terrible guilt like I had experienced with Professor Ravan. Cripes! What a horror show to feel all these noble feelings! Like some kind of pathetic human!

I pushed my emotions down with impatience. Then, with three swift steps, I approached the bed, grabbing the unwieldy silver stick in my right hand and the golden stick in my left. I swapped their positions, putting the golden stick at the girl's feet and the silver at her head. As I did so, I said, "Golden stick, silver stick, release this sleeper from your tricks." A jolt of power shot through me as I said the magic words.

In the next moment, the sleeping girl's eyes shot open. Her eyes were dark, like her hair, but they glowed with internal light. I started at a shape I thought I saw in them. No, that couldn't be right. I blinked, backing up, as the girl yawned, stretched, and then swung her legs around to stand up with a surprising sprightliness.

"My dear, sweet gumdrop girlie, Chandni, let me introduce you. This is my darling dumpling daughter, Pinki," my mother was saying. "You will be going with her. She will help you find your family."

"Do I have to go, Demon Auntie?" the girl said in her soft and tinkly voice.

Yagh! What kind of a prisoner didn't want to be freed?

"I'm afraid so, my cockroach cupcake," Ai-Ma said sadly. "It is not safe for me to have you here. The serpents are getting suspicious."

"In that case, I will of course go!" Chandni said

immediately, grasping Ai-Ma's hands. "I would never want to put you in danger! You've been so wonderful to me!"

Again, I had to choke back a gag. This girl was worse than those dainty heroines from stories who sang opera while they scrubbed floors.

"And as a gift, a thank-you for all the happiness you have given me, I present you with—"

Before Ai-Ma could finish, I jumped in. "These precious gold and silver kathi."

At Ai-Ma's squawk of protest, I hissed, "You won't need them anymore anyway! No more pets, remember?"

Ai-Ma sighed deeply, nodding. Then she took the sticks from my hands and, after reciting a shrinking enchantment, and handed them to Chandni in a smaller, manageable size. "Yes, please take my shonar kathi–rupor kathi."

As Ai-Ma and her pet swayed back and forth in a hug fest, I gave myself a mental pat on the back. Yes, I may have promised to get Chandni to her parents, but I'd also managed to secure the golden and silver sticks without Ai-Ma getting suspicious. They were in the girl's possession now, but I wasn't worried about convincing her to give them to me. And if I couldn't convince her, hey, I was about double her height and ten times as strong.

"Now, you both must go," Ai-Ma crooned. "Don't worry, dear lamplight girl, my Pinki will keep you safe until you get home. You will be great friends, I know it."

Chandni said something simpering and thankful that I promptly blocked out.

"Don't get the idea that I'm anything like my mother," I muttered to the girl when Ai-Ma wasn't listening. "We're not friends, and we're not going to be friends. In fact, I hate humans."

"Good to know," the girl said with a sticky-sweet smile. "In that case, we can be like sisters."

Rotten tarantula teeth! She was the worst. As I walked away from her, I tried to forget what I'd seen reflected in her eyes. It had to be a mistake.

Eyes on the prize, Pinki, I told myself. *No distractions.*

But as I walked back up the slippery secret stairs, I knew that what I had seen in Chandni's eyes. It had been nothing other than a reflection of the moon.

CHAPTER 9

In Which My Mom's Goodie-Two-Shoes Houseguest and I Almost Die a Horrible Midair Death

I feel like an idiot," I groused, running a finger across my totally dull and square teeth. I was glad I didn't have access to a mirror or any other reflective surface. I really didn't want to see what I looked like without my horns, fangs, and talons. The memory of having seen it once was enough.

"You look lovely, Didi," Chandni said again over her shoulder.

Blargh. Every time the girl respectfully used the word for older sister to refer to me, it made me gassy. I wished yet again I hadn't promised Ai-Ma I'd keep this ninny safe until I delivered her home. Every cell in me itched to stew her up for lunch.

"Your idea of lovely is shaped by your twisted human beauty standards." I tightened my grip around her waist. I couldn't believe I was flying again. My head spun from airsickness. "Power is lovely. Strength is lovely. Looking like a declawed potato—not lovely."

I was seated behind the girl on her black pakkhiraj horse, a moody animal whose name was apparently Raat. It was like the huge creature had known how much I hated flying—neighing and rearing up and trying to bite me when I went to mount him. The stupid thing had calmed right down when Chandni had approached him.

"He's very spirited," Chandni had explained, stroking his dark neck. "He's not even mine but borrowed from a friend."

"What friend?" I'd asked, but the girl had just laughed that annoying, tinkly laugh and let the flying horse soar into the sky. I almost screamed but stopped myself just in time.

To make matters worse, I was not only flying but flying disguised as a human. It had been Ai-Ma who'd insisted that I travel incognito, using my own warning to her against me. "You're right, my Pinki; if the snakes catch a rakkhoshi and human traveling together, there will be all goobledy-goo to pay!"

"Why do I have to disguise myself? Why can't we dress *her* up as a rakkhoshi?" I'd griped, pointing at Chandni.

"That's a good one, cousin-lady!" Mawla laughed. "But Miss Chandni don't look scary!"

Deembo and Kawla giggled in agreement, annoying me even further.

"What do you want me to do, dumpling butt?" Ai-Ma spread out her hands. "Stick some glued-on horns and fangs upon Chandni? Don't be silly, fairy fart! You're excellent at human transformation. And you have the top grades in Honors Transformation to prove it!"

My mother was right, of course. I was downright spectacular at human transformation. But that didn't mean I enjoyed looking like some round-faced, fangless, hornless *person*.

But there was no way for me to convince Ai-Ma that I wasn't in any real danger from the serpent patrols, not without admitting that I was working on the sly for Sesha. So I'd transformed into a human and set off into the sky with her pet. Or ex-pet. Or whatever. I'd also decided to leave Kawla, Mawla, and Deembo behind at Ai-Ma's. Deembo had been acting stranger than usual—which was saying a lot—since the day we'd met Sesha in the woods, and I wondered if a long weekend with her wacko but loving auntie wasn't exactly what she needed. Besides, I had no real desire to travel around the countryside anymore with the little ones, putting them at risk.

"I'll be back by the end of the weekend, and we'll all go back to school together, okay?" I'd told the sobbing Deembo. The tiny terror was attached to my knees again with a death grip and was so upset she was making the ground under our feet wobble and sway. "You'll have so much fun here catching rats with Ai-Ma!"

But all the girl did was wail. She didn't even calm down when Kawla and Mawla blew snot bubbles from their noses and batted them around like they were playing volleyball. Finally, Ai-Ma just scooped Deembo into her long arms and let her keep crying.

It was an awkward and earsplitting departure. "I'll come back soon, as soon as I . . . uh . . . make one quick stop and then get Chandni to her family," I shouted over Deembo's wails.

"Miss Chandni, please fly true," Mawla had said, his gaze so full of admiration for Ai-Ma's wispy pet that he looked like his eyes had been replaced with hearts. "With all our souls, we will miss you!"

"You're stho good, you're stho sthweet! I totally want to eat your feet!" Kawla had lisped, beaming with pleasure as Chandni bent to kiss each of the little ones on the head.

Even Deembo stopped crying long enough to hand the girl an egg from her pocket, which Chandni took with great gentleness. "Thank you, and I'm sorry for separating you from your cousin-sister," the girl had singsonged. "I hope to see you all very soon."

I already hated Chandni—that delicate glow, that tinkling laugh, those luminous eyes. But she made me hate her even more during the flying-horse ride to the bazaar. I'd had to tell Chandni at least part of the actual truth of my mission—that the Merchant of Shadows wanted the shonar kathi–rupor kathi in exchange for information important to the resistance.

"The resistance?" Chandni had breathed. "Of course! I'm happy to give up Ai-Ma's gift if it will help the cause of freedom!"

It had been too easy. The girl was so good, she made me want to puke.

"Didi, your mother is wonderful—kind and funny," Chandni told me over her shoulder. Her voice was delicate, yet it carried remarkably well on the wind. "I couldn't have asked for a better captor."

Why the suck-up girl should have been asking for any kind of captor, I couldn't tell you.

"She used to be a normal rakkhoshi, once." I moved

my head to avoid getting a nose full of Chandni's rose-and-honey-scented hair. "But two years in serpent jail for revolutionary activities kind of scrambled her brains."

"Your father died in prison too." Chandni was stating a fact, not asking me a question. Clearly, she'd heard all this already from Ai-Ma.

I stared for a minute at Raat's muscular black wings beating hard and fast through the air, tiny specks of human and rakkhosh villages below. I gulped, trying not to calculate how far we were from the ground or how fast we must have been flying. I closed my eyes but could still see the ground in my mind. I tried to calm down, telling myself this was my country. My home. The place for which one of my parents had given his life, and the other, her sanity. I let the rushing wind flick away the traitorous water from my eyes.

"It's not just them who had it bad, you know," I snapped, hating myself for all these darn *feelings*. "I don't know why Babu and Ai-Ma ever even adopted me from that well of dark energy. They didn't have time for me. They didn't care."

"That can't be true," Chandni began.

"You don't know what you're talking about!" I growled.

"Your parents were arrested during that raid—on the serpentine armory? The one that went so terribly wrong?" Chandni kind of tilted her head, and the horse changed direction midair even as the animal's reins lay limp in her hands. It was like the pakkhiraj and she had a telepathic connection. Gag. She probably talked to bluebirds too.

"Their freedom-fighting friends took turns to make sure I didn't starve. But they weren't exactly substitute parents." The memory was still sharp and painful this many years later. "Let's just say it's not nice to realize your parents love a cause more than they love you."

Chandni was quiet for a moment before speaking. When she did, her voice sounded a little choked. "It is hard when your parents' lives are larger than you, when they make choices different than you would. But it doesn't mean you can't find your own way. Anyway, you must be proud of the choices they made. I mean, you're following in your mother and father's footsteps."

"Oh, right, no, sure. Of course!" I backpedaled quickly. I'd almost forgotten to keep up my lie about working for the revolution. I'd gotten so caught up in all those memories and gooey feelie-weelies, I'd almost blown my entire cover as a freedom fighter. Honesty was the absolute *worst*. "No doubt they did so many things right. So right! They were great role models. Just took me a while to realize it. That's why I'm joining the revolution, after all!"

That was anything but the truth, naturally. When Babu

died, and Ai-Ma came home so damaged, I'd become even more resentful of anything to do with the struggle for liberation. Nothing good came of thirsting for some big, noble cause like freedom. I figured it was better to keep my head down and look out for myself. But I didn't need to open up my giant mouth and tell this human-ling any of that.

Then, out of nowhere, there was a jerking in the atmosphere that almost threw us both out of the saddle. It was as if the very air around us was reacting to my upset emotions.

"What was that?" Chandni exclaimed. "A storm?"

"Couldn't be, there are hardly any clouds in the sky." I gripped her waist a bit tighter. "It was nothing. We must have both been falling asleep."

But then it happened again. The air felt like it was shaking all around us.

"I'm not asleep now," Chandni said. "And I wasn't before either."

"No." I felt bile rising sharply in my throat. "Neither am I."

I could see nothing but some egrets flying by, but still I shouted out, "Who's there? Who's doing this? Come out where we can see you!"

But our enemy wasn't anything visible. Or anything that could answer us. Yet again, the atmosphere shook, and with a ripping sound, everything around us seemed to shift.

"What's happening?" Chandni yelled, keeping it together tolerably well for a human. "How can someone be tearing the sky?"

I didn't know either. It was as if some giant rakkhosh were shaking a globe inside which we were only play figurines. Raat whinnied in panic, skittering a hard left, his legs flailing as his wings tried to catch purchase on the wind. Chandni started to slip off the side of the horse, but I grabbed her elbow, helping her re-secure her hold on the horse's reins. But even as she cooed to the pakkhiraj, trying to steady him, the horse fell more out of control, plummeting downward in a free-fall death spiral!

"We're gonna die!" I wailed. I'll admit, I was not at my coolest or most collected.

"Raat! Boy! Up!" Chandni screamed. "It's all right, be calm and listen to my voice! Up! UP!" That last *up* was shrieked so loudly, I didn't think anyone hearing her voice could feel particularly calm. I certainly didn't.

Raat had barely regained some altitude, at least coming out of his free fall, when there was an earsplitting ripping sound, like a giant piece of paper being torn. It was as if everything around us were getting rent apart. As if the universe itself were a crudely painted stage backdrop now tearing under a callous actor's toes, and we mere stick figures drawn on it.

"What is going on?" I shouted. For whatever illogical reason, I felt furious at Ai-Ma's ridiculous houseguest, like this were her fault. Before I'd met the girl, the sky had never torn apart.

"It's got to stop soon!" Chandni cried. "It's got to!"

But she was wrong. Whatever was happening wasn't stopping. Right in front of our eyes, a flock of panicking kingfishers seemed to get caught by something in the air. They screamed like they were being ripped apart by invisible claws, and then they were gone. The place they disappeared was but a few feet from us, a magical tear in the sky. One by one, as each colorful bird flew into the atmospheric hole, it got decimated. Feathers and beaks flew everywhere. The death screams of the birds were seriously disturbing, as I knew that mere chance separated our fates from theirs.

I tried very hard not to bellow in terror again. I can't guarantee that I succeeded.

The horse too had no ears for anything but its own panic. He whinnied and cried, losing and then gaining altitude, frothing at the mouth and rolling his panicky eyes. As he—and we—half flew and half fell, I felt the air around us trembling more. Below, on the far-closer-than-before ground, brown blobs of land and blue bodies of water seemed to be shifting, like marbles on a giant checkers board. I watched as dots of land slid past each other and rearranged themselves into different patterns. But how could that be? How could any of this be?

"The land itself shifts!" I screamed. "As if it's adrift!"

The fact that I was rhyming was a true testament to how freaked out I was. I was lucky there weren't any snake spies around to hear.

Then, as suddenly as everything had begun shifting, it all stopped again. With a zipping sound, the air around us moved and settled, coming back together in a different pattern than it had been in before. Raat was able to regain control of his flying and was soon flapping his wings as normally as he had before. The ground below, which only seconds ago had seemed to be in motion, now was again still. Only, everything seemed to be in a slightly different place than it had been.

"What kind of magic was that?" I hissed. I'd never seen anything like it in all my days. My stomach churned with acid, and my chest burned with terror.

"I don't know." Chandni's voice was shaky. "Nothing good, that's for sure."

Raat just whinnied pathetically, which wasn't much help at all.

"You're all right, boy," cooed Chandni, patting the beast's sweaty neck. "It's all over now."

But was it? I wasn't sure at all.

That's when, out of absolutely nowhere, another one of those serpentine decrees appeared in midair.

Empire of the Serpent Overlords Decree #1619
All Lands and Bodies of Water in
the Kingdom Beyond Seven Oceans and
Thirteen Rivers Will Forevermore
Be Unfixed and Moveable.
This Geographic Reorientation by Order of the
Serpentine Governor-General.
Don't Even Think About Protesting Because
This Land Is Our Land to Do with What
We Will.
Have a Good Day.
#ComplianceOverDefiance

"Unfixed and moveable?" I breathed, trying to wrap my head around what that meant.

"It wasn't enough to come up from their undersea

kingdom and invade our land, then take its treasures and natural resources." Chandni sounded more serious than I'd ever heard her sound. "Now they want to turn the land itself against those who live on it."

"But how can they do it?" My stomach was still halfway up my throat. "That kind of magic is so advanced."

"Rulers afraid of losing their power will do any sort of dark magic to keep the reins of control," Chandni said in her overly wise way.

I thought about how the land and water below us had shifted, how the air around us had seemed to tear apart and then repair itself in a slightly different orientation. If this kept happening, how would anyone move from one part of the kingdom to another? I remembered what Chhaya Devi had said about snakes wanting to keep rakkhosh and humans apart. Maybe she was right.

"I wonder if this moving-land stuff is the snakes trying to control the movement of rakkhosh and people," I said. "Maybe they're trying to divide and conquer those who live in the Kingdom Beyond, make sure we don't band up against them."

"Why would you care?" Chandni asked. "I thought you hated humans."

"I do," I said, remembering my words to her when we

were still at Ai-Ma's. After what we'd just been through together, it seemed like a long time ago. Still, it wasn't my brand to back down. "I hate you all."

I was incredibly annoyed when Chandni just laughed at my words.

CHAPTER 10

Make New Friends, Don't Eat the Old, One Is . . . Yada, Yada, You Know the Rest

There it is!" Chandni pointed down toward the ground. "The bazaar!"

"Finally." After our near-death experience, I was pretty relieved to be landing on solid ground.

Raat landed to the side of Chhaya Devi's stall, and I leaped off his muscular back before Chandni could even settle the animal.

"I got this." I grabbed the golden and silver sticks from the girl, muttering the enlarging enchantment so that they grew long like swords again. I crisscrossed them over my back, where they magically attached, without need for any scabbard or holder. I had to admit, they looked very cool.

"Leave this dangerous stuff to me," I told Chandni with a wave. "I wouldn't want you breaking a nail or anything."

The afternoon was blistering, with the midday sun high and merciless in the sky as I began striding over to the Merchant of Shadows's shop. Luckily, that meant the bazaar was fairly empty. Few humans ventured out at this time of day, preferring to hide their weak bodies indoors, taking their after-lunch naps. Which was lucky for me, because it meant I had no audience.

Chhaya Devi peered out suspiciously from behind her counter at me, a foul-smelling bottle of who knows what in her hands. "Yes, miss, can I help you?"

Since it was too much effort to change my human features back to my own rakkhoshi ones, I ducked into the shade of her awning, then spoke in my normal voice, hoping she would recognize me. "It's me, the fire-demoness Pinki. Come with these for you." I held out the shonar kathi–rupor kathi but pulled them away when the shopkeeper tried to touch them.

"Not yet," I tut-tutted. "These are yours after you tell me about the stolen . . . thingamajigs I was asking about."

Chhaya Devi put down the stinky flower-scented bottle she'd been fiddling with and gave me a critical look. "You got these sticks from your mother's house, correct?"

"You know I did." I swiped at some sweat beading on

my forehead. I was still getting my sea legs after that awful flight. "Why?"

"Then you should know where it is, the thing you seek." The woman's dark eyes crinkled as she smiled.

"What are you talking about?" I demanded. "You said I had to bring the sticks here first, and then you'd tell me about the moonbeams."

The shopkeeper just stared over my shoulder. In a millisecond, her expression shifted from sly to shocked. I looked back to see that she was looking at Chandni, who had come walking up behind me. I guess I couldn't blame Chhaya Devi for her awe. Chandni looked like some kind of glowing goddess, lit up by the full light of the sun. It was almost as though she were a perfectly reflective surface, bouncing the golden rays off her own silvery body.

But, I mean, seriously. Like, puke.

"Namaskar, Auntie," the girl said to the shopkeeper, her hands in a respectful prayer.

"What foolishness is this?" The older woman practically leaped out from behind her counter. She stared frantically up and down the empty, dry street. "Get out of here this instant! You dim bulb of a demoness, why did you bring her here?"

"I came here to bring you the shonar kathi–rupor kathi,

like you asked." I was baffled by the merchant's panic. "What are you so worried about?"

"Is everything all right?" Chandni's voice was gentle with concern as she stepped under the awning next to me. "You didn't break a nail or anything, Didi?"

I stared at the girl. Was this puny pint of purity actually being *sarcastic* to me?

"You must go now! Go!" Chhaya Devi was wringing her hands, looking as if she was going to cry. "I just wanted you to get her away from your mother, not put her in more danger."

Then the merchant's expression changed from worried to downright terrified. It wasn't too long before I realized why. With trumpets and fanfare, booted stomps and slithery hisses, an entire serpent brigade was marching up the midday market road. They lifted the red dust into the air as they marched so that it looked like they were accompanied by a series of swirling tornados.

"Too late now!" Chhaya Devi pulled Chandni into the darkness of her shop and then tried to tug me back too, but the snake soldiers had seen me. One snake in particular, in front of the brigade, was all too familiar. Sesha.

"Hide those dratted sticks!" hissed the shopkeeper.

Without knowing why, I muttered the shrinking enchantment, then tucked the shonar kathi-rupor kathi behind my back, under the drape of my sari. I put my hand in front of my eyes to protect them from the gritty dust storm created by the serpents' feet.

"So, Pinki! We meet again!" Sesha called out, waving his hand like we were old friends.

The snake boy was flanked by dozens of soldiers, all in their human forms. Even in the punishing sun, they were wearing their heavy Empire uniforms, with hats low over their eyes and sharp-looking weapons over their shoulders. Their appearance was obviously meant to inspire fear and awe, which it mostly did, except for the fact that the soldiers had to break rank to avoid two bullocks sleeping in the middle of the road, not to mention the big plops of poop the animals had left behind, like some kind of checkerboard maze.

"How did you recognize me?" I asked, wishing I could do something about my hideous appearance. I was, after all, still in a human face, which was nothing short of mortifying.

"I would recognize you anywhere," the boy said smoothly. That sent a jolt of something exciting through my stomach. Sesha was wearing a spiffy red army uniform with shining buttons and tons of gleaming medals across the front. When he took off his hat, I saw his hair was swept up in a pomade-shiny back-combed hairdo way fancier than even Aakash's windswept locks.

"Besides, you still look like yourself, just without horns or fangs," the snake boy added, giving me a smart nod and heel click.

"Nice outfit," I said in what I hoped was a casual-enough voice. It was exciting to see him again, but I didn't want him to know that.

"Thanks, I'm fond of the medals." Sesha winked, fingering some of the dangling metal on his chest. As he touched each one, the metal reflected the sun's light, dazzling my eyes with its unnatural glow. What had he even done to earn all that? I wondered.

In the meantime, Chhaya Devi was nervously darting around the shop behind me, picking up and then putting down bottles, all the while muttering to herself, "Where did I put it? Where did it go?" I wasn't sure why she'd lost her mind so much since the last time I'd seen her.

Sesha joined me in the shade beneath Chhaya Devi's shop awning. As soon as he stepped out of the blazing sun, his blinking eyes locked on Chandni, who had been effectively hidden in the shadows.

"You? Here?" he whispered, his voice almost shaking with shock.

"Hello, my *prince*." Chandni's words were laced with that sarcasm again. I felt a spark of jealousy. How was she so darn confident all the time?

I looked from Sesha to her and back again. "You two know each other?"

But no one answered me. In fact, both Sesha and Chandni acted as if I hadn't spoken. I really couldn't care less about Chandni ignoring me, but after his attentiveness two seconds ago, it was insulting to have Sesha blow me off in favor of Ai-Ma's goofy human pet. I mean, what was I, chopped crocodile meat?

"I can't believe you're here," Sesha said. "I thought you'd be with your little friend."

"I don't even know where he is." Chandni's lips were pursed tight and her eyes narrowed. "But if you're so obsessed with him, then maybe *you* should go hang out with him."

"Well, you've obviously been busy," Sesha accused. "My spies tell me you've been up to your tricks."

What in the multiverse were they talking about? My eyes shot from one speaker to the other like I was watching a Ping-Pong match. Only, it was a Ping-Pong match in which I couldn't even see the ball.

"You're the one who's been busy." Chandni's eyes were flashing with anger. "What's with this new decree and making the ground itself move around?"

"You like that, do you?" Sesha ran his hand over his medals, making them ring against his chest. "I suggested that one to Father."

"Like it?" Chandni shoved an angry finger in Sesha's face. "We almost just got killed because of that little trick of yours. It's abominable! Disgusting! Besides, did you not think how shifting the land, water, and air around might kill those in mid-flight?"

"Well, if you'd told me where you were, I could have warned you," he said defensively. "Why'd you come out of hiding now anyway? I didn't think that demoness would find you."

"Hey!" I tried to interject. "Someone mind filling 'that demoness' in on what's going on here?"

"Not that you care, but it was getting far too dangerous for my host, and I had to close up shop," Chandni said right over me.

"Close up shop?" I echoed. But no one clarified. It was like I wasn't even there.

"I'm glad you're safe; you know I am." Sesha's voice was almost a growl. "But if you keep this stuff up, I don't know if I can protect you anymore. How many did you send down the river this time?"

At Sesha's words, I had a sudden vision of the clay pots all lined up at Ai-Ma's. Had Chandni been using my mother's house to stage some sort of illegal smuggling operation?

"A lot." The girl crossed her delicate arms over her chest. "But not enough. Never enough. Not until this thing is over."

"Over?" Sesha laughed, shaking his head. "It'll never be over."

"You didn't use to believe that," Chandni said sadly. "You don't have to be the dutiful son, you know. You can still come back to the cause."

"And betray my parents, like you betrayed yours?" Sesha's voice was scornful. "I don't think so."

My head felt so heavy, it was like a barbell on my neck. "What is going on here?" I demanded. My shout practically shook the walls of the shadow merchant's stall.

"I'll tell you what's going on," Sesha finally said. I would have felt better about him finally acknowledging my presence if he'd bothered to look at me. Sesha pointed at Chandni with an accusing finger. "What you're looking at here, my dear Pinki, is one of the most dangerous criminals in the entire kingdom!"

"Chandni? A dangerous criminal?" Glancing at the wispy creature with her button nose and pert, round face, I snorted. "If you believe that, I have a wormhole I'd like to sell you for real cheap."

When no one laughed at my sad attempt at a joke, I realized that Sesha was serious. "Chandni! What is he talking about?"

Instead of answering me, Chandni placed her delicate little hands on her delicate little waist. Her pretty face was flushed with passion. Regurg and reflux, I really hated this girl.

Chandni's voice tinkled like wind chimes as she spoke. "If you think I'm such a criminal, *Prince* Sesha, why don't you go ahead and arrest me?"

I looked to Chhaya Devi for help, but the merchant woman also seemed too mesmerized by Chandni to even remember I was there. Ugh. What was the hold this girl had on everyone?

"Why in doito dung cakes should he arrest you?" I demanded. "Is it, like, a crime to be too cloyingly cute? Is it illegal to be so adorably full of yourself? Although what am I saying, it probably should be."

"Listen, Chandni. It's too dangerous for you out here."

Sesha pushed back his thick hair with his ringed fingers, still staring at the girl as if his life depended on it. His voice had lost its playfulness and was deadly serious. "None of my soldiers know who you are. Just get out of here, all right? Skip galaxies, follow those kids into whatever that other dimension is where you send them. Just go before it's too late!"

"Fat chance. I'm staying right here in this dimension, thank you very much. This is my home, and I will fight for it." Chandni put out her hands, wrists together, in a dramatic gesture. "So if you want to arrest me, go ahead!"

"Oh, for demon's sake!" I rolled my eyes in annoyance. Of all the ninnies in the world, I had to get saddled with this one. How was I going to explain it to Ai-Ma if I let her precious pet get taken to serpent jail? I was supposed to be taking her back to her human family!

"I'm not going to arrest you, and you know that." Sesha took two big steps closer to the girl. "Just stop this ridiculous thing you're doing, and I'll look the other way. I can't say the same for my father. He's heard about your operation, and as you can imagine, he's not happy about it. And you know what he's like when he's angry."

"I don't care what he thinks. I just can't believe you're on his side," Chandni snapped. "There was a time when that would have been unthinkable!"

"Just stop this traffic to other dimensions down the River of Dreams, all right?" Sesha pleaded. "Don't worry about me, I'm doing fine."

The snake boy's mention of the River of Dreams confirmed my suspicions. What illegal activity had Chandni been up to while living at my demonic mother's? Had she been taking advantage of Ai-Ma? I suddenly remembered how my mother had said that Chandni had come to her of her own free will.

"Sesha! Chandni!" I shouted, stepping in between the two. "One of you tell me what is going on here, right now!"

And just then, in the moment that I finally captured both Sesha's and Chandni's attention, the Merchant of Shadows did something spectacularly bizarre.

"No!" Chhaya Devi yelled, like some heroic legend of old. "You'll never take her!"

With a giant heave, the shopkeeper threw the red vial she'd been holding down on the ground between Chandni and Sesha. As the glass vial shattered, the shadow she had trapped inside it slithered out, darkening the bright midday atmosphere immediately to a pitch-black.

The snake soldiers outside the merchant's stall hissed and spat as the shadow reached them. I could hear Sesha and Chandni somewhere near me, coughing. Even though rakkhosh, like snakes, can see in the dark, the sudden change was disorienting.

"What the fireballs?" I spluttered.

"Run, my girl, run!" the Merchant of Shadows yelled. I suppose she meant Chandni. No one seemed to care what happened to me around here.

I was fully expecting Chandni to have taken off by the time the darkness cleared, but unfortunately, Chhaya Devi's shadow must not have been very powerful because almost as soon as the darkness set, it began to lift.

"I knew that wasn't the right vial!" wailed the Merchant of Shadows. As if in sympathy, a couple of stray dogs down the alley began to howl.

"You've done all you could, Auntie!" Chandni said in her gentle voice. "Now go! Let my friends know what has happened."

"Friends! Hah!" Sesha coughed. "I knew you were still in touch with him!"

The Merchant of Shadows shot Chandni a worried look, but then did as she was bid, ducking out of the back corner of her stall. I thought Sesha would have his soldiers stop the shopkeeper, but he didn't. Probably because something else had distracted him.

As the darkness caused by Chhaya Devi's pitiful shadow

lifted, I saw the ranks of snaky soldiers stand at sudden attention, making a path between them as they split down the middle. A tall, striking figure was striding through the ranks right at us. A tall, striking, and very familiar-looking figure who didn't seem to care that he was stepping directly through the cow dung all over the road. The boa constrictor I'd met before slithered beside him, blowing a "Puh-puh-puh-*puh*!" fake trumpet fanfare with his mouth.

"Now the fun really starts," muttered Chandni.

"Father!" Sesha saluted, his body at immediate attention.

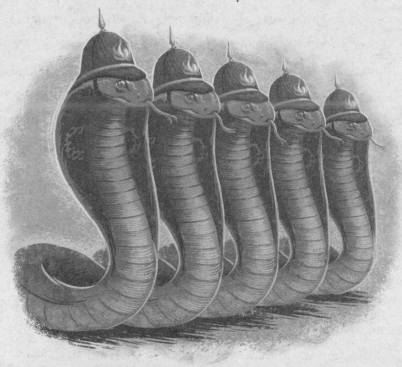

The snake soldiers all stood at attention too, slithering out their tongues in excitement. As the older snake saluted them back, the serpentine battalion erupted into a chorus of "For he'sss a jolly good general," ending with three cries of "hip, hip, huzzah!"

Oh, flaming doo-doo balls. This was not good. Not good at all.

CHAPTER 11

In Which Everyone Is Willing to Believe the Worst of Me, Which Is Mostly Unfair and Only a Little Justified

The Serpentine Governor-General was like an older, beefier version of Sesha, with the same green-black hair and piercing eyes, but an elaborate moustache and beard covering half his face. He was bigger and even more imposing in real life than in his propaganda photos. I tried to hide my nervousness, but I wasn't sure at all what was coming next. What did come next about bowled me over.

Like his son had been before him, the Governor-General seemed stupidly goo-goo-eyed by Chandni. He caught his breath, walking straight up to the girl.

"Isss what my ssspies tell me true, my boy? Is thisss

her?" Sesha's father spoke in a rough whisper. "Have you actually found the Moon Maiden?"

Sesha shot Chandni an "I told you so" sort of look, and she shrugged.

I, on the other hand, was flabbergasted. Agape. Aghast. Gobsmacked. All the surprised things. Jackal tongues! How could I not have realized!

"*You're* the Moon Maiden?" I stared at Chandni. "As in, the daughter of the Old Moon Mother? Did you forget to tell me or something?"

"Oops?" Chandni said. Which was pretty much the understatement of the year.

How could I have missed it? Her glow, her laugh, the way that the moon reflected in her eyes. Of course! There had never been any missing moonbeams stolen from the Moon Mother. There had only been her daughter, who had escaped from the serpents' clutches to unexpectedly somehow find refuge with my own ai-ma! She'd never been human at all! And Sesha had known the entire time, somehow. He'd known about her and hoped I would be able to find her.

"You've done very well, my boyo." The Governor-General actually licked his lips with his forked tongue as he stared at Chandni, like she was a juicy meal he was about to eat. "Very well indeed!"

The two bullocks who had been sleeping in the road lumbered to their feet, gave loud moos, and sauntered away, swishing their tails. One plopped out some dung as it walked. The flies who had been sitting on their hides did not go with them.

"Thank you, sir," Sesha muttered, staring at the ground now. "I . . . I captured her as a surprise. For you, I mean."

"You jerk!" Chandni shot him a look of pure hurt and betrayal.

I looked from the girl to Sesha and snorted. She was such a fool—could she not see the truth? Did she not remember how Sesha had been trying to get her away from danger only moments ago? I looked to the snake boy, assuming he would clarify, but in front of his dear old dad, he didn't seem to be able to do much speaking. Instead, he just stared at his father's boots. Which, were, of course, coated in dung.

"When will you learn, boy?" the Governor-General boomed, slapping his son so hard on the shoulder that Sesha kind of crumpled forward. "There are no sssecretsss from me. I have eyesss and earsss everywhere. I know everything."

Sesha shot me a desperate look under his long lashes, mouthing the word *help*. Which made me seriously want to punch him in the nose. He had convinced me to find him the stolen moonbeams, which had turned out to be

Chandni, but obviously not because he wanted to hand her over to his father. It was because he was worried about her, or obsessed with her, or something. Like everyone else seemed to be. Only now Sesha was stuck between keeping her safe and keeping up the appearance of loyalty to his dad. And so he wanted me to save Chandni and take the blame for it too. No, thanks.

I narrowed my eyes and shook my head at the snake boy. No way was I going to risk my neck to rescue his precious moon girl. I mean, let the snakes have her! After all, I had hated Chandni and all her sticky-sweet goodness before. Now that I knew all that goodness was wrapped up in revolutionary zeal, I hated her even more.

But then, why did this all feel so wrong?

I tried to tell myself it was just the promise I'd made to Ai-Ma. But in truth, it was also the gross gleam in the Governor-General's eyes. He rubbed his hands together, practically drooling as he commanded, "Sssoldiers, get that girl! Finally, we have captured the lossst daughter of our old friend the Moon!"

There was something about the disgusting way he said it, so oily and hungry, that made me want to bite off one of his limbs. I tried to catch Chandni's eye, but the girl just stood there, as cool as you please, staring off into the bright sky. I wanted to shake her. Did she not understand what was happening here? This wasn't her trading witty barbs with Sesha, this was the actual Governor-General of the entire Empire of the Serpent Overlords getting ready to capture her. You would think she would whimper or cry or plead for her life. Isn't that what maidens like her were supposed to do?

"Father, wait." Sesha looked flustered. He took a step closer to Chandni, like he wanted to protect her with his own body. "What are you going to do with her?"

I'm not gonna lie, even though I'd just been considering protecting the girl myself, Sesha stepping in to do the job made me seriously annoyed.

"Do with her?" Sesha's father actually laughed out loud, spittle flying from his lips at the force of his exclamation. He narrowed his eyes, saying in an initially mocking voice, "Well, I thought she and I could have a little chat, maybe over some herbal tea, talk about our facial poresss and favorite imported ssskin-care masksss . . . You moron! What do you think I'm going to do with her? I'm going to kill her!"

"And use her moon power to build a superweapon?" I demanded. At the sound of my voice, the Governor-General looked at me in surprise, like he hadn't even realized I was there.

"That old propaganda ssstory about a moon-powered sssuperweapon? Is that ssstill out there?" He began to laugh. As he laughed, the battalions of serpent soldiers began to laugh too. "There isss no moon-powered sssuperweapon, you gullible goon! You've been watching too many high-budget ssspace epicsss!"

Chandni turned to me, muttering, "The stories about the moon-powered superweapon were all just false rumors, Didi. To make everyone too scared to join the rebellion."

I stared at her. "Then why do they want to kill you if not to take your moon power?"

Sesha winced, shooting me another desperate look.

"They want to kill me because I'm the spark that will light the fire of the revolution," Chandni said simply. "And they are afraid."

Wait a minute. My brain whirred, putting the pieces together. There was no moon weapon, after all. I'd been right when I thought it sounded too wacky to be true. Except, of course, there *was* a moon-powered superweapon of sorts: this girl standing before me, this girl who claimed to be the spark of the revolution. But wasn't that what *I* was supposed to be? The spark of the revolution, I mean? It wasn't logical, but there it was in the pit of my stomach, a snake of a surprising feeling: jealousy. I mean, *I* was the daughter of two famous freedom fighters. *I* was the powerful demoness who should strike fear into the heart of the Serpent Empire. *I* was the one who was supposed to be the spark of the revolution, not this namby-pamby, luminous lightbulb of a girl. Never mind that I didn't want anything to do with all that. I just didn't appreciate her casting a shadow over what was supposed to be my light.

As I thought all this, Sesha seemed to get himself together. "Father," he started again, his voice only a little shaky. He squared his shoulders, facing his father down. "You can't kill Chandni."

His father responded like lightning.

"Shut up, you insssolent whelp! Don't tell me what I can do!" The Governor-General backhanded his son across the face with a wallop whose sick echo resounded across the empty market road. Its ugly power was evident in how his rings left open gashes in Sesha's cheek. The dogs who had been sunbathing by the open sewers growled and barked.

Chandni gasped, taking a quick step forward. But Sesha put up a hand in warning.

"Leave it," he snapped, holding his cheek with his other palm. "I'm fine."

"Don't wassste your lassst bits of life energy on my ssson, dearie." The Governor-General flashed his pointed teeth.

"Unlike you, he knowsss where his loyalty liesss! Unlesss you want to come over to our caussse and finally make your Moon Mother proud?"

"My Moon Mother was weak," Chandni said in a disgustingly brave way. She even stuck her chin out and everything. "She caved and helped you snakes because she didn't think she had a choice. But there's always a choice. And I choose to go a different way. I choose freedom."

But even as she said this, Chandni continued to direct all her attention to Sesha, as if her eyes were magic beams and she could compel him to look at her. But the prince of snakes kept his head turned away as he mopped the blood off his cheek with his sleeve. I could see where his father's rings would leave scars.

"Freedom?" the Governor-General snarled. "Little girl, the only choice you ever had wasss between life and death. And you just chossse the wrong door." He made the sound of a disappointed buzzer: "Mwah-mwahhhhh!"

Sesha looked up. He still looked so defeated, but I saw he'd pulled his hands into fists. I had a flash to what his childhood must have been like, cowering before his bully of a father.

"Don't talk to her like that!" Sesha said, gulping hard.

The Governor-General's eyes practically bugged out of

his head. "What did you sssay to me, boy?" He made as if he was going to slap Sesha again.

"Stop that!" I jumped before him. "You disgusting monster!"

"Look who'sss talking!" The Governor-General whirled on me. "Disguisssing your face doesssn't hide what you are." He turned his face up, sticking out his forked tongue in the air. "I could sssmell your ssstench a mile away, demonesssss!"

I put my own nose up, taking a long whiff. "Better than smelling like bull dung!"

"How dare you?" I thought the Governor-General was going to pop a blood vessel. "Do you know who you're ssspeaking to?"

"Back off, Pinki!" Sesha said, totally surprising me. "I don't need you to defend me!"

"Well, it kinda seemed like you did there," I began.

"No, you're wrong!" Sesha rubbed at his hurt face, and I wondered if he was somehow mad that I had seen him get slapped. There were angry tears shining in his eyes. "I don't need the help of a demoness who can't even control her own powers!"

"Oh, you make me sssick, you sssorry sssniveler!" The Governor-General narrowed his eyes at his son. "Don't think I don't know about the deal you made with this demonesssss here. My ssspies tell me everything! You were worried you couldn't you find the Moon Maiden by your wittle ssself, weren't you?"

"No, I mean, I just thought it would be easier to get her to find Chandni," Sesha began.

"You just thought it would be *easssier*!" the Governor-General mocked in a singsong tone. "You're alwaysss thinking of what would be easssier, aren't you, you weakling? Never taking the hard way!"

That shut his son right up. Even though he'd just been nasty to me, Sesha looked so small and powerless with his father looming over him that it broke something in me.

My father was dead, having died long ago for a cause he loved more than me. And every time I met someone whose father was alive, I hated them. Until today. I now realized that there were worse things than having a father who'd died as a freedom fighter. Like having an awful father with muttonchop sideburns, a mean temper, and a penchant for slapping you. That's when I decided I wasn't about to stand around and let this power-hungry old windbag demean his son and then kill a girl right in front of me, no matter how sickly sweet and annoying the girl was.

I turned around and around in a wide circle, removing the magic that hid my rakkhoshi features. In a moment, I was myself again, horns and fangs and talons and all. I felt the hot blood rushing through my muscles. I felt taller, and faster, and stronger. I was the entirety of me again, powerful and glorious.

"Sesha, I got you," I said. "Like it or not, I'm on your side." I made a move toward him but was stopped by the sound of a familiar, unexpected voice from the back of the shop.

"Traitor!"

I whipped my head around, and when I saw who it was who had joined us in Chhaya Devi's stall, I groaned.

"I knew you were no resistance fighter!" a familiar voice yelled. The voice of my roommate! "You've been working with the snakes this whole time!"

"Aakash? Kumi? What are you doing here?" I sputtered. They'd crept into the shop the same way Chhaya Devi had crept out, but how, and more importantly, why? Then I saw who else they had with them and felt my panic rising. "And why in the demon snot are my cousins with you?"

Kawla, Mawla, and Deembo looked like they wanted to run to me, but Aakash held them back with a quick tuck of his wings, which were wrapped around them. "Naw, little dudes, stay here. It's not safe for you to associate with dangerous snake collaborators, even if you are related to them!"

"I am not a dangerous snake collaborator!" I shouted. "And this isn't what it looks like!"

"Isss it not?" The Governor-General's face wore an almost-maniacal expression of glee at this new plot twist. "Did you not jussst bring usss the moonbeamsss my ssson asked you to find for us? Moonbeamsss that were actually Chandni, missssing daughter of the Old Moon Mother?"

"Is it true?" Chandni shot me a look of betrayal. "Were you working for the serpents this whole time?"

"I told you!" Kumi said triumphantly to no one in particular. "I told you Pinki wasn't looking for those moonbeams to help the revolution!"

"Aw, dip! I'm sorry you have to see what a traitor your cousin is to rakkhosh-kind," Aakash said to Kawla, Mawla and Deembo, who were starting to cry. He patted them awkwardly with his giant hands. "Growing up can be a real bummer sometimes, little demon-lings."

"I am not a traitor to rakkhosh-kind!" I insisted as my cousins began bawling even louder, snot trailing down their warty faces. "Kids, this is all a huge misunderstanding!"

"When I heard my son had enlisssted the help of not just a fire rakkhoshi but the daughter of sssuch legendary resisssstance ssscum, I was doubtful you had the gutsss to bring usss the moon girl." The Governor-General gave me a sinister smile and went on, "But now I sssee I was wrong."

"You were actually working for Sesha when you came to find me, Didi?" Chandni's eyes were round with hurt. "That's why we came to the market? You knew he was here?"

"No! I mean, yes," I fumbled. "Kind of! Not how he just explained it, though!"

"Then how?" Chandni asked. "I thought it was just a coincidence. But now, to realize you were meeting Sesha here to . . . what, hand me over?"

"It wasn't like that!" I insisted. "I didn't even realize who you were! Plus, I didn't know Sesha would be here!"

Confusion passed over Chandni's face as she thought this through, but before she had a chance to say anything, my roommate butted in.

"Oh, I had her number the whole time!" Kumi was so happy to be right about me, she seemed to forget she was potentially in a lot of danger from all these snakes. "Pinki was trying to make it seem like she was a revolutionary freedom fighter, but I knew she never could be!"

"Yo, don't hog the glory." Aakash fluttered his wings in protest. "We both suspected."

"Get over yourself, flyboy; it was me all along." Kumi

tossed her always-sopping hair. "Just wait until the head-mistress and Professor Ravan read the note I left them!"

Note? What note? I had a moment of panic, imagining Professor Ravan's disappointment and Surpanakha's glee that she'd been right about me all along.

"You two are pathetic!" I snapped. "Neither of you should be Demon King or Queen!"

"Do you want me to kill them for you, fire rakkhoshi?" the Governor-General said in an oily, amused voice.

"Kill? Who's talking about killing? Yo! That's way uncool, man!" Aakash protested, and even Kumi finally looked concerned.

The Governor-General ignored them. He was enjoying all this confusion far too much. "Murdering your classsss-matesss in some gruesssome and painful way is the leassst we sssnakes could do for sssuch a loyal ally, my dear Pinki."

"Stop saying that!" I whirled back to the Governor-General. "I'm not a snake ally, all right? Stop trying to make it seem like I am!"

"You could have fooled me," snarled a bitter-looking Sesha. "You seemed pretty eager to help me when I asked. All I had to do to was offer to help you control your power."

The sympathy I'd been feeling for the snake boy

vanished in a whoosh. What a two-faced, double-crossing weasel!

"Well, that's no surprise; she needs all the help she can get on that score!" Kumi laughed.

"How could you? After all your parents went through?" Chandni mooned her liquidy goo-goo eyes at me.

"Well, you're not exactly a chip off the old block either, moon girl!" This was all so unfair! I couldn't believe everyone was so willing to believe the worst of me. I mean, especially when only half of what they were thinking was actually true!

"I thought we were friends!" Chandni said.

"Well, you were obviously wrong!" I'm not sure I meant it, but my patience was pretty much at its breaking point. "I told you when we met that we'd never be friends!"

The Governor-General put back his head and laughed. "Oh, thisss isss all too good! I'm glad I didn't kill you both yet! I would have misssed watching thisss heartbreaking betrayal of your inter-ssspeciesss sssisssterhood!"

"Shut up!" Chandni and I shouted at the snake, almost at the same time, but he only kept laughing more.

In the chaos, a crying Deembo broke free of Aakash and ran to me. I caught the little rakkhoshi up in my arms, holding her as she nuzzled her wet, egg-smelling face into my cheek. I let myself feel the comfort of having her again in my arms, her sticky hands wrapped around my neck. No matter what any of these other jerks thought, she believed in me. She didn't have to say it; I could feel it. But I had never really appreciated what that meant and how much strength that gave me. Then I looked at Kawla and Mawla and made a decision.

"Come here, kids!" I put out my arms, and they ran to me too. I held all three of them close for a moment, finally feeling like all three of my hearts were back in my chest. I glared at Aakash and Kumi. "Look, you can hate me, but I wouldn't have thought the two of you would put three underage rakkhosh in danger like this!"

"Yo, we were just trying to help, yaar! I mean, sure, we were also secretly following you, which is how we ended up at your mom's house," Aakash explained shamefacedly. "But Ai-Ma said Deembo was making herself sick crying she missed you so much! So your mom asked if we could try to find you and bring the kids back to school."

"And now they can witness your humiliation!" Kumi said, but with less conviction.

"Oh, wake up already, Kumi!" I shouted, still holding my cousins close to me. "We have much bigger problems right now!"

"Bigger problems than disloyalty?" sniffed Chandni. "Bigger problems than a lack of honor?"

Oh, dirty demon butts. Of all the moralistic, do-gooding nonsense! This was really not the place or time for any of this. I seriously wanted to scream.

"Oh, my didi, can it be twue?" asked Kawla, her expression mirroring the confusion on Mawla's and Deembo's faces. "Can a twaitor's heart beat in you?"

Hearing Kawla rhyme chilled the very blood in my marrow. Too late, I put my hand over her mouth.

Then Mawla joined in too. "Loyalty to rakkhosh-kind, has it gone and left your mind?"

"Well, well. What have we here?" The Governor-General's eyes focused on my cousins huddling around my legs. His gleaming grin widened. "Oh, sssoldiers! Thessse ill-educated rakkhosh children need to learn how to ssspeak properly! Let's sssend them to our lovely retraining school, shall we, where they can have a proper education and forget thessse dirty demonic waysss?!"

At their leader's words, three snake soldiers marched forward toward my baby cousins, making as if to pick them up.

"No! Don't touch them!" I shouted. "Back off, snakes!"

But the snakes kept coming.

CHAPTER 12

Powee! Kazowee! Dhooshoom! Dhashooom! (A Lot of Fighting Ensues)

"Wait a minute." Kumi put herself between the snakes and the kids, as if only just realizing the danger she had put them in. "Why aren't those snakes listening to you? I thought you were working for the overlords!"

"I might have thought I was at one point, but I'm not!" I yelled as the serpent soldiers kept coming toward my now-terrified cousins.

"Get those little monsssstersss!" snarled the Governor-General.

"No!" I shouted. I shoved the kids behind Chhaya Devi's countertop, and then, without thinking about it, without worrying about it, without even realizing it, I sneezed out three wild fire streams from my nostrils. I don't know how, but I managed to curl the flames so each one twisted around one of the soldiers heading toward my cousins, burning their snaky skin. The snake soldiers fell to the ground, writhing and screaming.

"How dare you, you demon scum!" With another snarl, the Governor-General shot out a bolt of burning green lightning at me. I was so busy controlling my fire, I didn't see it coming.

"Yo, watch it!" Aakash threw a wind gust just in time, tumbling me out of the way.

"You're all wet, snakes!" Kumi pelted out a water cannon, throwing both Sesha and the Governor-General off their feet.

"Our deal is off!" Sesha spat through his flattened and sopping hairdo. "I'm not helping you control your power!"

"I don't need you to!" I snapped.

Unfortunately, what happened next totally proved me wrong. All this distraction made my nose flames go wide. My fire hit and exploded two nearby stalls, the lizard-roll shop and a hair-oil store next door. They were empty, but the small stalls were incinerated in minutes.

"You pathetic excussse for a rakkhosh!" the Governor-General growled as he shook water out of his eyes. "You really have no control over your power, do you?"

I felt my hearts tighten in my chest. "I'm getting there, all right? It's a work in progress!"

"Evidence to the contrary, my dear!" said Sesha's father, pointing to the still-burning buildings. Then he turned and barked at his soldiers, "Sssnakes, kill her!"

"Aakash and I will take the kids to safety!" Kumi was closer than I was to the countertop behind which Kawla, Mawla, and Deembo were hiding. In retrospect, I probably should have let her take them, but I just couldn't forgive her for bringing them in the first place.

"Forget it! They're my responsibility and I'll take care of them!" I shouted. Aakash made a sound of protest, but I cut him off. "If you want to take off yourselves, go!"

"They're not going anywhere!" The Governor General was practically purple with fury now, ordering his soldiers to surround the small store.

"Don't be ridiculous, Didi!" Chandni scolded. "Just like I am still angry with you, you may be angry with your friends, but that is no reason to put these young ones in danger!"

I looked in frustration from Chandni to Aakash and Kumi.

"No way!" This whole forgiveness thing was so not my scene. "Why should I trust those idiots after they brought my cousins here in the first place? If they want to leave, they should! Good riddance!"

"We can't go anywhere! They've got the door blocked!" Kumi was fighting off some approaching serpents by making it thunder and rain. Unfortunately, their green lightning cut right through her water.

"What do we do?" Aakash whirled around, sending tornados toward the battalion to stop more soldiers from coming inside the shop. But there were too many, and they just kept coming. "How do we get through this?" he asked in panic.

Then Chandni, that annoyingly delicate lotus blossom, raised her hands, saying, "We get through this by relying on each other." She generated a white light so full of power it made the air hum. "Teamwork makes the dream work, after all."

The snakes were all pointing their bayonets at us now, and green sparks were flying off the Governor-General's fingers like so much overripe lightning.

I took a deep breath, ready to blast the snake man and his soldiers with a plume of probably uncontrolled flames, but before I could even open my lips, Chandni held out her hands, shouting, "Moonbeam magic come to me! A staff of power you must be!" At these words, a glowing white staff appeared out of nowhere between the girl's clenched fists.

I was so surprised, I spit out a smoky puff of fire from my mouth, giving myself a serious coughing fit.

"Don't!" Sesha cried out, seeing her staff. "We'll guarantee your safety!"

"No, we won't!" sputtered the Governor-General.

With a sad smile to Sesha, Chandni took a running leap, then used her glowing staff to somersault over the entire battalion of snakes. As she flew, she twisted the staff in the air, letting loose a light so bright, so powerful, it shook the very sky. The atmosphere above the snake army darkened and shuddered, as if rocked by an earthquake or a silent explosion.

The snakes fell to the ground, clutching at their heads and hearts, the moonlight's power shaking them to their very core. Both Sesha and his father fell to their knees where they stood.

"She's no joke, dude," muttered Aakash as he took in the collapsed snakes. He looked reverently up at Chandni, soaring through the air on her moon magic. "Yo, I think I love her."

"Get in line, man," Kumi said, squinting up at Chandni. "She's mad impressive."

The truth was, I was just as amazed by Chandni's magic. She had felled the entire serpent army with one blast of her moon baton while keeping the rest of us standing. No wonder she'd been so unbothered before.

"We better get out of here while they're down." Kumi pointed to the fallen snakes.

Even though Chandni's magic had dropped all the serpents at once, the force of that initial blast was starting to wear off. The snakes were already struggling back to their feet.

"Sorry for getting the whole you-being-a-traitor thing wrong, yaar," Aakash said awkwardly. "Maybe we shouldn't have left that mean note for the headmistress about you."

"Just go! The little ones and I will follow you in a minute!" I made a shooing motion to the back of the shop. I didn't have time for any of their weak-livered apologies now.

Before they left, Kumi turned back. "Why not come with us, fire chick? That moon girl bought us some time. We could all get away!"

But I looked out at Chandni, across the market road now, facing down an entire battalion of snake soldiers alone. Snake soldiers who would be up and attacking her any minute. I knew I should let her fend for herself, but somehow, annoyingly, I couldn't. Blargh. Teamwork was dreamwork, and all that gross stuff.

"Just go. I'll be behind you," I said. "Right after I help that honorable ding-dong of a moon girl."

The snakes were beginning to struggle to their feet, Chandni's magic having almost totally worn off. Oh, blast. I needed a plan, and fast. As if in answer, the shonar kathi–rupor kathi tucked into my waist seemed to heat up.

"Hang in there, moon girl!" I yelled at Chandni, who was on the far side of the battalion, swirling her staff in complicated patterns over the soldiers.

I grabbed my mother's magic sticks and held them in my hands. Their power should be able to hold the snakes off long enough for Chandni, the kids, and me to get away too. I tapped the shonar kathi–rupor kathi together as I came up with a quick rhyme of enchantment. "Stick of silver, stick of gold, these serpents in your sleep enfold!"

The sticks grew automatically to their full, swordlike size. I placed the silver stick at my feet, on one side of the serpentine battalion. For the spell to work, the other stick had to be placed on the far side of the soldiers, where Chandni was standing. But I had no way to take the kathi over.

I thought about throwing the golden stick, javelin-style, and hoping that Chandni could somehow catch it, but I knew it was too far. And I didn't have wings or a magical moon staff to help me fly. There was only one solution. I gave the kids, who were still hiding behind the counter, a quick look. "Keep your heads down, okay? I'll be right back!"

Kawla and Mawla nodded, obviously too scared to speak. Deembo stared at me with frightened eyes and offered me an egg. I took it from her, ruffling her hair. "Don't look so worried, you three. It'll all be fine. I promise. Just stay hidden!"

Then I called out, "Raat!" hoping the pakkhiraj didn't hate me too much to listen. "Come on, horsey! Help me out here!"

In the meantime, the Governor-General was already rising from his knees. Oh, demon snot, this flying horse really needed to hurry.

"Get me up, boy!" shouted the Governor-General. "Where are you, you good-for-nothing son of mine?"

But Sesha wasn't there, so the old snake Governor-General started to rise by himself. "I'm going to kill you, demonesss, right now with my own handsss!"

"Not if we have something to say about it!" I heard Kumi's voice and then saw the waves of water she sent toward the Governor-General, making him stumble violently backward.

"Yeah, snake dude! Don't threaten our friend!" Aakash sent a torrent of wind along with Kumi's waves.

"You guys . . ." I couldn't believe what I was seeing. "You came back!"

"Yo, we weren't going to let you have all the fun!" Aakash hit the Governor-General with another blast of air.

"Stop that, you demon scum!" the Governor-General huffed even as he fell to his knees in the face of Aakash and Kumi's combined powers.

"Now go!" Kumi gestured to the recovering snake battalion. "Get that magic stick to the other side of the snakes!"

"Yeah, here's your ride, Pinks!" Aakash pointed to the flying horse barreling toward us.

Raat was in a rapid canter, still on the ground but hooves so light and wings so spread, he would take off into the air at any time. Oh, dung balls, I was going to have to do this—there was no other way.

"Here, boy!" I hitched my sari up in the middle, then ran alongside the horse as fast as I could, grabbing on to the pommel of his saddle just in the nick of time. I had barely gotten myself astride the horse when he took flight. I tried my best not to puke on the animal's mane.

"Ssstop, you demon ssscum!" the Governor-General bellowed. He raised his hands, ready to blast me with that terrible green lightning, but somehow Aakash got in the way, falling full-body weight on top of the older snake.

"Aw, dip!" said the giant air-clan boy. "I done tripped!"

"Get off me, you humongous collection of mussclesss!" gasped the Governor-General.

They were a tangle of limbs now, demon and snake, struggling over the ground. It was a ridiculous display. Not to mention ridiculously bad acting on Aakash's part. But it gave me some much-needed seconds.

I shot Aakash and Kumi quick nods of thanks before turning my attention to Chandni, all alone at the far side of the now-rising soldiers. Raat flew fast and low over them even as I gulped hard, fighting my own fear of flying.

"Here goes nothing." I leaned over the horse's back, urging him to fly faster. The animal rolled his eyes back at me. He snuffled his nose, heaving out huge, frothy, nervous breaths.

"Scared now that I look like a rakkhoshi?" I asked. "Well, you're not my favorite either. But none of that matters; you just have to get me to the other side of these snakes!"

Raat seemed to understand that we were on the same team and that neither of us had the time right now to indulge our delicate sensibilities. We were almost over the expanse of soldiers. We had only a few seconds before they would fully recover and attack us again.

"Chandni, catch!" I called. I was within yards of the girl now and hurled the long golden stick to her. She leaped and caught it in a dramatic twirl, then put the shonar kathi on the ground just beyond all the soldiers, completing the force field. In a voice so loud and musical it shook the dust from the marketplace ground, she shouted my rhyme again: "Stick of silver, stick of gold, these serpents in your sleep enfold!"

The moment the words left her lips, the snake soldiers began falling, row by row, like matchstick men. As each row fell, they joined the previous ones in a deep sleep. By the time the wave of magical sleep reached the Governor-General, now at the far side of the battalion by Chhaya Devi's stall, all his soldiers were already unconscious on the ground. Sesha, for some reason, still didn't appear anywhere nearby. Where was he? But I didn't have time to worry about that now, as I had more important things to think about. Like staying alive.

"You'll regret this!" The Governor-General's words turned into a giant, uncontrolled yawn. "I'll make you regret this!"

Aakash had just gotten up off the Governor-General, but it was a second too soon. Because as soon as his hands were free, the Governor-General managed to send a bolt of green lightning right at Raat's back.

I dodged the bolt barely in time, feeling its nearness prickle my skin. "That was close!"

"Wait, he's not going to sleep!" Aakash yelled. I realized that even though he was yawning and rubbing his eyes, the Governor-General seemed immune to the sleeping magic of the shonar kathi–rupor kathi. "Why is he not going to sleep?"

"It's not that easssy to magic me!" the Governor-General snarled, managing to get yet another green lightning bolt off in my direction.

"Watch it, Pinki!" Kumi yelled, sending some rain my way. But she was too late. The lightning came too fast.

I knew I should have sent a fireball to block it, but I hesitated. What if I couldn't control my fire? What if I incinerated Aakash and Kumi, or my cousins, in the blaze?

It was that moment of self-doubt that doomed me. The pakkhiraj horse, Raat, trying to evade the lightning, swerved sharply to the right. His actions saved my life, getting me out of the direct line of the Governor-General's deadly magic. But the animal himself wasn't so lucky. He caught the edge of the serpentine lightning with the tip of his wing, screaming with pain as his injured wing buckled and we both fell.

"No!" I screamed, desperately staring at the horse's hurt wing. "No!"

But then I heard a cry below me from the ground. "Don't worry, sis! I got you!"

Chandni twirled, using her staff almost like a propeller. She lifted off the ground, flying herself within the range of Raat's back. I reached out, grasping her elbow with my hand even as she grabbed my elbow with hers. Like that, arm in arm, I hauled her to safety on the back of the flying pakkhiraj horse.

The snakes below us were all asleep, except for the Governor-General, who was locked in battle with Aakash and Kumi. And even though they were fighting two on one, I'm not sure my classmates were exactly winning. Overcoming the magic of the shonar kathi–rupor kathi had only made the Governor-General angrier. Green bolts flashed, thunder crashed, and lightning and storms howled.

"We have to go help them!" I cried.

Unfortunately, Chandni's added weight to the back of the horse did not help our whole falling-through-the-air situation. We lost even more altitude as Raat tried his best to keep flying with a broken wing.

"Here, my friend, take my energy." Chandni put her small hands to his injured feathers.

As soon as she did, her hands lit up with a glowing white light that seemed to transfer to Raat's broken wing. She closed her eyes tight, her face strained, like the transfer of moon magic was costing her. But Raat stopped that terrible shrieking and seemed to be able to flap his wings a bit better.

"Let's go!" I cried, unable to take my eyes off the battle between the giant snake and my two rakkhosh frenemies.

"I thought you weren't into the whole teamwork thing," Chandni teased even as she urged the horse forward.

I was going to say something devastatingly witty in response, when a weird premonition washed over me. "Where's Sesha?" I asked.

"I don't know." Chandni seemed exhausted after healing the horse. "I don't see him."

And then my question was answered. But not in a good way.

"Do you see what I see?" I pointed ahead of us. My hand was actually shaking.

"What?" Chandni raised her head and rubbed her bleary eyes.

"There!" A few yards before us was a chariot flying in midair. It was the kind Ravan had used to kidnap that long-ago queen. The thing that really made me freak was who was flying it.

"It's Sesha," I said in a strangled voice, not wanting to believe what I was seeing.

"Oh no, Didi, look!" Chandni squinted where I was pointing. There fell through the air a boiled egg, thrown down by someone in the chariot. It cracked as it hit the ground, smushing down to almost half its original size. Just as that long-ago queen had thrown down her jewelry so that her husband might know she'd been taken, one of the prisoners in this chariot was doing the same.

I really hoped that Aakash and Kumi were going to be able to take care of themselves, because I was definitely not going back to help them.

CHAPTER 13

In Which I Do Something Really Brave and Also Really Stupid and Almost Die in Midair (Again)

Deembo?" I screamed.

My cousin's little face peeked over the flying chariot's edge. Even though she looked terrified, at the sight of me, the tiny nincompoop actually waved. Oh no. Oh no no no!

Raat was still not flying like normal, and there was no way we were going to catch up with that chariot.

"Sesha! You dirty snake! What are you doing? Why are you kidnapping my cousins?!" I felt heat rising in me, but I couldn't release any fire. No matter how much I wanted to murder Sesha, I couldn't risk hurting Kawla, Mawla, and Deembo inside the carriage.

"I'm doing these demon-lings a favor!" Sesha's voice was thick, and his eyes were shining in a completely manic way. "That school of yours isn't educating them properly! They'll get a much better education in our snake retraining academies!"

"What is wrong with you?!" I yelled. "Let them go!"

Chandni clicked her tongue, urging poor Raat on. The injured horse was flying as hard and fast as he could, but the distance between us and the chariot was still enormous.

"This is the next phase of our schooling plan, to include rakkhosh kids. I'm just speeding things along." Half of Sesha's face was swollen up where his father had cut him with his rings. "It's what my father would want me to do."

"Who cares what he wants you to do!" Chandni's hands were still shaking a little after healing the horse's wing. "You can make your own decisions! This isn't like you!"

"What do you know about what I'm like anymore, Chandni?" shouted Sesha from the rising chariot. "You just tried to knock me out with your moon magic, then put me to sleep! You just didn't know my father taught me how to make myself immune to the shonar kathi–rupor kathi!"

"No wonder the Governor-General didn't fall asleep," I muttered.

Sesha was still ranting. "You don't care about me, especially now that I'm not a part of your precious cause! So I'm doing what I have to do, okay?"

Really, at some point, I wanted to know all the tea behind Chandni and Sesha's history, but right now, I couldn't have cared less. He had my cousins and I wanted them back.

"Didi! You muthst us fwee!" Kawla's face appeared next to her younger sister's in the back of the chariot. Her face was dripping with tears. "It's Kawla, Mawla, and Deembo, your cousins twee!"

"I'm coming!" Oh, blooming dung balls, this was a nightmare. "Hang in there, guys!"

I had to free my family. They were my responsibility, and even though all three of them were annoying weirdos, they were *my* annoying weirdos.

"I can't get a clean shot over their heads!" Chandni cried, trying to aim her magical moon staff. "Tell them to stop moving!"

I brushed aside a strand of hair that had been whipped into my eyes by the fierce wind. "Are you aiming for your boyfriend?"

"Hopefully just to injure him," she said grimly. "And he's not my boyfriend."

I shook my head. "If you hit Sesha, he could lose control over the entire chariot, and then they'll all come crashing down!"

"What else can we do?" Chandni's eyes had dark circles

under them, and she looked exhausted. "We can't let him just kidnap the little ones!"

"There is one thing." I took a big breath, leaning forward low over Raat's neck. "Steady, boy." I brought one wobbling foot up to the saddle, then the other. I sat there, squatting on the horse's back, summoning up all the courage I had.

"But, Didi, you're afraid of heights!" Chandni said, guessing what I was about to do.

I gave her a look. I don't know when she'd figured out how much I hated flying, but it wasn't exactly helpful to bring it up now. I gulped, trying not to glance at the ground so far below. "Will you help me?"

"As much as I can, but I'm a little weak right now, I'll give you fair warning," she said.

"This is really not a time for your honesty-is-the-best-policy nonsense, moon girl." I tried to think stable, steady, non-midair thoughts. I'm not 100 percent sure I succeeded.

Chandni's mouth was set in a grim line, and I saw her eyes darting up from Raat to the magic chariot and back again. "I think I can get you enough height."

"You better," I said. "I don't fancy being a rakkhoshi pancake."

With one big exhale of breath, I surged up to my feet, standing precariously on the flying horse's back. It was wobbly, and seriously scary, but I felt the fire of my bravery lighting up my insides, keeping me strong.

"On three!" Chandni's hands were on my ankles, steadying me and also transferring a continuous stream of pure moon energy into my every cell. I felt filled with nighttime comforts, silvery illumination, and the power of the tides.

"Steady, boy," I muttered. "Don't let me fall." My legs were shaking and my breath was coming out in gasps as, for a moment, I felt connected to both the horse and the girl, all three of us sharing our strength for a greater cause. Then I bent my legs, trying to get as much power as I could, and jumped.

For what must have been a few seconds, but what felt like a few thousand, I was flying through the air. Scrambling, clawing, reaching, boosted up by Chandni's moon energy and my own rakkhosh power, I jackknifed myself up from the horse's back. It was impossible, it was unthinkable, it was terrifying, it was ridiculously stupid. And still, I did it.

"Ahhhgh!" I yelled as somehow my extended talons touched one of the back wheels of the chariot, and I grabbed on. Of course, that was just before Sesha gave the machine a burst of speed, dragging me like a monstrous kite behind him.

"Hang on!" Chandni cried from Raat's back. "Don't let go!"

"Really? Ya think?" I screamed as I scrabbled to get a better grasp on the chariot wheel. Only, my weight was making the entire chariot tip dangerously. The shrill voices of Kawla, Mawla, and Deembo pierced the night as they slipped toward the lower side of the flying contraption.

"You're going to flip us, you traitor of a demoness!" Sesha cried, feet scrambling for purchase. "Let go, or your cousins will fall too!"

"You wish!" I snapped. But it was true, I had to get myself to the center of the chariot or risk tipping us all. I closed my eyes and summoned my magical energy. The wind was whipping through my clothes, and the effort of hanging on to this wheel in midair was wrecking my strength. But somehow, with a fearsome cry, I let go of the chariot wheel, did a 360-degree turn without barfing, and then grabbed the central part of the chariot platform. As soon as I had transferred my weight to the middle, the chariot evened out.

"Cousin-lady! You actually did it!" Mawla's face appeared at the edge of the chariot so that all three rakkhosh kids were leaning over at me. "Now get us away from this snaky idiot!"

They put out their hands, as if to pull me up, but I didn't take them. With our relative weights, it was far more likely that instead of me getting pulled into the chariot by them, I would pull my baby cousins out and send them hurtling to the ground below.

"Sesha! Help pull me in before I fall!" The wind was whipping through my hair and making me gulp big lungfuls of air. My entire body felt wracked with nausea—although whether it was from the aerial acrobatics I had just pulled off or the height, I couldn't be sure.

"I don't think so, you demonic betrayer!" said Sesha, peering over his shoulder from the front of the chariot. "You made me look bad in front of my father and Chandni! You never wanted to help me; you just wanted to undermine me!"

"Yeah, sure!" I was struggling to hold on to the chariot by my fingernails. "My entire agenda back there was to make you look stupid. Never mind that it was you who never told me that the moonbeams I was looking for were an actual living being!"

I snuck a peek over my shoulder, almost losing my lunch as I did so. Chandni and Raat were flying up behind us but were still too far away to reach. The air whizzed by my ears, swirling around me dizzyingly. "Get me in the chariot already, you slimeball of a snake!"

"Or how about I don't and say I did?" Sesha snapped,

making no move to help me. "Honestly, I'm surprised at myself! I should have known you would do something like this. You're selfish through and through."

"Me? What about you, you no-good baby kidnapper?" The entire flying contraption lurched to the right, and Kawla, Mawla, and Deembo went sliding in that direction. "Hang on, kids!" I shouted.

"This is your fault as much as mine! How do you think I got my hands on your cousins anyway?" Sesha went on as he tried to stabilize the chariot. "If you'd let those loser rakkhosh friends of yours take them, they'd be on their way to your Academy by now. But no, you can't trust anyone! You had to put them all in danger because of your own issues."

My hearts froze. Was Sesha right? Was this my fault? It was true, Aakash and Kumi had offered to take the kids, and I'd refused. I'd always been a loner, thinking I had no other choice. What if I was wrong? Argh! If there was one thing I hated, it was having to challenge my long-held opinions!

"What about you? I mean, you and I were supposed to be in this together!" My fingers were cramping from holding on to the back of the chariot. "I agreed to work with you, didn't I—and look where it got me!"

"Yeah, we were supposed to work together!" Sesha's voice was full of venom. "Only you don't know what being on a team means! You almost blew up your headmistress's classroom after calling out her bad taste in boyfriends! If that isn't burning your bridges, I don't know what is!"

"How did you know about that?" I shrieked.

Kawla, Mawla, and Deembo were watching this exchange between us like they were watching a demonic cricket match, swiveling their heads from where Sesha stood at the front of the chariot to where I precariously hung at the back.

"When a rakkhoshi does something legendarily villainous like that, word gets around!" Sesha spat. "I should have realized that someone like you, with no loyalty to your own kind, couldn't be trusted even with the villains' code of honor. I mean, the first chance you got, you planted poisonous stories about me in Chandni's head!"

I looked over my shoulder at the moon girl and Raat, who were still chasing us. The animal's hurt wing seemed better, but it was still affecting his ability to rise into the air with enough speed.

"I didn't need to tell her any stories about you, dude! If she's mad, that's all on you for siding with your dad!" I was trying my best to hold it together as I bobbed and swayed in the wind. Kawla, Mawla, and Deembo were crouching near my face, their three sets of luminous, worried eyes watching my every move. "Don't even use that as an excuse! You're the one who decided to become a kidnapper!"

"I don't want to hurt your small, hairy cousins," Sesha said grimly. "But I will. I will if you don't tell Chandni to stop her revolutionary activities!"

"What?" This guy was totally off his rocker. "You can't hurt some innocent kids because of that!"

"Oh, really? Just watch me!" Sesha looked behind the chariot, saw Chandni's approach, and put on another burst of nausea-inducing speed.

"All right, I get it, you want to keep her safe from your dad, but this isn't the way to do it!" I desperately hung on to the chariot as Sesha now banked a hard left. The kids all went "Whooooa!" as they fell the other way. "Not unless you want her to hate you!" I added.

That got Sesha's attention. He looked back at me, his face pained. "I . . . I can't fight my father, you know? I tried, but I just can't do it!"

"You have friends," I said desperately, swinging my legs and trying to find a toehold somewhere. My hair was whipping around my head like a spiky halo. "Chandni would help you if you wanted to break away from your father. I know she would."

"Not you?" Sesha asked, his expression a mix of anger and vulnerability.

"Are you serious right now?" I couldn't believe this guy was asking me this as I hung on for dear life to the back of his flying chariot. To make matters worse, the merciless sun was making me sweat, and I felt one of my hands slipping.

"Yagh!" I yelled, and my goofy cousins each grabbed me and held on with all their might.

"Didi, howd tight!" Kawla cried as all three little rakkhosh clamped on to my wrists. "We won't let you go without a fight!"

The chariot was clipping along, making their fur stand on end.

"Don't fall for our sake!" Mawla yelled. "And get smushed to a pancake!"

"I'm trying!" I yelped.

"Hang in there, Didi! I'm coming!" I heard Chandni shout from below me.

"Hurry, moon girl!" I shouted. "I'm not sure how much longer I can hold on!"

Sesha looked back from the front of the chariot. "I'm sorry about this, Pinki. I really thought we could have been friends."

"Don't let me fall, Sesha." My three hearts were

hammering in my chest. "I mean, you must have felt like you could trust me back there in the woods. Why else would you have asked me to help you find Chandni? Get me into the chariot already and we'll talk!"

"I chose you because you were supposed to be a villain, just like me. None of this do-gooder stuff." But even as he said this, Sesha moved toward me, his hands outstretched. "I chose you because you would know better than to place your trust in someone like me!"

Sesha reached out to grab my wrist with his strong hand. "No tricks, Pinki! Honor among villains!" he snarled, even as, without a driver at the helm, the flying chariot lurched, making me almost lose my hold and all my baby cousins lose their balance.

"I'm going to fall!" I shouted as I entirely lost my grip with my other hand.

"No, you're not!" said Sesha, using both arms now to grab my one. He was strong, and when he finally met my eyes, his gaze was fierce. "I'm pulling you in!"

Kawla, Mawla, and Deembo all cheered.

"Thank you!" I breathed, not daring to look down.

That would have been the end of that, if not for Chandi being particularly brave and heroic.

"Let her go!" shouted the Moon Maiden, now suddenly closer than ever. I saw that she was standing up in Raat's stirrups, her staff glowing fiercely in her hand. "I don't want to kill you, Sesha, but I will!"

Sesha gave me a devastating look. Both his hands were holding on to me, so he couldn't generate any lightning bolts. He was going to die, and it was going to be my fault.

"Let me go!" I whispered to him, meeting his green-brown eyes square on.

I thought he'd argue. I thought he'd say or do something noble. But do you know what that slimeball did? I still can't even believe it. That no-good double-crossing fink. He just nodded and said, "As you wish."

And then he let me fall.

Which just goes to show you that I really needed to start making better decisions with my life.

I screamed as I fell, because there is only so long that someone can hide their fear of heights. The only problem was, someone else was screaming too. Someone else who was falling right alongside me. As I'd feared, my weight had pulled one of my cousins out of the safety of the flying chariot. The one cousin who didn't let go of me when everyone else did.

It was, of course, Deembo, that little pickled egg of a rakkhoshi. She might not have been able to speak, but boy, could she scream.

I had told Sesha to let me go to stop Chandni from killing him. And that part of my plan worked. I fell right onto Raat's back, Chandni grabbing me to steady me as the animal dropped several dozen feet from the force of my weight. This all meant, of course, that the Moon Maiden couldn't shoot at Sesha, since her hands were occupied with both (a) saving me and (b) making sure Raat didn't plummet down to all our dooms.

"Deembo!" I pointed desperately to where someone was still falling like a tiny meteor from the sky. "My cousin!"

"I see her!" Chandni leaned low over Raat's back. "Come on, old friend, I know you're hurting, but we've got to get that kid!"

As we dived for Deembo, Sesha got clean away. He didn't even seem to look back to see we were okay but instead just flew off into the sky with Kawla and Mawla in tow. I could hear the twins screaming in terror.

My three hearts pounded in my ears and my breath was coming out in hot rasps. Deembo was so small in the blazing afternoon sky that it was near impossible to see her.

"Where is she?" I screamed. The sun was making me

see spots everywhere. Or was that my own panic? Which one was my falling cousin? "Chandni, can you see her?"

"I can't!" she yelled.

And for that millisecond, I was sure Deembo was done for. I was sure my egg-loving little cousin would be splattering on the ground any moment, her insides spilling out like so much runny, reddened yolk.

CHAPTER 14

I Agree to Crash a Royal Lawn Party but Draw the Line at Singing Harmonies with Bluebirds

I see her! Raat! Fly to the left! She's right under us!" Chandni pointed to a speck of darkness against the land.

"Hurry! She's so near the ground!" I yelled.

I reached around Chandni's shoulder to pat Raat's mane. "I'm sorry I got you hurt in the market, horsey. Really. Please help, and I'll owe you forever!"

As if he could understand, Raat let out a fearsome snort and put back his dark ears. He gave two hard beats of his wings and then dived.

Unfortunately, just as he did so, the sky decided to do some moving of its own. As it had done before, I felt everything around me rending, shifting, and splitting apart like paper in a giant child's hands.

"Stinky camel cakes! Not now!" I screamed, unable to help it, my fear for myself mingling with my fear for Deembo.

Like before, the ground and water below us started to shift and rearrange themselves like pieces on a game board.

"This is not the ideal time for this to be happening again!" Chandni really was the queen of the obvious statement.

I felt the atmosphere tear, somewhere near us, the pressure of the air shift making my ears pop and skin crawl. If Deembo fell into that hole in the sky, she would be gone forever. If we fell into that hole in the sky, we would have no hope of saving her and we'd all be goners.

"Down and to the left, horsey!" I yelled, reaching around Chandni to yank at the pakkhiraj's reins. "Down and to the left!"

Before me, Chandni was muttering, "Come on, come on, come on." I could see her hands were glowing silver again against the horse's neck, as if she were transferring more of her own energy to the flying pakkhiraj.

Even with his hurt wing, Raat was a champion. With an

otherworldly scream, he dived under the little rakkhoshi, allowing me to grab her arm as she almost fell by us. With a ferocious heave, not caring if I broke her arm, not caring about anything, I yanked her to my chest.

As if the multiverse were on our side, the shifting of the air, land, and water stopped almost as soon as I had plucked Deembo out of her deadly free fall.

"Oh, Deembo, oh, Deembo, are you all right? Are you all right?" I kept asking as I squeezed her small frame to me. I was breathless and dizzy, hearts pounding from our horrible close call.

Not able to answer me with words, Deembo nodded, her eyes big and frightened as they looked into mine. She was sitting backward on the horse, between Chandni and me, with my arms tight around her. Not able to stand the thought of almost having lost her, I crushed her trembling form into me, wanting to hold her but wanting to rail at her at the same time.

"You egg cream! You quiche butt! You soft-boiled ninny!" I screamed as Raat rose again, gaining altitude after saving two falling passengers midair. "You almost killed me from fright! Don't ever do that again!"

It seemed she understood that my fury was coming from my love for her, Deembo just nestled her furry head harder into my chest. She was crying and snotting into the front of my sari, but I didn't care. I held her tight as her tiny body racked with sobs, as if she couldn't shake the feeling of that terrible fall.

Chandni turned her face over her shoulder, concern in her eyes. "Is she all right? Why doesn't she answer?"

"She doesn't speak," I explained even as I had to catch my breath a little from the force at which we were flying.

"She doesn't speak? But—never mind," Chandi said in a tone that implied she wanted to ask more. But she cut herself off and said nothing else.

I didn't have the energy to find out what the moon girl had been about to say anyway. "Thank you, both," I said to Chandni and the pakkhiraj. "Thank you for saving my cousin."

"Well done, old friend." Chandni patted Raat on his neck. "Well done."

Even through her tears, Deembo fished out an egg from her pocket and handed it to Chandni, making a gesture like she should pass it forward to Raat. The pakkhiraj accepted the offering with a satisfied gulp.

"All right, so let's go! We've got to save Kawla and Mawla!" I couldn't keep the worry out of my voice. "They could be anywhere by now, especially since they were on the other side of all the shifting that happened."

"There's no way we can catch up. Especially since we have no idea where they went," Chandni argued. "We're going to have to get some help."

"We don't have time to get any help," I protested. "We've got to go after them now!"

"This is no time for individual heroics," Chandni said. "How will we find them? You said it yourself that they could be anywhere—the rip in space that just happened almost guarantees that. If you want to save them, we can't do it alone."

She was right, of course. It felt horrible not to take off immediately, but I thought about how much trouble my loner instincts had gotten us into in the market. If I'd just accepted Kumi and Aakash's help, my cousins might not have been kidnapped in the first place.

"Well, then, who is going to help us find them?" I felt a wave of desperation as I did a quick mental run-through of all my potential allies. It ended up being a very short list. I mean, Aakash and Kumi were probably dead, killed by the Governor-General. I should have gone back to help them, but I hadn't. Which was a guilt I'd have to deal with later. Of course, because of the note they'd left, everyone at Ghatatkach undoubtedly hated me and thought I was a serpent collaborator. Which was actually true, in part. So I'd probably never be welcomed back at school again. Ai-Ma would give her life to rescue her niece and nephew, but she was a prisoner, under serpent cave arrest. Who else did I have? The truth was, no one.

"Who's going to help us?" I repeated, frustration lacing my voice.

Chandni's answer was firm. "We're going to get help from the resistance."

Once we were flying a few moments, and Deembo had settled into my lap in a deep, exhausted slumber, I tapped Chandni hard on the shoulder.

"You know, Sesha was about to pull me into the chariot." I was feeling completely annoyed with her. "He only let me go because you were going to whack him with your weapon."

Chandni pursed her lips. "I'm not sure, Didi. He's so changeable. He might have pulled you in only to push you out again a few minutes later. I don't trust him at all."

"Well, if I'd gotten into the chariot, I could have saved all the kids," I persisted.

"Maybe," Chandni agreed. "But also, maybe not."

"Where are we going anyway? Where are we going to find the resistance?" I gritted out. My nerves felt like frayed wires. "Will they agree to help us get Kawla and Mawla back?"

Instead of answering any of my questions, Chandni did

her ESP trick with the horse again. Without her doing anything, Raat changed direction, banking right and flapping hard toward the horizon.

I gulped. "I hate it when you do that!"

Chandni answered with a perfect little laugh.

Argh! I couldn't understand how chill the girl was in the face of danger. You would think someone that delicate and wispy would be screaming or swooning, depending on me to solve our problems. But instead she was the one with the plan, and I was the one with all the worries. I desperately wanted to shake the girl, or maybe bite off one of her perfect toes. Every time she laughed like that, all I could think of were helpful bluebirds and perfect sunrises and flowers that bloomed under her feet as she walked. All of which was so gross. I tried not to think of Kawla and Mawla and how afraid they must have been right then.

"So what kind of smuggling operation were you running out of my mother's house anyway?" I asked, my irritation making my tone snappy.

"So why'd you make a deal with Sesha to trade me for lessons on how to control your power?" Chandni shot right back.

"I told you already, I didn't know you were a person when I made that deal—a lunar person anyway," I explained.

"But it was otherwise okay to make a deal with the same oppressive overlords who have been ruling our land now for decades—plundering and killing and taking away all our freedoms?" With a nod of her chin, Chandni directed Raat to fly lower, toward the ground. The sun was finally getting a little less intense in the sky, but it was still hot on the horse's back.

"You have no idea why I made that deal, all right? There were . . . extenuating circumstances," I said, not wanting to explain the embarrassment of being strung upside down over the forest floor, or the shame of having almost burned down the school banyan grove.

"I don't get you at all, Pinki." Chandni shook her head. Her use of my name rather than the respectful, familial *Didi* kind of hurt. "You are born from the most legendary freedom fighters of the past generation—"

I cut her off. "I told you what it was like for me growing up. Anyway, what's your deal with Sesha? You guys seemed pretty enemies-to-love-interests meet-cute back there."

Chandni made a scoffing noise in the back of her throat. "We used to be in the resistance together, that's all, before he convinced himself that he was being a bad son to that monster of a father."

Her answer kind of shocked me. "Sesha was in the resistance? But he's a snake!"

"Who someone's parents are doesn't matter," the Moon Maiden said. "They can still decide for themselves what's right or wrong."

For some reason, her words reminded me of that human -teacher I'd seen in the woods, Shurjo. He'd been talking about culture and tradition being our hidden sources of strength, but he'd also said something about leaving behind those beliefs that didn't serve us.

"You still haven't answered my original question." I wasn't ready to let Chandni off the hook just yet. She was so smug and superior it set my teeth on edge. "Were you running a smuggling operation out of my mother's house or what? How could you do that to her?"

"Oh, she knew what I was doing."

Chandni's reply startled me so much, I almost lost my balance. With a little half scream, I righted myself on the horse's back. Deembo grabbed my arm and mouthed something in her sleep. "What do you mean she knew?"

A flock of quacking ducks flew right by us, making Raat whinny.

"Ai-Ma didn't know who I was, but she knew what I was doing," Chandni said. "You underestimate her way too much.

I mean, she's a legend in the resistance. Why do you think she chose to live on top of that underground part of the River of Dreams?"

"What, exactly, were you smuggling down the river?" I demanded, envisioning drugs, weapons, poison spells. "Did it never occur to you Ai-Ma might be put in danger?"

"That's why I agreed to leave." Chandni sighed. "As for what we were smuggling, I'd rather show you than tell you." She pointed down to the rapidly approaching ground. "We're here."

"Please tell me I'm seeing things," I said. "Because if my eyes aren't deceiving me, we're heading toward a . . . palace?"

"You're not seeing things!" singsonged the Moon Maiden. "And since it's already evening, I think we'll get a good reception!"

"Oh, just great." I squinted at the marble structure surrounded by rolling lawns and lush woods. Its turrets and towers reached toward the sky, and it had the romantic air of something out of a fairy tale. "I'm going to assume this palace is full of royal humans of some sort?"

"Well, obviously," the girl said in her bell-like voice. Then she coughed. "Just promise me you won't try to eat them."

I snorted. "Why do I have to promise?"

"Because if you don't, then I can't take you there, and we have no one else who can help us find your cousins." Chandni's tinkling voice had an edge to it again. "Or do you want to just forget about rescuing them?"

"Fine, I won't try to eat your friends," I grumbled.

"Or scare them either," Chandni insisted, gripping my wrist. "Promise!"

"Ouch! Loosen up!" I griped. "Fine! I promise! But there better not be any princes down there," I groused as Raat descended farther toward the palace. If my knowledge of storybooks told me anything, it was that a prince plus a princess usually equaled trouble. Cloyingly, sickly sweet trouble, but trouble nonetheless.

"Sorry," said Chandni, not sounding sorry in the least. "There are actually seven princes. The Seven Brothers Champak, as they are known."

"Seven princes!" Ugh. Just terrific. "Well, there better not be a ball. Or talking chipmunks or something. You better not start acting all princessy and, like, singing harmonies while you're cleaning toilets!"

"Well, not exactly a ball." Chandni squinted through the evening darkness. "I think it's more like a fancy lawn party."

"A what?" I looked where Chandni was pointing and

saw that the extensive lawns in front of the marble palace were lit up with lanterns and torches. Even from our distance and height, my rakkhoshi eyes could see small dots of partygoers milling around, and my acute ears could hear some kind of stringed instrument being played.

Chandni went on, "I'm fairly sure our hosts aren't going to ask either of us to sing harmonies while cleaning toilets, but if you really want to, I suppose you could."

Again with the unnecessary sarcasm! For a delicate and fragile maiden type, this girl had a mouth on her. "Why are your resistance friends having a big palace party? I would have thought having canapés wasn't as much their scene as painting protest signs and planning marches."

The moon girl sighed even as she directed Raat to land in a secluded area out of view of the palace lawns. Then she said something that made no sense to me at the time. "Sometimes the best way to hide something is to leave it right where no one would suspect it to be."

As soon as we three dismounted, Raat, who was apparently the property of the eldest prince of the realm, trotted off in the direction of the palace stables. Chandi, Deembo, and I were left to walk slowly in the direction of what was obviously a happening soiree. Even from our distance, I could hear music, laughter, and the clinking of glasses. I felt my skin tingling with anxiety at the thought of having to walk into a big human party. I hated small talk almost as much as I hated meeting new people. Especially if I wasn't allowed to eat or scare them.

Chandni turned toward me kind of awkwardly. "Oh, and there's one more thing."

"I have a feeling I'm not going to like this one more thing." I adjusted Deembo in my arms.

"It might be good for you to be in your human form again." At the sound of my protests, Chandni butted in, "Just for your own safety. At least right away."

"I knew it." Humans were so boringly predictable. "Those fancy party people are going to start chasing me with pitchforks and flaming torches, aren't they?" I looked down at my sleeping cousin. "I suppose you want me to magic Deembo too?"

Chandni shrugged. "If it's not too much trouble?"

"If this wasn't about getting Kawla and Mawla back, I wouldn't even consider it." Saying the words of the transformative incantation, I swirled around, changing my own form back into the human one I'd inhabited before, and Deembo into, well, something slightly different.

"She looks like a baby . . . cheetah!" Chandni's surprise

only took her a second to get over, and then she was coo-
ing and cuddling with the sleepy, extra-furry girl. Deembo,
predictably, kind of purred and gurgled, turning up her
tummy to be petted.

"She's so hairy, it was easier than making her look like
a human," I admitted. "I haven't had a lot of practice in small
humans, but I aced Mammalian Transformations last year."
I caught Deembo's gaze. "I hope you don't mind, kiddo; I'll
get you transformed back to yourself as soon as I can."

Deembo grinned and scratched her ear with a spotty
back paw.

Chandni gave us both a critical look. "Maybe just a tad
fancier too," she mumbled. And with a wave of her hands,
she transformed my ordinary cotton sari into one made of
silver-embroidered silk. I felt my ears heavy with jhumko
earrings and my wrists jingling not with my normal glass
bangles but with stacks of thin silver ones. Even poor
Deembo had a bejeweled gold necklace around her spotty
neck. I was annoyed, but my cheetah cousin purred with
pleasure, so I guess she liked it.

"Good," Chandni murmured. I noticed her own sari
had gotten even sparklier than usual, and her ears, neck,
and arms were adorned now with delicate jewelry that

shone like they were made of diamonds—or maybe, on closer inspection, stars.

"This is ridiculous!" I protested, feeling like an imposter in my fake skin and borrowed finery. "I need to save my cousins, not get all fancied up for some trifling human party!"

We were almost to the edge of the lawn now and in a few steps would be in full view of the partygoers. The music of a stringed sitar and the rhythms of the tabla reached my ears. On top of the music was the cacophony of too many voices, too much fake laughter.

"Okay, so here's the thing." Chandni turned to me, another apologetic expression on her face. "It's probably not just going to be humans."

"What do you mean, not just humans?" In my arms, Deembo meowed as if wondering too.

"Well, you know how there are at least fifty minor the Raja in the Kingdom Beyond, all basically powerless kings of small principalities?" Chandni asked.

"I guess." I swatted at a mosquito buzzing by my ear. "So?"

Chandni looked even more uncomfortable. "Well, the thing is, those royal human titles are actually granted by the Empire of Serpent Overlords—"

"Yeah, I know," I cut her off. "Just like the title of Demon Queen or King. No real power, just scrappy morsels our snake rulers hand out to keep us all quiet and satisfied."

"Right." Chandni nodded, taking a minute to scratch Deembo under the chin, just above her neck scar. "So, the thing is, the Raja of this particular principality, my friend Prince Arko's father, he's, well, made himself quite a favorite of the Serpentine Empire."

"Your friend's dad is a snake collaborator?" I was kind of shocked. "And I'm supposed to trust him to help me find my cousins?"

"Arko's not like his dad," Chandni reassured me. "But the thing is, there very well may be, uh, snakes at this party."

"What?" I wished I still had fangs to snap in her direction. "Do you not remember that we literally just escaped from a bunch of snakes? And now you're telling me that we're about to walk into a party full of them?"

"Kind of?" Chandni twisted her face in half smile, half grimace.

Oh, perfect. My day was just getting awesomer and awesomer. "Then we better find this Prince Arko as soon as we can and get going. I'm not here to play royal court games or make nice with a bunch of slimy snakes. I need to rescue my cousins from your maniac boyfriend as soon as I can."

"Not my boyfriend," Chandni muttered through gritted teeth just as we came into view of the royal lawn party.

"Plus, you better hope the Governor-General isn't here." I felt my own insides quake at the thought. "Or we're all dead anyway."

CHAPTER 15

Oh, Yippee! A Shindig Full of Evil Snakes—I Mean, What Could Possibly Go Wrong?

It was a seriously fancy shindig, fancier than anything I'd ever seen. The perimeter of the lawn party was guarded by thick men with curved swords, and for a second, I was worried. But then the silly humans let us in as soon as they saw us in our fancy clothes.

"That was easy," I muttered, cuddling cheetah Deembo closer. Her body was soft and hummed like she had an internal purring engine. "I guess they couldn't imagine that two girls in saris and jewels could be revolutionaries."

"That's sexism for you." Chandni spoke stiffly through the artificial smile she had pasted onto her face. She waved cheerily at the guards, who smiled, goo-goo-eyed, back at her. "Just keep walking and try not to make any more eye contact with anyone."

I tried. For about thirty seconds. I really tried. Then I realized there were waiters running around the party with plates piled high with fragrant tikia, kebabs, and bhajis. I hadn't seen delicious food like this—and in this kind of quantity—in my entire life. The mouthwatering treats were quite a change from simple Academy dinners of rice, daal, and liver curry. I stopped one waiter after another, shoving the fried finger food and meat into my mouth with some serious speed until Chandni stopped me.

"Chill, Pinki!" she said through her smile. "People are starting to stare."

I picked some onion bhaji out of my front tooth. "What, I'm not supposed to eat?"

I snuck Deembo a couple more chicken kebab pieces before wiping my hands on the floating back section of Chandni's beautiful sari. That would serve her right.

The palace lawns were packed. There were silk-clad ladies wandering around whose entire job seemed to be putting flower malas on the necks of guests, and others who simply walked around, smiling, with lighted incense holders that made the evening air thick with the smells of jasmine and sandalwood. There were fire jugglers and high-wire acrobats, dancing girls and magicians. What there wasn't, however, were any snake charmers.

And me having a tiny cheetah wasn't even a weird thing at this party, because there were mischievous monkeys, golden deer, and thick-plumed peacocks mixing freely among the guests. Plus, near the top of the lawn on a small palace terrace, there were two large cages that housed half a dozen tigers and lions. Next to these cages lounged seven beautifully dressed but sleepy-looking human women, probably members of the royal family, on various divans and couches. Even though the women didn't have any visible cages around them, it was obvious they were expected to just sit up there, looking pretty. It was hard to tell who was more caged—the women, the animals, or both.

I had an almost-uncontrollable impulse to free those lions and tigers, letting them feast on the terrible partygoers milling around the lawn. Because let me tell you, the party guests were ridiculous. The human women wore such heavy brocade saris and jewels they looked like they were about to sink into the grass, while the men wore elaborate silk turbans and had moustaches that reached out stiffly from the sides of their faces. The snakes were even worse.

The serpents attending the party were in human form but recognizable by the greenish tints of their skin, their forked tongues, and their medal-laden red uniforms. The soldiers had brought their snake spouses, who each looked more annoyed than the next and turned up their noses at the human food, demanding bland puddings and bottled water. There were even dressed-up snake children chasing the human ones.

"You don't know how to ssspeak right!" snapped one nasty snake girl to a smaller human boy. "My daddy sssaid they're going to take all you mongrelsss away from your familiesss and sssend you to sssnake retraining ssschool until you get ssstraightened out. They're going to pluck the voicesss right out of your throatsss!"

At this, the human boy started crying, and I noticed the snake girl give a triumphant grin to her mother. The snake woman was close enough to hear the whole thing but did nothing to stop her bully of a daughter.

"Please, can I eat that one?" I muttered to Chandni. "Just that one little girl? Nobody would miss her."

"Just keep your head down and try not to make a scene," Chandni said. "We've got to find Arko as soon as we can."

I nodded, but I didn't stop cheetah Deembo when she jumped out of my arms to twine herself around the bullied boy's legs. He stopped crying and bent down to pet her, to which she mewed in pleasure. When the snake girl tried to reach down, though, Deembo started hissing and scratching at her so much, I had to intervene.

"I told you not to make a scene!" Hurriedly, Chandni yanked both Deembo and me away.

"I didn't do anything!" I protested. And then, when Chandni wasn't looking, I gave Deembo a juicy kebab as a reward.

As we crossed the lawn, I realized the dynamic of the party was seriously strange. The humans, servants and nobles alike, were absolutely tripping over themselves to see to the serpents' needs, bowing and scraping, laughing at their terrible snaky jokes. I also noticed that the snakes seemed to have commanded all the best seats, the cushy ones nearest the musicians and the cozy ones farthest from the smoking lanterns.

"My dear Lord Sssshaputon!" said an older human noble, so subservient he bobbed like a cork in water before a red-coat-clad snaky officer. I noticed the graying man drew out his *s*'s in a poor imitation of the serpentine accent. "I'm so sssorry the Governor-General is delayed, but I hope you're enjoying the party before our guest of honor arrives!"

At the mention of Sesha's dad, I quaked. He was still

alive, which wasn't a hopeful sign for Aakash and Kumi. Worse, he was expected at this very party. Which meant Chandni, Deembo, and I seriously needed to find Chandni's resistance buddy and skedaddle before he showed up.

"You humansss and your tediousss affairsss!" drawled the snaky officer, swiping an aloo tikia from a passing waiter with a white-gloved hand. "But we do what we mussst, Your Royal Majesssty!"

I felt my eyes go round. Wait, this human was the Raja of the realm? This guy who was bowing and scraping to serpent officers, imitating their accents?

The Raja laughed in a falsehearted way. He was a king, and he didn't even have the guts to respond to the snake soldier's rudeness! "Of course! I mean, of courssse! The august condessscension of the ssserpents is ssso very, very appresssiated!"

I suppressed a strong desire to bite someone as the powerless king and rude soldier passed out of earshot. The son of this ridiculous raja was going to help me save my family? Chandni's brain was obviously made of cheese if she thought this was a good plan.

"Hey, moon girl," I called out.

"Shhh!" Chandni whirled around furiously. "Are you trying to get us killed?"

I felt bad for about half a second, but then the feeling passed. Like gas. "I'm getting out of here. This was a ridiculous plan. These humans are all serpent bootlickers! And besides, the Governor-General is supposed to be here soon!"

"What?" She looked around in concern.

"Yeah, he's like the guest of honor or something! So we better get going before he shows up." I pulled at her arm.

"I don't see Arko anywhere," Chandni said. "Maybe we should look inside."

But before we had gone more than a few steps toward the marble palace, we were approached by a slim young man with a bejeweled turban. "Lady Chandni!" he cried, clasping her hands. "I didn't expect to see you here! But a pleasure, as always!"

"So nice to see you! This is my friend Pinki!" Chandni introduced me, only looking slightly flustered. "And, Pinki, this is Prince Aadil, the second son of the realm!"

I gave the handsome Prince Aadil an awkward wave and what I hoped was a normal human smile. From his confused expression, though, I'm not sure I succeeded. This pretending-to-be-human stuff was hard.

"A pleasure, Lady Pinki!" Prince Aadil gave Deembo an affectionate scratch. "Welcome to you both!"

And then, suddenly, we were surrounded by more

princes all vaguely of the same height and build, the same thick hair and same dark eyes. The funny thing was, even though they were all dressed up, everyone had a sleepy look about them, like they had just woken up after snoozing all day.

"Our days are so tedious, Father has decided to throw a party every night when we are all awake!" said a prince whose name was Ishan. Even as the handsome prince grinned at me, he swallowed a yawn.

I wanted to ask Chandni what Ishan meant, but I didn't have a chance, because then I was meeting the fourth, fifth, and sixth princes of the realm, smiling young men of about the same height and looks named Uday, Umran, and Rishi who were eager to show Chandni their new pakkhiraj horses.

"She's a lovely white foal named Tushar Kona!" said Rishi. "But I think I'm going to call her Snowy!"

"Maybe we'll walk down to the stables later. I've only just sent your eldest brother's horse there myself. It was so kind of him to let me borrow Raat," Chandni said.

As she talked, I took a quick look around the party. No sign of Sesha's dad still, but that didn't mean he couldn't arrive at any second. I raised my eyebrows, shouting, "We've got to hurry up!" with about every facial muscle I possessed.

Chandni seemed to understand what I was saying, because she asked, in a voice that only slightly betrayed her tension, "By the way, where is Prince Arko? I haven't seen him yet."

"Oh, you know how much Bor-da hates these parties!" said Uday, referring to Arko as "biggest brother." "He's up in the astronomy tower, as usual!"

"Astronomy tower?" I asked, glancing at the many turrets of the palace. Good. The sooner we were off this exposed lawn, the better.

"The work our eldest brother has been doing is actually kind of amazing!" Ishan said to me. "He thinks he's discovered something about rakkhosh that's quite remarkable!"

"Rakkhosh?" I cursed my voice for getting so loud. Chandni gave me a huge-eyeballed look, and I tried to calm down, adopting a more human tone. "Why, whatever can you mean about rakkhosh?" I batted my eyes in that simpering way I'd seen Chandni do, hoping I appeared like a normal human girl.

Apparently, I didn't. "Is there something in your eye, my lady?" asked Umran, handing me an embroidered handkerchief. Not knowing what I was supposed to do, I took it with thanks and blew my nose in it.

I heard some titters and saw that groups of young

women—human and snake alike—were giving us the stink eye (or rather, multiple stinky eyes) for monopolizing so many princes. I waved my snot-covered handkerchief at them until they made disgusted faces and turned away. I know I've said it before, but it's worth repeating: Titterers are the absolute worst.

Chandni's own voice was pretty loud as she said, "So what were you saying about Arko discovering something about rakkhosh?"

"He has a theory from studying black holes," said Prince Rishi, whose hair sprouted in shaggy waves practically over his eyes. "He thinks there is a relationship between rakkhosh and this interstellar phenomenon—this space in which energy gets both created and destroyed."

"We think of rakkhosh as destructive, but if Bor-da is right, they are creators too!" added Uday, enthusiastically showing me a page full of incomprehensible calculations in a notebook he pulled from his pocket.

"He's not sure yet what it is," said Umran, "but he thinks that rakkhosh have an important role in the movement of stars and planets, the very foundations of our galaxy!"

"Fascinating!" said Chandni, who was obviously impatient to get on our way too.

I was about to start in on our good-byes when a new voice piped up from my elbow.

"With all respects to our eldest brother, I think he must be incorrect about this," said a boy who I realized must be the seventh Brother Champak. He was dressed in the same sorts of clothes as the older princes but with a bit more bling—extra rings, necklaces, and turban clips. At his elbow hovered a palace servant holding a tray overfilled with sweets, including sandesh, rasagolla, and mishti doi that the prince was happily sampling from. "Rakkhosh cannot be anything but evil! Indeed, they kill and plunder and commit all sorts of unpleasantries!"

"Well, maybe they have their reasons," I began, until Chandni poked me in the side with a bit more force than necessary and I shut my mouth. Still, I smarted at the prince's words, not only because I couldn't rip off his head but also because I sensed something true in them.

The boy went on. "I sssay, old thing, fear-mongering or violence without cause is very unsssportsmanlike!"

The young prince was wearing a cricketer's knee and elbow pads over his silk clothes and carried a cricket bat with him to the party. I noticed he dragged out some of his s's, like his father had. He was obviously a snake-o-phile, and even though I myself had until recently been in cahoots with the prince of snakes, it kind of grossed me out.

"Lay off your cricket talk and your sweet tooth for once, Bhai?" Aadil gave his brother a frown. "Lady Pinki, may I present to you our youngest brother, Rontu."

Despite his dessert-sticky face, the boy bent low over my hand. "A true pleasure, my lady!" As his eyes looked up at mine, they went huge. "I am awed to be in the company of sssuch ressssplendent beauty!"

It was all I could do not to yank my hand away with an "ew," even as the other brothers immediately began ribbing their sibling. "Ore! Sweetie Rontu-re!" "Ronts!" "Baby Rontu-shona!" "Ole Chhoto Rontu-baba!" they shouted and cooed.

"Ssstop that! I'm only a few months younger than all of you!" Rontu said huffily. "A year younger than Bor-da!"

I raised my eyebrows at Aadil, at first not understanding how this could be, until the second eldest prince indicated the bored women on the dais, explaining, "We all have different mothers—the seven ranis of our kingdom—and we were born all rather close together."

Of course. It was a custom among royal humans that rakkhosh didn't share. Plus, it explained those bored-looking, lounging women.

"You all are just jealous because I'm the only one who was brave enough to tell Lady Pinki the truth!" Rontu announced, and I almost jumped out of my skin. What did this kid mean by "the truth"? But then he shot me another admiring look. "I hereby declare ssshe is the most beautiful creature I have ever seen!" He made a chivalrous bow to Chandni. "With the exssssception of Lady Chandni, of course!"

"Prince Rontu seems quite taken with you." Chandni's voice was thick with amusement.

Her words irritated me more than I liked to admit. Of course Chandni would think that anyone liking me was funny. She probably couldn't wait to reveal to these princely brothers that I was really a rakkhoshi—hairy and violent and unworthy of their attentions.

Rontu was still waxing poetic about my qualities, laying on the serpent accent thick. "Sssuch sssparkling eyes, sssuch sssquare teeth, sssuch radiant ssstrength, sssuch resplendent hair, sssuch tall height . . ."

Since he didn't seem eager to let it go, I forcibly pulled my hand out of Rontu's grip. "Uh, thank you." I thought of Kumi threatening to feed flirtatious Aakash's gallbladder to her hench-crocs but didn't think that sort of thing was considered appropriate among humans. "For the . . . uh . . . compliments. But really, it's time we got going. Don't want to monopolize you when you have all these guests!" I gestured to the groups of tittering girls.

"Yes!" Chandni agreed enthusiastically. "Time to go visit the astronomy tower and learn all those cool things about black holes and rakkhosh!"

With a quick set of good-byes, Chandni, Deembo, and I started fast-walking toward the palace and away from the party. It would have been a little more than awkward if we'd still been there if and when the Governor-General arrived. And by awkward, I mean, guaranteeing of our gruesome deaths.

CHAPTER 16

Are All Cute Boys Extra Complicated, or Just the Royal Ones?

When we knocked on the front doors of the palace, it was opened not by any royal servants but by the eldest prince of the realm himself.

"Prince Arko!" Chandni said, practically clapping her hands. We were standing in the darkness, the boy a tall shadow before the light.

"I saw you coming across the lawn." The prince pointed at the long telescope sticking through a top turret window of the marble palace. "Or running, rather."

"Well, we heard that a certain important official might be the guest of honor tonight," said Chandni with a significant look. "And we thought it might be best if we weren't hanging around to greet him. Especially since our last encounter with him wasn't exactly the best."

Arko, still a shadow before the lights of the palace hallway, yanked the door fully open. "You've had an encounter with the Governor-General?"

"I'm afraid so, in the marketplace," Chandni said. And then, at the sight of a passing servant, she made her tone light and breezy. "Thank you so much for loaning me Raat!" she blathered. "What a good horse, a wonderful flier!"

With tense gestures, Arko ushered us inside, shutting the front doors behind us. But as we stepped into the lit palace entryway, I almost screamed. Arko's face was startlingly familiar.

"Wut!" I practically clapped a hand over my mouth but stopped myself just in time. Chandni gave me an odd look but then, as we were still in full view of a number of sleepy-appearing palace servants, formally introduced me to Prince Arko.

"Lady Pinki, you are most welcome!" The prince made a gracious gesture that caused my three hearts do an uncomfortable flip-flop. He raised his eyebrows at the sight of cheetah kitten Deembo, awake and mewing enthusiastically from my arms. "As are any friends of yours!"

"Um, thank you, Your Princeliness!" I said, even as my hearts began beating wildly in my chest. Because I knew this prince but not as Arko. I knew this prince to be the forest schoolteacher Shurjo!

"Forgive me, my lady." The boy gave me a thoughtful look that made my face warm. "But your voice, it seems so familiar."

At this, Deembo started mewing even louder, like she wanted to tell Arko why he recognized my voice. I gave her a stern look, then coughed. With an effort, I made my voice breathier, like how I imagined all those swooning princesses from fairy tales must talk. "Gee whiz, I must just have some of those common-sounding vocal cords!"

Arko-slash-Shurjo opened his mouth as if to say more, but then Chandni began babbling again about how wonderful Raat had been and how thankful she was that he had loaned her the pakkhiraj horse, blah, blah, blah, magic hearts, rainbows and friendship, etc. As she dithered on, I studied the prince from under my lashes. He looked the same as he had in the woods, muscular and broad, confident and sure-footed. He still had that golden glow about him too. But now, instead of rags, he was clad in silks. Instead of a simple stick, his hand rested on the hilt of a curved sword he wore at his waist. I noticed there

was a jeweled scabbard on his other side, undoubtedly holding a sharp dagger. He looked like he knew how to use his weapons, which was something I could respect. It had to be the same guy; I mean, his face was utterly imprinted in my mind. But what in the multiverse was he doing here?

Luckily, Chandni was so occupied with babbling, she didn't seem to notice Deembo's or my reaction to Arko. As she embraced the prince, I noticed how the two seemed to glow in each other's presence, his aura golden and warm, hers silver and cool.

"Too bad it was already dark when you arrived," Arko was saying in a low voice. "We wouldn't have had to be so secretive."

"We couldn't help it," Chandni said in just as low tones. "Something has happened, and we need your help."

"Let's go up to the tower, where we can talk more comfortably," the prince said.

"My cousins—" I began, but Chandni cut me off with a gesture.

"Arko's right, let's talk upstairs," she said. "It's not safe here."

Arko gave me another confused look, and I realized that he must be finding something familiar in my human features. Hadn't Sesha said that even in human disguise, I looked like myself, just without the horns and fangs? But of course, the only time this human prince had seen me was when I was in full rakkhoshi mode, chasing him and his students out of the forest.

As we walked toward the tower stairs, I wondered for some weird reason what the prince thought of me. Even in my human disguise, being next to delicate Chandni made me feel like a towering giant created entirely of muscles, elbows, and knees. My voice felt too loud, my footsteps too broad. Even my nostrils felt too big, with too much hair inside them. Did he think I was grotesque? Or did he admire my strength, like his younger brother had? But what would he think when he realized I was a rakkhoshi?

We walked together down a long palace breezeway, passing courtyards dotted with marble fountains, arched doorways covered with flowered vines, and sparkling pools decorated with sculptures in the shapes of peacocks. As we did, we passed even more curious palace servants, who bowed and smiled at Arko. Some of them were yawning and bleary-eyed, as the others had been, like they had just woken up.

"You must think all this very odd, Lady Pinki," Arko said as we climbed up the narrow tower steps. "That my entire household seems to be just waking up, after having slept all day."

"Not really." I felt a silly eagerness to show him how fast my mind could work. "Your brothers said something about how tedious their days were. So I figure, what, the entire palace must be under some sort of sleeping curse, right? That everyone falls into a magical sleep all day until it's dark?"

"I'm impressed," Arko said, and I felt myself warm at the compliment. "Although sad that you are familiar with such curses."

My fuzzy feelings were entirely quashed by a warning look from Chandni. Ah, right, time to act more human. Which meant, I guess, stupid.

"Well, the curse can't be that terrible, since you're all together?" I suggested in a fake hopeful voice. My fingers trailed the cool banister as we climbed.

"Not really," Arko said. "My brothers and I, well, we're not exactly in human form during the day."

We were approaching the top of the tower as I asked, "Not in human form? What form do you take during the day?"

It was Chandni who replied. "The princes are cursed to be champak flowers during the day. That's why they are called the Brothers Champak."

Wait, what? The seven brothers were cursed to be flowers all day, and their household was cursed to sleep? That all sounded like a serious bummer, sure, but I couldn't understand how that could actually be true. Because I'd seen Prince Arko during the day—as Shurjo the schoolteacher. He was obviously lying.

"That can't be right," I blurted out before I had a chance to think about the words.

Both Arko and Chandni shot me looks. "What do you mean?" Chandni asked.

"Wait." Arko shook his head. We'd gotten to the top of the tower, and he was just opening the door. "Wait until we're inside."

The prince pulled out a heavy key from his pocket and unlocked a set of double doors, ushering us into the rounded astronomy tower at the top of the turret. As he shut and relocked the doors behind us, I studied the stunning room we had entered. There were twisting stairs leading to increasingly high indoor balconies. On these balconies were windows through which seven separate telescopes

protruded. Some of the telescopes were so big, they began at one level and ended a few levels up, crisscrossing the room above our heads. On the main floor, there were low tables and sofas and desks loaded with scrolls, inkwells, rulers, protractors, and pens. There were giant potted plants everywhere that gave the room a lush green feeling. Through the one main-floor window that did not have a telescope leaning through it, a cool night breeze flowed into the room. Half the window was obscured by a growing vine, from which drifted the smell of champak flowers. The most amazing thing about the room were the scores of bookshelves that lined every wall, at every level.

"So many books," I breathed, unable to help myself. The library at the Academy was falling apart, and I'd read almost every book in it. But here was a wealth of books that could keep me reading for months, if not years. The sight of them gave me goose bumps.

After quickly going around to shut all the windows on this floor of the tower, Arko gave up any efforts at secrecy. "All right, I want to hear what happened at the bazaar."

Chandni quickly filled Arko in on our battle with the serpents in the marketplace and was going to say more, but Arko cut her off with an apologetic smile and a distracted shake of his head. "I'm sorry but, Lady Pinki, I hope you won't mind me saying so, I really do have the feeling we've met before."

"Oh?" I said vaguely. At random, I picked out one of the volumes from the shelf. It was called *The Adventurer's Guide to Rakkhosh, Khokkosh, Bhoot, Petni, Doito, Danav, Daini, and Secret Codes* by someone named Professor K. P. Das. I opened it, skimming a chapter about ghosts and their strengths before flipping forward to one about rakkhosh. That's when I put the book carefully aside again. I was usually down to read anything, but a book treating rakkhosh like we were some kind of animal specimen to be studied and understood? No, thank you.

"You seem so familiar," Arko insisted. "But I can't place where we could have met."

Chandni looked curiously from Arko to me, obviously annoyed at being interrupted. "You're mistaken, my friend. I guarantee you, there's no way you've met Pinki before."

I bristled at the moon girl's words. She was always so darn sure of herself, wasn't she? "Maybe we have met before." I gave Arko a winning smile. "Could it be . . . oh, I don't know. A ball? A royal soiree? Or maybe when you were on a walk, say, in the woods?"

Chandni seemed to puff up with irritation. "Pinki, don't be silly, there's no way you could know . . ."

But Arko's expression changed suddenly. He met my eyes, and his own widened. "Wait a minute, I know where I've seen you before . . ."

"I'm telling you, Arko, you must be mixing her up with someone else," said Chandni.

Oh, the nerve of that girl! That's what sealed the deal for me. I just couldn't let Miss Moony-Two-Shoes have the last word.

"Oh, yeah? You think so? He's mixing me up, huh? No way he could have met someone as lowly as me?" I asked as I turned in a wide circle, saying the words of the reversal incantation. As I did so, Deembo and I transferred once again to our original rakkhosh forms.

"Remember where we met now?" I stretched my taloned arms and cracked my neck, shaking my thick hair over my gloriously restored horns. I gave the prince my raised-eyebrow look. "Or have you forgotten, Shurjo-da?"

There was a shocked silence that filled the astronomy tower as we all just looked at each other.

"You're that rakkhoshi from the woods!" The prince looked, as the serpent's say, gobsssmacked.

"I can explain!" Chandni cut in. "She's an ally—the daughter of two revolutionary rakkhosh leaders from the armory raid . . ."

"My goodness, you don't have to tell me. I know she's an ally!" Arko suddenly laughed—a big, warm sound that melted the tension in the room like fire on ice. "Your friend here saved my students and me in the woods—warning us away before the serpents came. She did us an invaluable service, and we certainly owe her our freedom, if not our lives!"

"She did what?" Now it was Chandni's turn to look gobsmacked. She sat down on a cushion-lined divan. "So you two actually *do* know each other?"

"I believe we do." Arko's handsome face was full of gratitude. "In fact, I owe Lady Pinki a great debt."

He kissed my hand, and unlike when his brother Rontu had done it, I didn't feel like pulling away. Of course, I'd saved him totally on impulse, practically by accident, but he didn't have to know that. I'd take the compliments without complaint. Plus, the jealous look on Chandni's face was a major bonus.

"So I guess you don't turn into a champak flower during the day, like your brothers?" I asked. "I mean, you didn't look very flowery that day I saw you."

Arko laughed again. "You've got me there. I use the days to do my work as a freedom fighter, and some days, that work is as simple as teaching young ones to love their language and culture." He tweaked Deembo's nose, and she laughed, offering him an egg from her pocket. He accepted her gift with an elaborate, theatrical bow.

My mind was putting the pieces of everything Arko had just told me together. "Don't tell me you put your own family under that curse yourself so you could be a revolutionary without them noticing?"

"No, hardly that," Arko protested. "It's a coincidence I'm immune from the curse put on them. But it turned out to be convenient when my father, and then some of my brothers, became so enamored with our snake rulers."

"How are you immune from a curse that affects every other person in your household?" I began, before answering my own question in my head. I remembered Arko-slash-Shurjo's names—both of which were other words for the sun. I thought of how he glowed golden, and how the sunny energy in him seemed to reach out to the fire in me.

"You're a sun child?" I asked.

Arko shook his head. "No, just a human boy whose mother managed to ask a celestial being to give him a boon at his birth ceremony. I am blessed with certain powers from the sun and, well, know I need to use those powers to make a difference."

I stared at the prince. He really was too noble, too pure.

In all normal circumstances, I should find his ooey-gooey goodness the ultimate in grossness. But somehow, I didn't. Not entirely, at least.

"By the way"—I studied my talons in affected casualness—"you totally do owe us, dude. You know, my cousins and I got trapped upside down by our feet in serpent traps after you escaped the woods that day."

Deembo nodded, pantomiming how the ropes had come and ensnared us. Chandni made a sympathetic noise and put her arms around the little rakkhoshi.

"Oh no!" Arko ruffled Deembo's hair. "I'd heard rumors the snakes were setting traps for human children."

"Why are they so set on kidnapping kids? I mean, I get that they want to train them to forget their language and culture . . ." I trailed off as I noticed the frozen expression on Deembo's face. "What is it, cuz?"

Deembo just stood there, still as a statue for a moment, until Arko bent down so he was eye to eye with her. "Do you have something to tell us, small one?" he asked in his gentle schoolteacher's voice.

Touching the scar on her throat, Deembo nodded.

"She wandered off school grounds a few months ago, came back with that scar," I explained. "They said it's probably from an animal . . ."

My words trailed off again, because Deembo was looking at me with giant, watery eyes. Slowly, carefully, she shook her head no.

"Do you want to tell us what actually happened to you?" Then, as if re-creating how he had drawn letters in the dirt that day in the woods, Arko walked over to one of the potted plants and scooped out a couple big handfuls of dirt that he spread on the floor in front of Deembo.

"What are you doing?" I asked. "She doesn't know her letters; she'll just make a mess."

"You're a land rakkhoshi, right?" Arko said, focusing all his attention on Deembo. "And there's no animal who walks the land who would dare hurt you, isn't that so?"

As Deembo nodded again, the prince looked up at me, lowering his voice to an anguished whisper. "That's no animal that did that."

"Then what?" I demanded, but Arko put up a hand, asking for my patience.

"Do you remember that day how I drew in the dirt?" Arko turned his attention to Deembo again and was talking in that quiet, patient, teacherly way. "I know you don't know how to write, but do you think you could show us with pictures what happened to you?"

Deembo shrugged, rubbing her nose in concentration.

Then, instead of actually touching the dirt, she reached out, her hands hovering inches above the soil Arko had spread. With the force of her land magic, she began creating a dirt painting of the day she had wandered off the school grounds. There, in the simple pile of soil on the floor, I saw Ghatatkach Academy, the banyan grove, the Thorny Woods. I saw Deembo herself, chasing what looked to be another warbling bird, but this one real. Then, with a quick motion of her hands, the scene changed. Deembo showed us how she had stumbled upon another human patshala at play between their lessons. How she'd hidden until one shy human child had wandered away from the other pupils' games, and how Deembo had given him an egg in friendship. They'd been building tiny fairy houses of sticks and leaves when the serpent patrols came. With a wave of her hands, Deembo erased the scene again, whipping the soil into yet another set of images—snake men with sticks and small cages, a magic boat that dived under the sea to the serpents' kingdom, an assembly line of crying children being bathed and getting their hair cut and their old clothes burned. When the cruel line had come to Deembo and her friend, she'd fought, biting and snarling. It was then that the snake soldiers had discovered she was a rakkhoshi child, taken by mistake in a human raid. They'd bundled her back into a cage and sent her home above the water. But this was not before they'd magically sliced her throat, along with all the other children's, taking her speaking voice.

After Deembo was done, we three stared at her a moment, as silent as she was.

"I should have guessed." Arko ran a distracted hand over his eyes. "We've been looking for the location of that retraining school for so long and now it's so obvious why we couldn't find it! It's back in the snakes' undersea kingdom!"

"Their voices," breathed Chandni, her own voice breaking on the words. "I thought it was just a rumor, but the snakes really are stealing the children's voices!"

I felt a burning fury exploding in my chest. "None of what happened to you is your fault!" I said to Deembo, my tone fierce. "Those are cruel adults doing cruel things, and they are wrong to have hurt you. Do you understand?"

"Pinki . . ." said Arko, as if trying to diffuse my anger.

But Deembo understood what I meant. When she nodded, I took her in my arms and held her very, very close.

"I'm going to hunt down those snakes who did this to you," I promised. "We're going to shut down that jail of a school under the sea. Not just shut it down. We're going to get Kawla, Mawla, and all those kids out of there, and then we're going to destroy it!"

Unfortunately, even as I said these words, there came a thunderous noise from outside. A cheer went up from the guests down on the lawn, and a brass-and-drums band began to play.

"The Governor-General," Chandni breathed. "He's here. We're too late."

CHAPTER 17

The Jig Is Seriously Up and I Have to Save Everyone's Butts with a New, Possibly Not-Very-Well-Thought-Out Plan

Almost as soon as Arko ran to the window to look out, there came a pounding on the tower door.

"Bor-da! Brother!" It was Rontu's voice, calling out even as he clattered at the locked door handle. "Our guest of honor is here—and he's specifically asking after Lady Chandni and Lady Pinki! It's so funny, but apparently the Governor-General knows them!"

Chandni and I exchanged panicked looks. Arko's brothers had obviously spilled the beans about our being here!

"There's no way out!" I hissed, looking frantically around the closed tower room with its one door. "What do we do?"

"Tell our honored guest we will be right down!" Arko

called through the locked door. He looked over at Deembo, who was balanced on my hip, and he gave her a wink and a finger-on-lips shushing gesture.

"Father says we can't keep him waiting!" Rontu rattled at the door handle again. "Why is the door locked anyway? He's saying to come down this instant!"

"Of course, Brother! We'll be a moment!" called Arko again. As he talked, he gestured for Chandni and me to follow him up the room's winding stairways to the topmost balcony.

"Should I wait?" Rontu asked through the door, his voice seriously whiny. "Father said I should bring soldiers up if you didn't bring the ladies down right away, although I can't imagine why. I guess the Governor-General isss apparently very eager to meet them!" Rontu dragged that last *s* as if remembering to put on his snaky accent.

"Come on!" urged Arko in a whisper. "We've got to get you out of here!"

"Bor-da?" asked Rontu again through the downstairs door. "Come on! I mean, I left an entire plate of uneaten rasagolla down there!"

But Arko was too busy to answer him anymore. We sprinted up the winding staircases until we arrived at the topmost of the inside balconies that circled the tower room. There, we dashed behind Arko to the largest telescope, the huge one that spanned all the floors of the tower. Arko unscrewed a piece of it, then showed us the hollow tunnel it hid inside.

"It's an escape route to the underground river passage," he whispered, pushing Chandni forward. "Go! I'll hold them off as long as I can."

Chandni looked down the narrow shoot, which was just wide enough for us to slide down, one at a time. "We'll meet at the resistance headquarters?"

Arko nodded. "I won't be more than a day or two. I'll send word through our networks. We'll regroup, then we'll plan the raid on the undersea retraining school."

"You're not coming with us now?" I was surprised at my own disappointment.

"I'll follow as soon as I can," Arko said. "I'll have Raat waiting for you by the riverside."

"I can just call him with my mind, you know." Chandni put on a brave smile as she climbed, feetfirst, into the chute.

Arko nodded, giving her a quick hug. "I know, but I have to tell you that it always weirds me out when you do that."

"Right?" I couldn't help but snort in agreement. "Like, next thing, you expect her to start talking to bluebirds."

"Singing while she's cleaning," added Arko, to which even Deembo giggled.

Chandni shook her head. "You two are the worst."

But then there was no more time for chummy chitchat, because the pounding at the tower door was getting louder. "Bor-da? Brother? Are you coming out, or do I have to bring the soldiers like Father says?"

Without another word, Arko gave Chandni a push and sent her sliding. Then it was Deembo's and my turn.

"Bor-da? I can't hear you! I'm going to get the soldiers!" Rontu called, rattling the doorway with impatience. And then there was the sound of heavy, booted feet on the stairs. "Never mind, Father already sent them!"

"Prince Arko?" a deep voice boomed. "Are you there? Are Lady Chandni and Lady Pinki in there with you?"

"I'm afraid they left already!" Arko called down, faking a yawn. "I'm rather sleepy. Do tell my father I'll be down after a short nap."

"They left? I didn't see them go! I thought you just said they were with you!" called Rontu. "Um, Brother? Lady Pinki—did she say anything about me before she went?"

Arko raised his eyebrows at me, and I shrugged, trying not to meet his eyes. "I think I made quite an impression on your brother—even in human form."

"I commend his taste!" Arko whispered, and I felt my cheeks warm.

"I'm afraid His Royal Highness will want to see you immediately, regardless," the soldier's voice was calling out. "Please, my prince, open this door immediately!"

"You better go!" Arko whispered. "It looks like we're about to get company."

The soldier from the doorway was shouting now. "I'm afraid His Royal Majesty has ordered us to knock this door down if you do not open it."

I clambered into the slide with only a bit of difficulty. It was a tight squeeze for me, and I worried about getting stuck. Plus, I didn't fit that well with Deembo in my arms.

"You might have to send her down alone," Arko said.

I was about to argue with him, but I realized he was right.

"Are you okay to go down by yourself?" I asked Deembo as I climbed back out, putting her on the slide alone. "Chandni will be waiting on the other side."

She nodded bravely, and I smacked a kiss on her nose. "Just like on the playground," I whispered. My hearts were frantically beating, and I felt like I couldn't breathe, but I let her go.

"I'm going to count to ten, Your Highness." The soldier was saying. To his credit, the man sounded unhappy. "I really don't want to batter down the door. Please, won't you open it?"

"Now your turn." Arko helped me climb back up to the tube.

"Ten . . . nine . . ." counted the soldier at the door. It might have been my imagination, but he seemed to be counting pretty slowly.

I turned to Arko, a thought making my hearts freeze. "What if they hurt you?"

Arko shook his head. "They might hurt Shurjo the schoolteacher, but they would never dare hurt the crown prince of this realm."

"Seven . . . six . . ." the voice went on.

I adjusted myself in the tube, looking with concern at how narrow it was. "You know," I blurted out suddenly, "there was something in me that recognized you that day in the forest. As if you were my clansman."

Arko's face lit up. "I felt it too. I suppose the sun and fire are made of the same stuff."

"Four . . . three . . ."

I had so many of those annoying feelings zooming through me again that I almost couldn't bear saying good-bye. I made my voice as harsh as I could, muttering, "If I get stuck in this wack escape slide, you better come get me."

Arko smiled, kissing my hand again. "It would be an honor, my lady."

"One! Sir, I'm breaking down the door!" shouted the soldier.

And then, without any warning, Arko pushed me, and I was sliding down, down, down at breakneck speed. The light above me immediately dimmed as Arko refastened the cover of the fake telescope, and then I was plunged into darkness. I kept my hands folded over my chest and my head back, trying not to panic. Some might have loved it—by the happy squeals we heard before, Deembo obviously had—but for a control freak like me, it was a complete nightmare. Worse than flying, because it was faster and in the dark. My hearts pounded in my ears, and I felt the fire roil in my belly as the slide shot me down the many floors of the palace, on and on seemingly without end.

At a point when I thought I could no longer stand it, when I thought I might explode with flames of fear, I finally popped out the other end, where Chandni and Deembo were waiting for me. I fell with a thud on a hard stone floor at their feet.

"You all right?" Chandni asked, looking at my nauseous expression. I doubled over, coughing out smoke rings.

"I'm fine. Grand." I rubbed the shoulder on which I'd landed, then hugged Deembo, who seemed bubbly and none the worse for wear after her adventure. I took a deep breath and looked around at our underground surroundings.

We were in a dim, echoing cavern deep beneath the palace complex, at the edge of a river that flowed under the marble stones. I recognized its familiar smell and the vivid color of its blue water. "This is another part of the River of Dreams?"

"It is. The same river that runs under your mother's home, the same one that links our dimension to the 2-D realm," said Chandni, mentioning the other parallel universe that we had long-ago discovered was magically connected to ours.

The waters of the river rushed by at such speed, their echoes bounced off the cavern walls. "Can we get to Ai-Ma's from here?"

Chandni shook her head. "Unfortunately, we're downstream from her caves." Then she pointed at some clay pitchers I hadn't noticed at first, floating down the river. They were identical to the ones I had seen at Ai-Ma's. "But I can show you why Sesha was so upset about my smuggling operation."

Using her moon staff, which she made appear magically in her hands, Chandni pulled one of the bobbing clay pitchers out of the river's current and toward the shore. Lifting the lid, she revealed not weapons, not poisons, not jewels, but a small and frightened-looking child, only a year or two older than my cousins.

"You're smuggling children?" I hadn't been expecting that.

At the sound of my voice, the little passenger of the clay pot looked up with fright.

"Hello, sweeting," Chandni said in that gentle and soothing voice, the one that sounded like wind chimes. "Are you all right? Do you need any more water or food?"

The child shook her head no, looking a bit calmer at the sight of the moon girl. "You're the lady Chandni, aren't you? You and that nice schoolteacher Shurjo-da helped us get away when the snakes tried to take all us village children."

"And do you remember what I said then?" Chandni smiled kindly. "That you must be very brave and that your parents would be waiting for you in the other dimension?"

The girl nodded solemnly, giving Deembo and me frightened looks. "Are those rakkhosh going to eat me?" she squeaked.

"No, darling, they're friends! Just like that lovely grandmother Ai-Ma!" Chandni said. As if in proof of this statement, Deembo produced an egg from her seemingly endless supply and offered it to the girl.

The child accepted the egg with a grin. "Ai-Ma was so funny. I liked her a lot."

Something inside me warmed at my mother's name. "She's my mother, you know."

"She is?" The little girl wrinkled her nose in delight. Then, unexpectedly, she popped up to stand inside her clay pot. Before I could even stop her, she gave me a quick kiss on the cheek. "That's for Ai-Ma. Tell her I'll come visit her again when I can. I want to hear more of her stories."

Chandni the sap looked like she was about to burst into tears. Or maybe song. I, on the other hand, really wanted to wipe my face of the girl's spittle. I mean, this was a little human being, for demon's sake; who knew where that mouth had been! But Deembo and Chandni were looking at me with such gooey, approving expressions that I just let the icky germs stay where they were.

"I'll tell her," I said gruffly. "Now, Lady Chandni shouldn't hold you up anymore. The sooner you go, the sooner you will be back with your family again. I know what it feels like to be without your parents and alone."

On a whim, I breathed out a fire ember, holding it tight until it grew cool to the touch but still glowed bright. I gruffly handed it to the girl. "Here, take this. I know it can be scary to be alone in the darkness. Let this ember be your light."

Without looking at either Chandni or Deembo, I refixed the lid to the clay pot and gave it a firm push back into the current, where it joined its many companions, bobbing and swaying in the force of the river's run.

I took in just how many clay pots there were floating down the speedy river. "You're putting them in danger, you know."

"We haven't lost one yet," Chandni said. "Arko helps transport the parents whose children have been taken, via wormhole. And we have allies in the other dimension who help the children find their families and settle into their new lives."

"But smuggling children like they were goods!" I protested. "In clay pots of all things!"

"I can control the run of the river with my moon magic. And what's the other option?" Chandni asked sadly. "Let them get taken underwater by the snakes like poor Deembo was? Have their voices ripped away?"

At this, Deembo made a small moaning sound, and I held her close, glaring at Chandni. "What about my mother?"

"Ai-Ma is wonderful with the kids. She tells them stories, gets them calm and ready for the journey," Chandni said, and I felt jealous that she had shared such an experience with my mother.

"But skipping dimensions," I persisted. "You're sending them away from the only home they have ever known."

"What kind of home is there without safety, without freedom, without their families?" Chandni asked, and I had no answer. "Their families are desperate to keep them safe. I mean, who would ever skip dimensions unless they had no choice?"

There was the sound of clip-clopping hooves as Raat and another, white pakkhiraj made their way through what must have been underground tunnels from the royal stables. "Arko never fails to think of everything," Chandni said with a smile. "Look, he even sent a second pakkhiraj. That must be Rishi's new horse, Tushar Kona."

At the sight of the pakkhiraj horses, Deembo wiggled down from my arms and ran over to them. They snuffled the little rakkhoshi's hair as she buried her nose in their velvety skin.

I looked at the smaller white horse with skeptical eyes. "You ride that one," I said. "Raat and I have gotten used to each other."

"It's not too far to the resistance meeting place anyway." Chandni busied herself checking the horses' saddles and tack. "Once Arko gets the word out, it won't take but a few days for us to assemble everyone. Then we'll come up with a plan of how to rescue all those children from the undersea retraining school."

"That may be what you're going to do, but I'm not waiting." I lifted up Deembo, then hoisted myself onto Raat's back. "It's been too long already. I'm going to get my cousins now."

"Don't be ridiculous," chided Chandni as she mounted the other pakkhiraj horse. "You're being all diva-ish again. This isn't the kind of thing you can do on your own. Think about what happened last time."

"No time to argue strategy right now." The two of us whirled around at the familiar voice.

"Arko! How did you get away from the party?" I took in the prince's mussed hair, his harsh breathing, his reddened face.

Chandni had clearly noticed the same things. "What happened?"

"Let's just say my cover might be a little blown," Arko said, indicating that he wanted to get on Raat too. I scooched Deembo forward and helped the prince up behind me. The horse danced and neighed, welcoming his owner.

"Are you sure you weren't followed?" Chandni glanced down the long tunnel through which the prince had come.

"I'm pretty sure. But when I say my cover is blown, what

I mean to say is that our cover is blown." Arko's voice and face were tense. "The Governor-General didn't even pretend at niceties. He accused me of smuggling the two of you out."

"Which of course you did," I added unnecessarily.

Chandni clicked her tongue at me and Arko went on, "He was about to arrest me and would have if my father hadn't protested. There was enough confusion then, and my brothers ran interference so that I could get away. Apparently the snakes have rounded up almost all our resistance friends already. And I think our meeting place has been compromised. We've got to get out of here now!"

"What about the smuggling operation?" Chandni indicated the pots floating on the river.

"Aadil will look after it," Arko said shortly.

Chandni's mouth was a grim line as she turned to me. "I guess we follow your plan, Didi, and storm the stronghold sooner than later."

"Plan?" I hesitated.

"You don't have a plan?" yelped Chandni. "You seemed so confident."

"Of course she has a plan," said Arko at almost the same time.

"Of course I have a plan!" I agreed, my mind a total

blank. Raat danced under me, ready to go. I cast my memory around, trying to think of something, anything. I couldn't go back to school to get help from any rakkhosh, since Kumi and Aakash had left that note and everyone probably hated me for being a serpent conspirator. And all of Chandni and Arko's resistance friends were captured, so that wasn't any help. Then I remembered the book I'd seen up in Arko's astronomy tower. The one about monsters, demons, and ghosts of all kinds. A rough idea began to come together in my mind.

"If we can't pull together an army of either humans or rakkhosh to help us storm the undersea serpent stronghold, maybe there is another type of army we could use," I said.

"What kind of an army?" Arko asked, his voice at my shoulder.

"Well, here's the thing," I said, my voice as innocent as I could make it. "You don't have anything against the dead, do you?"

The prince groaned, but it was Chandni who spoke. "Please don't tell me you're suggesting what I think you're suggesting."

"Oh, I'm not!" I said.

"Really?" Arko seemed doubtful. "What are you suggesting?"

I gave a bright smile. "Oh, just gathering an army of ghosts together to help us storm the snake stronghold!"

"Yeah, that's exactly what I was afraid of," Chandni sighed.

CHAPTER 18

Great, Just What My Raiding Party Needs: Some Ghosts with Bad Senses of Humor and a Bird Who Makes Poor Jokes

I didn't tell Arko and Chandni the rest of my plan until we were already flying toward the closest ghost community, which hung out in a tamarind tree grove at the edge of a putrid bog. The night sky was lit by a sliver of moon, and I pointed up to it.

"We're going to need her help!" I shouted across the distance between the two flying horses. "Your moon mom, I mean."

"No," said Chandni immediately. "She's a traitor to our entire homeland. I don't want to talk to her."

"People change," said Arko. Then, clearing his throat, he amended, "Non-people too. I mean, we can all change."

"Give her a chance to make up for her mistake," I said, adjusting a snoring Deembo against my chest. "Maybe she felt like she didn't have a choice but to help the snakes."

"No," said Chandni again. "I won't go beg her."

"It's not about begging," said Arko, raising his voice to be heard above the beating horse's wings. "It's about giving her a chance to make it right."

"And besides, if you don't ask her to help us, we're all going to drown on our way to the undersea kingdom," I snapped. "We need her."

"Fine!" Chandni rubbed her hands together, producing a shining silver chain of moon energy, which she handed to me. "Here, so that I can find you again."

She kept holding one end of the silvery chain, and as soon as I grabbed the other, it magically disappeared. "It'll keep us connected," Chandni explained with a grave look to me.

"We are connected," I agreed, surprised at how much my feelings had changed about her.

Then, without another word, Chandni guided her white pakkhiraj toward the moon and took off straight up. I saw her hands glowing silver against the horse's flanks, giving it extra power. They zoomed like a rocket toward the face of her mother, the moon.

"We did the right thing," said Arko, almost like he was trying to convince himself.

"Totally," I agreed. "I mean, it's not like her mom's going to kill her or hand her over to the snakes or something, amiright?"

"Completely." But Arko sounded worried. "It'll be fine. For sure."

"Well, let's just focus on what we have to do. We're almost there!" I pointed down.

After landing a few yards away from the haunted bog, we decided to leave Raat at a distance while Arko and I did some reconnaissance. We had to take Deembo with us, of course, which was not ideal safety-wise, but I wasn't willing to leave the little rakkhoshi alone either. Although because of Arko's celestial powers and our rakkhoshi blood, none of us were that vulnerable to ghostly magic, it still wasn't the smartest decision to stumble upon a large group of bhoot without some proper planning.

We crept through the tamarind trees toward the flickering blue lights coming from the wetlands. The air was thick and rank, and my ears buzzed with the angry sounds of mosquitoes. The prince and I stepped carefully, me balancing Deembo on my hip, not wanting to alert the ghosts too early to our presence.

"They don't need to breathe air, so they can't drown," I muttered. "It makes complete sense to take a ghostly army to the serpent stronghold."

"Stop feeling like you have to justify it," said Arko in just as low tones. "I don't like it, but I get it. It's a good plan."

"Or rather, the only one we've got," I said, and Arko sighed in agreement. Deembo offered me an egg from her pocket, as if in sympathy.

That's when we heard them. Something we hadn't counted on at all.

The terrible, terrible jokes.

"How did the ghost travel from floor to floor? By scarecase!" boomed someone with a high, squeaky voice.

This ridiculous line was met with cackles of ghostly laughter.

Arko gave me a "what the heck is going on?" look and I shrugged. Deembo giggled and I put a hand over her mouth to stifle the sound. "Shhh!"

"Thank you, thank you!" said the same squeaky voice, booming as if through a microphone. "Here's another classic, folks. Why do ghosts hate rain?"

"Because we get all wet?" screeched a different voice.

"No, because it dampens your spirits!" announced the

squeaky performer, adding, "You're a great audience! A little see-through and scary, but a great audience!"

Arko and I exchanged looks again and crept cautiously forward. Hiding behind two large trees, we peeked out to see that a makeshift stage had been set up at the edge of the bog, with rows of logs, tree trunks, and stumps lined up in front of it. There were seated a few hundred or more ghosts of all varieties—sari-clad petni and shakchunni, the ghosts of unmarried and married women, identifiable by their bizarre, backward-facing feet. There were mechho bhoot devouring piles of stinking fish, and gechho bhoot hanging upside down from the surrounding trees. There were begho bhoot, the ghosts of those who had been eaten by tigers and still looked a bit feline. And of course there were the easily identifiable skondokata, or headless bhoot, walking about with bloody stumps for necks. Most of those carried their heads under their arms.

The audience was encircled by magical blue flames that the bhoot burped out of their mouths, replacing the old flames when they burned out. The atmosphere smelled putrid, and a layer of pollution hovered about the ghosts—a smog so thick you could almost taste and touch it. A chorus of bullfrogs set up an earsplitting croaking from the bog. Mosquitoes buzzed everywhere, as well as tiny nipping gnats and larger biting flies. Neither Deembo, nor I, nor the unnatural audience, seemed affected, as opposed to a slap-happy Arko, who looked positively tortured.

"What is this?" he hissed.

"A really bad comedy show," I whispered back. "Obviously. With a super-tiny performer."

"Really, you're a lovely audience," said the little yellow bird who was holding the attention of all these ghosts. The microphone-wielding, cravat-wearing bird took a hit from a portable oxygen tank on the side of the stage before he

approached an audience member in the front row. "Now, madam, tell me what you were when you were alive."

"I was a married woman and, of course, died with unfulfilled desires," said the shakchunni in a nasally voice. "So now I capture village housewives and mothers as they are passing by the tree where I live. I stick them in the tree and then it's off to their households to impersonate them and take over their lives!"

Arko slapped a giant mosquito on his forehead, earning himself a scowling "Shh!" from me. Deembo wiped the bloody thing away, patting Arko on the head in sympathy.

"What usually gives you away, dear lady?" the bird was asking the shakchunni audience member in a sympathetic voice.

"I forget to gather kindling in the morning, so I stick my feet into the fire to boil rice." The ghostly shakchunni sniffed a couple times, then began wailing in gulping, messy sobs. "Or I feel too lazy to gather lemons from the tree the human way and so I stick my arm all the way out the window and around the side of the house to pick one. That's when they realize I'm not who I appear to beee."

"Let it out, dear lady, let it out," cooed the bird, plunking a wing on the crying shakchunni's back. Then, with a sudden change of tone, he cried out, "Well, enough with the gloomies and doomies. How about we keep the laughs rolling, folks?"

Despite the fact that the shakchunni was still crying, the rest of the crowd sent up a loud cheer. Deembo cheered right along with them.

"Hey, what's the favorite amusement park ride of the formerly alive?" chirped the yellow bird to the crowd.

"The tree branch!" yelled out a hanging-upside-down gechho bhoot.

"That's not an amusement park ride!" shouted a fish-eating mechho bhoot.

"When's the last time you were at an amusement park, you shutki-eating stinker?" shot back the gechho.

Ignoring the argument in the audience, the bird performer shouted into the microphone, "A roller ghoster!"

There was a rising cheer from the audience, and the bird warbled back, "Thank you, thank you. I'll be performing here all week, midnight and two a.m.! Come for the jokes, stay for the psychotherapy!"

"No listening from behind trees, even for the magical and living," said a nasal voice. Arko and I started to see a salwar kameez–clad petni with a swinging braid. She operated a cash register that floated in midair, and she appeared to be popping some chewing gum into her half-rotted mouth. "You've got to pay for tickets, just like everyone else."

"Um, sorry," Arko mumbled, fumbling in his pockets. "How much for two regular tickets and one, um"—he snuck a look at Deembo—"child?"

As Arko and the ticket-selling petni exchanged rupees and paisa, I decided it didn't make any sense to keep pretending we were hiding. Obviously, the ghosts knew we were here, so I might as well step out and start making friends. I walked slowly down the aisles of bhoot audience members, who, now that the show was over, were gathering their handbags and walking sticks, umbrellas and skateboards. I tried to nod pleasantly as I passed them by. "Great show, wasn't it? Hilarious! Such a sense of humor for a bird! I was in stitches!" I said almost at random to the ghosts as I passed. I coughed, waving my hands, as I walked through a smog as thick as chhanar daal. For her part, Deembo high-fived ghosts, handing out eggs like she was a candidate running for office.

"Toto is the funniest act we've had down here for a long time! The mechho bhoot were in favor of eating him, but he's hilarious!" said one petni with boiling red eyes.

"He's the bomb!" said an upside-down gechho bhoot from my shoulder level, almost startling me out of my wits.

I was starting to realize that this tiny yellow parakeet of a performer might be the key to getting the ghosts on our side. With a gesture to a freaked-out-looking Arko, I made my way down to the stage, where the tiny bird was still signing autographs, a giant pen in his beak.

"So you're Toto, huh?" I asked after pushing to the front of the autograph line. The ghosts behind me were seriously unhappy about it, but I didn't care.

"Who's asking?" said the bird, startling when he looked up and saw Deembo and me. "See here, your rakkhoshiness, Toto doesn't want any trouble. I know that this is usually the territory of that gang of land rakkhosh swordswallowers, but I heard they were on an international tour and I didn't think they would mind if I took their slot here at the stage by the bog. But obviously that was my mistake! Listen, it's no big deal. I'll leave town right away! You don't have to break my legs or eat my toes or anything."

On hearing this, the autograph-seeking ghosts began to protest even more. "The sword-swallowing rakkhosh were terrible! No sense of humor! And their act had no audience psychotherapy in between sets! It was a rip!"

The compliments from the bhoot made the bird's chest swell with pride. "Toto's adoring fans," chirped the parakeet even as he slipped a surgical mask over his beak to beat the smog. "They can't get enough of me!"

"I can see that," said Arko dryly. Not only were his nose running and his eyes red from the ghost pollution, but he was developing some serious welts on his face from all the mosquito bites. He also looked more than a bit worse for wear after his walk through the ghostly crowd. Even now, a skondokata bhoot kept shoving his cut-off head in Arko's face, trying to freeze Arko in place.

"Human boy, you are mine!" hissed the skondokata rather ominously, blood dripping freely from his severed neck.

Man, bhoot were goofs. Clearly, since he wasn't freezing in place, Arko wasn't a susceptible human, but they didn't seem to be able to get that through their transparent skulls.

"I told you, that trick doesn't work on me!" snapped Arko, apparently at the end of his tether. He itched a mosquito bite on his neck with frenzied fingers. Trying to help, Deembo made a rude face at the skondokata, sticking out her tongue and wiggling her hands in her ears.

"Blast them with some of your sun juice," I whispered. Obviously, Arko had been hanging out with his fully human family for too long. "No need to pretend you're something

you're not. Being superhuman doesn't have to be something you're ashamed of. Don't hide it, enjoy it!"

"Okay, why not," agreed Arko, putting up his hands and
letting a golden arc explode from his palms.

"Ooh! Aah!" shouted the ghosts. "Impressive!"

"You see he's not fully human, so stop crowding us,
okay?" I shooed away the bhoot who had been standing
basically on top of Arko, pulling at his hair and clothes in
an attempt to enchant him. "Give us some room, please?
We've got to talk to the comedian bird here."

As the formerly-alive backed off a bit, I turned again to
the little yellow parakeet who had so captured the ghosts'
collective attention. "So, Toto, where were we?"

But while I'd been talking to the bhoot, the bird had
been throwing what appeared to be all his belongings into
a small suitcase and was trying his best to exit stage left, his
oxygen tank tucked under his wing.

"Wait a minute, birdbrain," I snapped, grabbing the
parakeet back by a wing.

"Oh, your demoness-ness, Toto wasn't trying to escape
from your evil clutches or anything! Really!" declared the
bird with earnest unbelievability. Deembo grabbed him
from me, rocking him back and forth like a tiny baby in
her relatively giant arms. "I just . . . um . . . got a call from

my auntie in Schenectady. It's the gallstones, terrible they are! She's in terrible shape! Moaning and groaning and suffering something terrible! Those gallstones are making her wings swell up to the size of cabbages!"

"Your aunt has gallstones in her wings?" Arko said, obviously trying not to laugh at the bird's terrible lies.

"Where is Schenectady anyway?" I added.

"Tell this giant monster baby to let me down!" Toto squawked. I noticed Deembo was trying to force-feed the bird pieces of egg. I shook my head at her, and she sighed, putting the bird back on his little birdie feet.

"Well, what is it Toto can help you with, your monstrousness? I am entirely at your service, I am!" said the bird, shooting Deembo a nervous look. I noticed there were pieces of egg hanging limply from his beak.

"All these ghosts seem to really like your act, Toto." I indicated the audience of watchful bhoot.

"I am a fan favorite!" chirped Toto proudly. "What can I say? If Toto's jokes can ease the boring days and nights of these immortal, disgusting beings, then their five-rupee admission tickets won't have been for naught."

"Five rupees! That petni at the front charged me fifteen!" Arko bellowed.

"Not relevant right now." I scowled at the prince. "Stop

being such a cheapskate. We're trying to save children's lives here, or had you forgotten?"

"What, wait, I wasn't being cheap." Arko's handsome face turned a brown red.

"You kind of were," I told him, and even Toto nodded his agreement.

"As I was saying before I was so rudely interrupted," I continued, "the bhoot here seem to trust you, Toto. So what say you use your leadership skills for some legendary ends?"

"What do you mean? Is this for some kind of a new act? Maybe at a proper venue—a theater with a greenroom and ushers!" Toto flew around in an excited circle. "I'll have to talk to my booking agent of course, and Toto will want a fair percentage of the overall revenue."

"I'm not trying to book your act," I spat out. "I'm trying to get you to help in the revolution!"

"The revolution?" sputtered Toto. "Against the Serpent Empire? Oh, no, no, no. Heroism? Sacrifice? Honor? Death? No way! That's *way* above Toto's pay grade."

"You don't have to fight," I wheedled. "Just use your considerable powers of persuasion to convince these bhoot to help us raid the undersea serpent retraining school!"

"A school? Why're you hitting a school?" Toto lowered his voice to a confidential whisper. "What are they hiding there? Is it gold? Jewels? A secret map you're stealing? What's Toto's cut?"

"No cut!" I snapped. "And no jewels!"

"What's there that's so important, then?" asked Toto.

"Something much better than jewels," said Arko, finally getting with the program. "Hundreds of children!"

Deembo nodded in vigorous agreement.

Toto considered this, and we watched him with bated breath as he did. "Little ones, huh? I've always wanted some tiny backup dancers. Do you think they'd be willing to be a part of my show after we rescue them? Toto would give them a decent cut of the profits!"

CHAPTER 19

In Which We Get the Band Together Again Only to—You Guessed It—All Almost Die

It took some convincing, but Toto did it. Except for the begho bhoot, who had a mind of their own and staged a meowing protest, all the other audience members agreed to come with us.

At first, he tried to appeal to their sense of patriotism. "You bhoot are the key to unlock the Kingdom Beyond's independent destiny! You will bring forth a new dawn, a new dawn of freedom!" announced the bird, his yellow chest all puffed out in revolutionary pride.

The ghosts booed, hissed, and threw their limbs, which we took as a bad sign.

"I tried my best to convince them, my fierce lady." Toto

spread his wings in an imitation of a shrug. "What more can Toto do?"

But I wasn't bothered. "I guess they don't love you as much as you thought they did," I drawled.

"Not true!" the bird sputtered. "Toto's fans adore him!"

"Prove it." I snapped my teeth at the bird, my arms crossed fiercely over my chest. Deembo snapped her teeth too and imitated my crossed-arm stance.

Toto's giant ego forced him to accept my challenge. It was like taking candy from a very feathery and annoying baby.

The bird threatening to move his act to another venue is what eventually clinched the deal with the bhoot. "This prince here is offering Toto a great nightly gig at his royal palace," the little yellow bird announced. "Huge percentage of the profits, my own opening act, bouncers with dark glasses, and a fully stocked greenroom with a drinks fridge!"

All the ghosts let up a shocked boo. Deembo booed right along with them.

"You know I'm actually offering you none of those things?" Arko muttered to Toto.

"You will, you will!" said the bird with a ridiculous level of confidence. "By the time this is all said and done, you'll be asking me and all my descendants to be your royal ministers!"

"Keep dreaming, bird." I couldn't suppress a laugh.

"However, do not give up hope!" Ignoring me, the bird continued talking to the ghostly crowd, "If you come with us now to storm the stronghold, Toto will keep his comedy act here in the Great Bog!"

So with that, things were finally all going according to plan. We went back to where we'd tethered Raat, but before we mounted the huge pakkhiraj again, I turned to my little cousin.

"Deembo, you've got to show us the way, okay?" I said to her. "Do you remember the location of where the snakes took you and those other kids underwater?"

She nodded, waving her hands over the ground like she had with that handful of dirt up in the astronomy tower. Under her hands, the soil began to move and create structures—a map of sorts, guiding our way to the Ruby Red Sea and the entrance to the underwater serpent homeland.

Arko and I both noted the route and nodded. I wrapped a handful of soil in the handkerchief that Umran had given me and tucked it into my pocket, just in case Deembo needed it later.

The moon was starting to fade, as dawn was breaking

soon. I was tired from having been up all night but not as tired as mostly human Arko looked.

"I hope Chandni had good luck too," I said to Arko as we got on Raat's back and took off into the sky.

"She doesn't need luck," said Arko with something like reverence in his voice. "She can do anything when she sets her mind to it."

I'm not going to lie, his words gave me some jealousy-induced heartburn.

The ghosts all around us cackled as they flew, their undead energy transforming the previously clean air into a clammy, foggy soup. Every breath I took burned as it went down my nasal passages and throat, and despite the morning already coloring the sky, it was near impossible to see very far forward.

"Can't you do something, Toto?" Arko's voice was all choked up, and even Raat seemed to be snorting uncomfortably. "The smog is so much worse up here! I can barely breathe!"

"Give us some space!" Toto coughed, shooing at his adoring, if ghostly, fans. "You guys always make the air quality the pits!"

The bird, whose face mask had slipped below his beak, was sitting on a very nervous Raat's head. "Alpha squadron, to the right! Beta squadron, the left!" Toto shouted in his shrill voice. "Faster, horsey!"

As the ghosts flanked us, I felt my breathing ease up a little. "I don't think we divided them into squadrons, Toto," I said.

"Well, we should have!" I don't know where he got it, but Toto had a tiny army hat on his head, which bobbed up and down a bit as he talked. Deembo giggled and clapped, popping a celebratory egg into her mouth.

We had more than a hundred ghosts with us, ghosts who not only were fearless but couldn't be hurt, stopped, or killed by any mortal weapon. Or could they? With a sinking feeling, I thought back to Professor K. P. Das's book and what it had said about ghosts. As I recalled the page, it gave me a queasy feeling.

"Hey, Arko?" I asked.

"Hmm?" he responded.

"What kinds of weapons can be made with iron?" I had a bad feeling I knew the answer to this question.

"Any kind. Pellets. Swords. Blades. Axes. Lances. Why?"

"No reason," I muttered. Okay, so there might have been a teensy-weensy problem with my plan. But I wasn't willing to let Arko in on my realization, at least not yet. I'd just have to make sure the snakes never figured out our soldiers were ghosts. But how was I going to manage that?

That's when I heard something that startled the demon snot right out of me. It was a shrill, familiar voice yelling, "I see them! There they are, straight ahead!"

"Toto, was that you?" I asked the yellow bird. "Did something happen to your voice?"

But of course it wasn't Toto at all. As Deembo glanced over my shoulder, she gave a squealing cheer.

Arko turned back and looked out behind us into the wind. "I guess some rakkhosh have come to join us!"

"Aakash! Kumi!" I had never thought I'd be so happy to see those two. "You're alive!"

"Hey, dude! Dudette! Yo, Pinki!" Aakash swooped up next to Raat on his giant insect wings. One of his hands was bandaged, and he was missing some hair on one of his eyebrows, but he looked otherwise his usual doofy self.

All around Aakash swirled his murder of hench-crows. I was so happy to see him, I didn't even mind when one of them pooped on my shoulder.

Tiny Toto puffed himself up, squawking, "Stay away from me, you murderous magpies!"

"You didn't think we were going to let you have all

the fun?" Kumi was riding on a helicocroc and sported, I noticed, a whopper of a bruise over her cheek and a serious black eye. "Not to mention take all the glory?"

"How did you two find us?" I had to admit, seeing my two frenemies actually lifted my sagging spirits.

"Um, so like, back when Professor Ravan told us to keep an eye on you . . . I mean, I'm not saying we put a tracker under one of your shoes," began Aakash.

"But we put a magic tracker under one of your shoes," concluded Kumi. At my glare, she shrugged. "Sorry not sorry?"

I didn't have the energy to be mad. At least they were two more fighters to help us raid the serpentine school.

"I was sure you guys were goners!" I said. "How did you make it away from the Governor-General?"

"It was because of our superior skills and prowess," said Kumi with total seriousness.

"I sat on the old dude, and Kumi basically made him drown in a thunderstorm," Aakash said at almost the same time. "Then, before General Snaky could get his lightning powers dried off, we made a run for it."

Kumi rolled her eyes. "Yeah, I guess it was something like that."

"I'm sorry we didn't come back to help you, but Sesha kidnapped my cousins, and we had to go after him," I said by way of apology. "We rescued Deembo, but the other two are being held in the serpents' undersea retraining school—alongside hundreds of human children."

"So you're going to rescue them with all these ghosties?" Aakash asked.

"Something like that," I agreed.

"All right, we're in." Kumi cracked her knuckles. I looked at her in surprise, and she shrugged. "It was our fault the kids got kidnapped in the first place."

"Pretty cool you got a ghost army with you! I mean, gnarly!" Aakash flipped his wavy hair over his horns and pointed at the bhoot. "Not sure what use ghosts are going to be against snakes, though. All the snakes have to do is pull out some iron weapons! And it's not like bhoot magic works on anyone but humans."

Behind me on the horse, Arko groaned. "That's why you were asking about the iron weapons!"

Kumi went on, "All righty, then! Storming the serpents' undersea retraining center with just a bunch of human haunters! That's gutsy! Sure to fail, but gusty!"

"Just what we needed, some cheerful optimism," Arko muttered.

Aakash squinted at the prince. "What's with the human dude? Is he your lunch or something?"

"Sitting right here!" Although his voice didn't betray any nervousness, I did notice Arko's sword hand clenching and unclenching at his waist. "Can totally hear you!"

"He's an ally, not a meal!" I said firmly. "Lay off!"

"Well, he is kinda cute, for a pet!" Kumi spit a bunch of seawater through the air in Arko's direction. "It's adorable how loyal he is to you!"

"I'm not a pet!" Arko wiped his face off with his sleeve.

"She's annoying but harmless. Mostly anyway," I reassured Arko before making a fierce face at my roommate. "Behave!"

"If I can't eat your human, what about that bird?" Aakash snapped his teeth in Toto's direction, flying closer to Raat to get a better look. "It's small, but I'm starving. I wouldn't mind an appetizer."

"Toto doesn't want to be a rakkhosh appetizer!" wailed the yellow bird, putting a dramatic wing over his head. "I'm all wings and bones! I'd taste terrible!"

"Chill, guys. No eating the bird either," I said.

Deembo scooped Toto up in her arms, giving Aakash a warning glare with teeth bared.

"All right, all right, small fry, no need to get all protective. You want to eat the bird all on your own, I get it, that's cool," Aakash said.

"No one is eating the bird!" I was practically shouting. "Or the horse! Or the human!"

"All right, message received!" Kumi said, acting like I was the one being unreasonable. "No need to be so touchy!"

We flew on, the ghosts to the far sides, then Aakash and Kumi flanking Arko, Toto, Deembo, and me, all on Raat's back. I noticed Arko kept looking up to the sky, and

I too kept my eyes peeled for Chandni. But I didn't see her anywhere.

Unfortunately, right as we were getting to the shores of the Ruby Red Sea, the land, water, and air did that terrible stomach-flipping, shape-shifting thing again.

"No! Not again!" I felt my insides threatening to come rushing to the outside. "We're almost there!"

But as if the very environment were working against us, everything shifted.

"What's happening?" Toto shrieked, flying out of Deembo's arms and onto my shoulder. "Toto doesn't like this!"

"It's some kind of new serpent magic," I yelled. "They put out a decree saying that they can shift around the land, water, and air whenever they want!"

It was like being in a jigsaw puzzle that gets dropped on the floor. The edges holding reality together seemed to come unglued, shifting away from each other in jagged disconnections. Below us, bodies of land and water wiggled in an unnatural dance as above, the air too wobbled in a near-invisible undulation.

"Hold on!" Arko yelled as Raat gave a violent jerk to the left and then dropped a few feet. The air all around us was ripping, like giant hands tearing a piece of paper in two.

"Everyone! Bank right! Hard right!" I yelled, trying to

make sure no one fell through the chasm in space that was now stretched out in the middle of the air, like a gawking, hungry maw ready to devour us all.

In front of us, the ghosts paid no attention to my warning, following each other like sheep into the dark space in the air, screaming, then vanishing from our sight.

"What happened to them? Where did they go?" Kumi looked desperately in the direction the ghosts had last been.

"I don't know! But I don't want to find out!" I hung on to Deembo, determined not to lose her again. In the meantime, Toto dug his claws into my shoulder, drawing blood.

"We're gonna die!" shrieked the little yellow bird. "We're all gonna die!" We were kind of flying sideways, with Raat scrambling for purchase in the air, his poor wings beating irregularly, his sides heaving from effort.

"Tell your ghosts to change course!" I yelled. "They're not listening to me!"

"I didn't sign up for this! There better be some seriously A-grade refreshments in that palace greenroom!" Toto dug his claws even deeper into my skin. "I'm talking flavored fizzy waters! Full-sized candy bars! Organic gluten-free birdseed!"

As the bird babbled, more of the ghostly army got sucked into the dark vacuum opening up like an otherworldly portal to nowhere. But they just kept flying forward, each following the one in front, no one willing to think for themselves or change course.

"The ghosts!" I tried to pull the bird from my shoulder but failed. "Tell them to change direction! Or they're all going to die! Or die again! Or whatever!"

"What's happening? Oh, what's happening?" Toto squawked before flying in such a speedy circle, he hit his own head on Raat's saddle and passed out cold. Okay, so he wasn't going to be of any help.

"Now what?" I held the limp bird's body in my arms, but no matter how much I shook him, he didn't open his eyes. Luckily, he was breathing, but he wouldn't be for long if we couldn't stop whatever was happening.

"We've got to stop that ghost army from following each other into the void!" Arko exclaimed. "I can't believe the snakes have this kind of hold over the land, water, and air."

"Well, at least they don't own fire!" Aakash was desperately beating his wings, trying to right himself in the air.

"What did you say, flyboy?" Kumi tried to keep control over her panicking helicocroc.

"He said at least they don't own fire," Arko repeated, looking at me with huge eyes. "Pinki, it's up to you!"

"What do you mean it's up to me?" I shrieked as Raat fell at a sideways angle.

"Breathe your fire! Breathe your fire!" Kumi snarled. "Stop being afraid! Half your army's getting decimated! Stop the shifting already!"

My hearts were hammering, but I knew Kumi was right. Half the ghost army was already getting sucked into the void made by the magic shifting. If we didn't stop this soon, they would all be gone. I felt my panic bringing my inner flames to a quick, roiling burn. Imperfect though they may have been, I needed my ghost army to help me save those kids. The fire within me sparked and screamed, exploding with power.

"Watch out!" I aimed at the ripped space that had opened in the air, letting my fire fly. Flame balls shot from my mouth through the air, filling and somehow stabilizing the tearing and shifting happening all around us.

"It's working!" Arko yelled. "You're doing it!"

Was I? I looked around at Aakash and Kumi, at Deembo and Toto, at our flying animals, at the ghosts. What if I hurt them because I lost control? I'd never been able to tame my fire; what made me think I could now? I stopped breathing flames and instead huffed clouds of smoke.

"Don't stop!" Kumi shouted. "I swear, Pinki, if you chicken out now . . ."

"What if I can't?" I shouted back. "What if I burn you all up instead?"

"You, like, totally won't!" Aakash said with such conviction I kind of believed him. "You gotta believe in yourself, Pinks! Don't be afraid of your own magic!"

"Think about what the snakes did to your cousins, what they're doing to all of us!" Arko added. "They're not just taking away our homeland; they're breaking it apart! And you're the only one who has the power to stop it!"

It was scary. I had to fight everything in me that told me I couldn't, I shouldn't, that there was no way I'd be successful. But I had no choice. I had to save my cousins and those other kids. I shot flame after flame out of my mouth and nose and toward the void. The fire seemed to fill the emptiness, stitching together the rents in our world created by the serpents' magic. The ground and water below us stopped shifting with so much speed. My fire was like glue, or an anchor, giving everything that had been ripped apart and destabilized a sense of weight and connection again.

I didn't worry about harnessing my power or limiting myself, like I had back in the forest with Sesha. Instead, I let my passion and fury fill up all the spaces within me and around me. The fire danced about us, encircling us in its warmth but never touching us. Instead, it launched itself into the holes in the sky, the rents in the ground, the disruptions in the water. It healed and hardened and reforged the connections that had always been there—but undermined by the snake's decrees.

And then, just as the shifting had begun, so too did it suddenly come to a stop. Raat, Aakash, and Kumi's helicocroc corrected themselves in the air. The ghostly army, what was left of it at least, stopped throwing themselves off the invisible atmospheric cliff. Everyone looked hassled and harassed but grateful too.

And that gratitude was all directed at me.

"Yo, dudette, you did it!" Aakash flew over to high-five me.

"I never doubted you for a minute!" said Kumi, bumping her fist in the air. But when I raised my eyebrow in her direction, she looked a little sheepish. "Okay, I doubted you for a lot of years, but not just now."

"I knew you could!" Arko squeezed my shoulder. "But we don't have time to celebrate! These snakes have got to be stopped! However we can, we've got to get them out of the Kingdom Beyond."

Delicately picking something out of her teeth with a

talon, Kumi gave the prince an appraising look. "You may be a tasty snack, but you're right. They've gone too far this time. We've got to get them out."

"I thought Pinki said the human prince wasn't up for grabs." Aakash sounded vaguely miffed. "That we couldn't snack on him."

"I wasn't talking about that kind of snacking." Kumi snapped her teeth in Arko's direction.

I saw Arko's face darken a bit, but he ignored Kumi's comment. "We're going to have to band together—rakkhosh and human and everyone else who lives in the Kingdom Beyond. It's exactly what the snakes are afraid of. It's exactly what they're trying so desperately to stop."

When Arko spotted one of the skondokata bhoot who had fallen behind the others on account of being headless and therefore not being able to see where he was going very well, he amended, "Everyone alive and dead in the Kingdom Beyond."

"Small and large! Feathery and not!" Toto added suddenly from my arms, to which Deembo raised her fist, obviously in agreement.

"Oh, look who decided to wake up!" I said, my voice dripping with sarcasm. "Or was it that you were never really knocked out in the first place?"

Even Raat snorted, like the pakkhiraj horse too was throwing in his lot with the revolutionaries.

"All of us!" Arko said. "Air and fire, earth and water."

"Plus sun," I added.

And then a very welcome voice piped up. "And moon!"

CHAPTER 20

Teamwork Makes the Dream Work, Blah, Blah, Rainbows and Unicorn Farts and All That Sappy Stuff

As we all landed on the shore of the Ruby Red Sea, I took stock of our numbers. We'd increased our forces manyfold since leaving Arko's palace. We had ghosts, a bird, and air and water rakkhosh with us. And now a moon girl too.

As the six of us—Chandni and Arko, Aakash and Kumi, Deembo and me—held a council of war, Toto kept the ghostly crowd entertained, holding an impromptu comedy show at the shoreline.

"What's a monster's favorite dessert?" the bird squawked.

"Gulab jamun?" guessed a backward-footed shakchunni lolling in the sand.

"Rasagolla?" asked a gechho bhoot as he dangled from a tree.

"No, I-scream!" shouted Toto, collapsing in a fit of silent giggles. To my surprise, Arko, Aakash, and Kumi all laughed alongside the ghosts, who were in absolute stitches. Deembo was rolling about on the ground in hysterics.

"Thank you! Thank you! You're a great, if terrifying, crowd!" burbled the small bird.

We walked a few steps away from the riotous laugh-a-minute ghosts and began to talk.

"Chandni, what happened?" Arko's face was lit up by the full rays of the morning sun. "Did your mother agree to help us?"

"Also, any chance you remember me, from before? In the market? Big guy who was kicking serpent butt?" Aakash leaned not very casually against a palm tree, flexing a huge bicep. "I wanted to ask, uh, are you free to, like, hang out anytime? No big deal. But are you?"

"Really?" Kumi made a little wave from the shoreline splash Aakash up to the waist. As he sputtered, protesting, Kumi turned to Chandni, flipping her wet hair smilingly over a shoulder. "Seriously, though, are you, like, free to hang out anytime?"

Chandni's expression was tired, but she didn't seem to

mind Aakash's and Kumi's attention. She didn't, however, answer either of them. Instead, she turned to Arko, eyes shining with moonlight tears. "The thing is, my mother won't help us."

"I'm so sorry." Arko touched her arm. "She just flat-out refused?"

"I don't know why I'm so disappointed." Chandni scrubbed angrily at her face. As she continued to cry, Deembo snuggled up in her lap. "I know who she is, what she's done. But it still didn't stop me from hoping."

I felt for the girl. I really did. I recalled my many nights spent crying by myself, wishing that my parents would somehow break out of jail and make their way to me. I'd known it wouldn't happen, but there was a part of me that had thought if they just loved me enough, it could.

"It's not about you, you know that, right?" My words came out harsher than I meant them. "It's not that she could do it if she loved you more or anything like that. She is who she is. It's not your fault. Anyway, we're going to get those kids out of the serpent stronghold without her help."

Deembo hopped down from Chandni's lap, then waved her hands and made an image appear in the soft sandy soil—a giant bubble under the Ruby Red Sea containing some buildings spread out in a big U shape. She made the sand move again, showing a passage from the water to the bubble.

Kumi looked at the little girl with impressed eyes. But it was Aakash who said, "So, like, you were hoping that the Moon Mother would help us get under the sea?"

"Turns out it was the Moon Mother, with her power over water and the tides, who first helped the snakes create a path from under the sea to the land," Arko said. "She's the reason we got invaded by snakes in the first place."

"Aw, dip!" Aakash whistled through his teeth. "No way! And we thought the moon lady was a prisoner and stuff!"

"The moon's a traitor?" Kumi muttered, shooting Chandni a few sideways glances. "I can't believe it."

In the distance, Toto's overloud voice floated into our conversation. "What position does a ghost play in hockey?"

"I don't know, what?" asked one of the petni ghosts, who then proceeded to laugh with such violence she knocked over an entire row of other bhoot like they were nothing more than bowling pins.

"Ghoulie!" answered Toto, much to the amusement of the crowd.

"Yo, that was a good one," muttered Aakash. "I'll have to remember that. Ghoulie!"

I studied the see-through bhoot, with their detachable

limbs and ghoulish smiles. Along the edges of the crowd, some of the skondokata were trying to play soccer with their own heads, a feat made near impossible by the fact that the headless bodies couldn't see and therefore kept missing the ball. Next to them, some petni and shakchunni were trying to give themselves pedicures but failing, what with the turned-around feet and all.

"No snakes—especially snakes with a ready access to iron weapons—are going to be afraid of them," Arko muttered, following my gaze. "I'm not even afraid of them anymore."

Again, Toto's voice drifted over the sand. "Say, here's a good one: What's the rakkhosh's favorite subject in school?"

When no one could answer correctly, Toto answered, "Spelling!"

The ghostly crowd basically collapsed in laughter, but Toto's joke actually gave me an idea. We rakkhosh *were* good at spells. Maybe there was something there I could work with.

"Well, what if they weren't ghosts at all?" A grin spread over my face. "Bhoot can take on the characteristics of the humans whose lives and faces they take over, right?"

"Sure," said Arko. "They, like, capture their human victims, put 'em in the trunks of trees, and then take over their lives, disguising themselves as human."

"Well, what if we could have them transform and take

over someone else's powers without having to capture them?" A totally impractical plan was forming in my mind. Totally impractical, but worth a shot.

It took a bit longer than I'd hoped to help all the ghosts transform into rakkhosh form. Aakash, Kumi, and I had to donate a lot of hair, which made Aakash in particular very grumpy.

"Quit whining, you air baby, it's just a few strands," snapped Kumi, plucking the hairs from his head.

"Stop! I need every hair on my head! You think it's easy to achieve this look?" Aakash put protective hands over his swirly-whirly coiffure. "Do you know how many hours and how much product it takes to appear this good-looking?"

"I can only guess," Prince Arko said dryly. "Listen, it's for a good cause."

Aakash wasn't moved by any of our explanations. He tried desperately to feel if his elaborate hairstyle had been damaged in any way.

"Do one of you at least have a comb? A mirror? Some anti-frizz, anti-humidity gel? Some electromagnetic volumizer mousse? What about some soft-hold touchable hair spray?" he asked, naming hair products I hadn't even heard of. "Listen, yo, I need to scrunch out the crunch. Rewet and plop! I use the curly rakkhosh method!"

"We don't have any of those things," Chandni said. "But if it's any consolation, your style looks pretty much the same as it did before your hairs were pulled out."

"Really?" Aakash's eyes got a little shiny. "You're not just saying that?"

"Really." I could tell Chandni was trying not to laugh.

I stepped in before Aakash could freak out more. "Listen, we've got to distribute these hairs to all the ghosts. Get to it!"

We made quick work of getting each bhoot at least one strand of rakkhosh hair. And as soon as they did, I shared with them the spell to transform themselves into rakkhosh. They spun in place, each bhoot taking on the form of Aakash, Kumi, or myself. I had considered also passing out Deembo's hairs, but with her tiny size, it didn't seem like we would be doing ourselves a favor by making any of the ghosts look like her.

"Well, *that's* a little disturbing," Arko muttered, looking out at the replicas.

"I think it's kind of cool," I argued. A third of the ghosts looked like me—long haired and shiny horned, with honestly the most fabulous sets of gleaming white fangs. But was that really what my resting rakkhoshi face looked like? "The important thing is, they don't just look like us. They can reproduce our powers too."

We tested my theory, and it worked. The ones that looked like Aakash could control the air, the ones that looked like Kumi could control water, and the ones that looked like me, well, let's just say the shoreline of the Ruby Red Sea was minus a few palm trees by the time our experiment was over. Luckily, Kumi and Aakash just had to splash waves from the nearby sea to extinguish the burning trees.

"They're your duplicates all right," drawled Kumi, staring at the ashen remains of the burned-up trees.

"They're a work in progress." I didn't add but thought, *Like me.*

"The ones who are me look totes fabulous—their hair is really a masterpiece." Aakash touched his own complicated locks. "All the mes are so fine!"

"I should have thought of getting ghostly clones of myself a long time ago!" Kumi seemed equally in awe of her replicas. "It's a good look for me!"

"Anyway, back to the problem," I said louder than necessary. I was still a little embarrassed by the whole incident of my ghostly duplicates burning down those trees. "None of us, except you, Kumi, and of course the ghosts, can breathe under water."

"I mean, we might drown, but we might not." Aakash scratched his neck thoughtfully, staring at the bobbing surface of the Ruby Red Sea. "Like, depending on how long it is and if the actual bubble place the kids are being held has any oxygen, or whatever."

"It has to," Chandi said. "How else are the children breathing?"

"Regardless," said Arko. "I think it's safer to assume that some of us might drown getting to the serpent's kingdom. It's better to actually have some sort of an alternate plan."

There was a lull in the conversation, and I looked around,

realizing that everybody's eyes seemed to be trained in my direction. "Why are you all looking at me for?" I snapped, running my hand over my nose. "Is there something on my face?"

"No, Pinki, we just wanted to know about the plan," Arko said.

"Ugh, didn't I just come up with the ghost plan?" I indicated the groups of Aakashes, Kumis, and Pinkis milling around the beach, staring in wonder at their own hands and feet, feeling their new horns and tusks and talons.

"But how are we getting to the snakes' underwater kingdom, boss lady? We going to go kick some serpent butt and become legends, or what?" Kumi came over and draped her arm over Arko's shoulder, taking a long whiff of his hair. "You smell good," she purred.

"Stop smelling my friend!" I none-too-gently pushed Kumi off the prince.

"Seriously, though, what's your plan?" Arko asked, trying to ignore Kumi's attentions.

"She probably doesn't have one," said my roommate with a huge fake yawn. "'Cause she's obviously not Demon Queen material."

Deembo, bless her furry heart, proceeded to try and kick Kumi in the shin, but she fell over in the process.

"Relax, little watchdog!" Kumi laughed, tossing my

tiny cousin up playfully on a spout of water. "I was only kidding!"

"Who needs a plan, yaar? Let's just hold our breath and dive, like I said!" Aakash flew up a few feet in the air in his enthusiasm.

"That doesn't make sense!" Arko argued.

"Whatever, snack boy." Aakash flapped back to the ground. "You're just mad 'cause you're the one who's probably not going to make it."

"I wouldn't either," Chandni reminded Aakash, at which the air rakkhosh balked.

"Oh, well, then, obviously, no. I mean, seriously!" he spluttered, turning a funny dark brown. "Yo, obvi we need a different plan! Pinks, what's the plan? We can't let Chandni drown. I mean, hey, seriously, we need a plan!"

"Stop talking nonsense, I have to think." I looked around at all the ghost rakkhosh and real rakkhosh waiting for my orders, at Chandni, Arko, and Toto, all depending on me to solve this problem. I had a moment of passing dizziness. How had I gotten here? I'd always thought I wanted nothing more than to be a loner.

I took a deep breath of the sea-salty air and sized up my assets as Professor Ravan had taught me in Honors Thievery. Besides our rides, we had four rakkhosh, a bunch of bhoot, a prince who could command the rays of the sun, a girl descended from the moon, and a tiny yellow bird who told bad jokes.

"All right." I dug my toe into the sand. I couldn't believe what I was about to say and where I'd gotten the inspiration from. "I have a plan, but it's going to involve all of us working together."

Everyone nodded, still looking at me expectantly. I remembered how, in the woods, Sesha had worked with me and therefore somehow focused and sharpened my power. I hoped that we could do that now for each other. Only, our partnerships would be equal and fair—bolstering each others' powers rather than limiting or thwarting them.

"Chandni, you have at least part of your mother's powers, so you can partially control the tides, can't you?" I asked.

"Sure," Chandni agreed.

"Well, what if you had a water rakkhoshi to help you harness and amplify the powers you have?" I gestured to Kumi, who came to stand beside the moon girl.

"I think we could make that work," said the water rakkhoshi.

"Wait, how come I don't get to team up with Chandni?" Aakash whined. "I want to team up with her! It's not fair!"

Kumi looked like she was about to get into it with our classmate, so I stepped quickly between them. "We'll each partner with someone, to help to shape or strengthen each others' powers. This is no time to be a diva."

Everybody gave me funny looks, but luckily, no one pointed out that until recently, I had been the most diva-ish diva of them all.

We gathered solemnly at the shores of the sea. The first team up was Chandni and Kumi, who held hands to try and move back the tide from the shore.

"They're doing it!" Arko whispered so as to not break the two girls' concentration. In fact, the two had pushed back the waters so much, we could see the bottom of the sea. "Okay, Deembo and Aakash, it's your turn now!"

The huge air rakkhosh helped my little cousin kneel on the shore at the feet of the moon girl and water rakkhoshi. Closing her eyes, Deembo placed her hands on the soil.

"Concentrate, wee demon kiddo." Aakash crouched next to her, channeling his wind power through her land magic. "I know you can do it!"

And she did. Soon, the ground began to quake, making a split in what had been the bottom of the sea. With his wind, Aakash helped Deembo push aside even more ground and swirled away the last of the water so that now there was a dry space created where there once had been sea.

Finally, it was Arko's and my turn. Combining our powers like the others had, we burned through the remaining soil with our fire and our sun. It felt totally different than working with Sesha. Then Sesha had hemmed in my strengths. Now I was working with someone who appreciated my fire, whose powers complemented and uplifted my own.

I let my fire rise up and soar out of me. My flames danced with Arko's sunlight, and together we dried up the water, cracked the ground, and created a doorway and stairs down to the undersea kingdom.

We had decided to leave the horses and the helicocroc on the shore—underwater was no place for creatures of the sky. Then we each held our positions as Toto led the ghostly army down the stairway we'd created. Next, it was Chandni and Kumi's turn. Kumi picked Deembo up and let her ride on her shoulders. Aakash went after them, keeping the wind up and swirling away the waters. Finally, it was Arko's and my turn. We kept our inferno burning, sun sparks and flames, molten heat and shimmering light. We dried up any waters that threatened to come our way, lighting the path beneath the sea.

The hardest part was keeping the entryway steady. We all kept concentrating, keeping the forces of the waters above us at bay as we clambered down to the serpents' undersea kingdom. Chandni moon-magicked open the entryway into the bubbled-off area, and then we were through. With a crash and a splash, the sea closed in above and behind us. But we were in. We were breathing. We had done it!

We stood with our rakkhosh-ghost army in the oxygen-filled bubble under the Ruby Red Sea, somewhere near but outside the walls of the retraining school. We all exchanged worried looks. It was dark and quiet under the water, and although we were alone, I had no idea if we were about to be caught by serpent patrols. I breathed out and cooled down some fire embers, like I had for the little girl on the River of Dreams, and handed them out for everyone to use like glowing torchlights. It was time for me to formulate the next stage of our plan—how we were going to attack the serpent retraining school and rescue all those stolen children!

I took out the handkerchief full of dirt and spread it before Deembo. "How far away are we from the snake school, kiddo? Can you remember?"

According to the soil picture that Deembo whipped up for us from the dirt I'd brought along, we were closer than I'd thought.

"We're almost there." I gathered our troops around, pointing to the map Deembo had drawn. "It's straight ahead for a few hundred yards, then over in that direction, to the right."

"And now, my loyal ghost-rakkhosh fans!" Toto whisper-shouted. "It's time to storm the castle . . . er, palace . . . er, stronghold . . . er, school!"

Air, water, fire, land, sun, and moon, we were all prepared, all united, and all ready to go to war.

CHAPTER 21

In Which More Fighting Ensues, Sesha the Snake Turns Out to Be a Serious, Well, Snake, and Then Something Really, Really Bad Happens

The snakes knew we were coming. I don't know how they knew, but they did. And they were waiting for us.

The school was set up like Deembo had shown us, a semicircle with buildings all around and only the narrowest of entryways on one end and an open space on the other. When we got to the outskirts of the greenish brick school buildings, serpentine flags hanging high over the ramparts, everything seemed quiet. No soldiers, no sentries, no voices of children either inside the classrooms or in the yard. There was only a flickering green-blue lamplight to illuminate the undersea darkness. We extinguished our handheld fire embers and kept going. I should have known then that something was wrong. But I was so focused on finding and rescuing Kawla and Mawla, I ignored the signs of trouble.

As quietly as we could, we took our ghostly rakkhosh squadron up to the school's one narrow entry passage.

"You and Arko circle around the other side," I told Chandni. "Kumi, Aakash, and I will take the ghosts through the passage. Since they look like us, and all."

I felt the weight of everyone's expectations, not to mention their lives, on my shoulders.

"You'll keep Deembo safe?" I asked Arko as I handed my cousin over to him.

"Of course. We'll go around the back. It's too dangerous to all go in the same way." Arko gave Deembo's nose a bop, but she didn't laugh. Her eyes were huge as she studied the retraining school rising up a few yards ahead of us. I could tell she was remembering the last time she was here and the things that were done to her.

"We're not going to let them hurt anyone else like they hurt you," I whispered, kissing the little rakkhoshi's forehead. "We're going to free Kawla and Mawla, and all the other kids too. And then we're going to finally take back our homeland from the snakes."

"Together," said Chandi with a teasing smile.

"Yeah." I nodded. "Together."

Before I could protest, the moon girl wrapped me in a tight hug, which I'm only a bit embarrassed to say that I returned.

After Arko and Chandni had taken off with Deembo around the buildings, Aakash, Kumi, Toto, and I led our ghostly army through the long entry alley of the retraining school. It was like walking through an abandoned city. The square brick buildings had an architecture totally foreign to the soft curves and marble filigree work of most Kingdom Beyond buildings. They were like ugly sores, a jail more than a school. I peered up at the building walls, wondering exactly where in those hidden depths the children were being kept.

"Where is everybody?" Aakash muttered, flapping his wings like a nervous tic. "All inside? Why don't we hear them?"

I didn't know. Like him, I was constantly looking around, on alert. I noticed that the shakchunni, petni, and other bhoot glided along, wearing our rakkhosh bodies and faces but kind of floating a few inches off the ground.

"Can they make it look more realistic?" I whispered to Toto. "Make it look like they're actually walking?"

"Method acting, ghosties! Inhabit your rakkhosh characters! *Think* like a rakkhosh! *Feel* like a rakkhosh! *Be* a rakkhosh!" Toto spread the message down the line, and soon the bhoot were at least pretending to walk on the ground. They weren't the best actors, I'll admit, but it was better than nothing.

"At least we have the element of surprise on our hands. There doesn't seem to be anyone guarding the school at all," Kumi murmured. "Let's just find those kids and get out pronto."

"Something feels wrong," I muttered. The silence was too quiet. "I don't like it."

"Yeah, something's wrong all right." Aakash flexed his wings again and cracked his knuckles. "We're gonna make something go seriously wrong with all those snakes!"

My stomach gave a flip. Maybe Aakash was right. Maybe I needed to stop worrying about what felt wrong and pay attention to what felt right. I mean, being poised like this, ready for battle, made me feel fierce and alive. Even if I wasn't entirely sure I really wanted to go to war with Sesha.

"Ready to give the command?" I whispered to Toto.

The yellow bird puffed up with pride. "On my command you bhoot, I mean, rakkhosh, I mean, warriors!" Toto made a tooting sound through his beak. "Charge!"

As the small yellow bird's wing descended, we all swarmed the courtyard. Only it wasn't unguarded at all. Because as soon as our army of real and ghostly rakkhosh entered the central area between the buildings, snaky soldiers appeared from all the doors, weapons peeked out from all the windows, and serpent sharpshooters emerged all over the roof. They swarmed around the opening of the courtyard, blocking our way out. But that wasn't even the most disturbing sight that greeted us.

Because from every single one of those many rooftops and balconies, there hung cages. Gilded cages, like the kind you might put pet birds into. Only the things trapped inside these cages were not birds at all. Rather, each of the hundreds of cages housed a frightened child. Aakash took in a huge breath at the sight of them, and Kumi's eyes went round. Even Toto, on my shoulder, squawked in horror.

But I had my eyes on two cages in particular. Two cages whose familiar prisoners made my hearts feel like they were burning to ash in my chest.

"Kawla and Mawla!" I cried, pointing to my two cousins hanging from beneath a central balcony railing. Terribly, they didn't answer, at least not in words. Rather, my two rakkhosh cousins reached toward me, crying.

"Their voices have been taken," whispered Kumi, looking around at all the other silent children. "They can't speak."

She was right. I felt such a fury, such a fire in me that I could have burned down the entire kingdom or dried up every drop of the Ruby Red Sea. But as much as I had learned about my power recently, I knew that to use it here, with all these children hanging about, would be madness.

"Behind!" shouted Aakash, and I whipped around. Now the alley through which we'd entered and the one other exit pathway were blocked by serpent soldiers. We were sitting ducks in this cordoned-off courtyard. It was a trap.

"Fools!" scoffed a familiar voice. Sesha came out to stand at the center balcony above where Kawla and Mawla hung. He was wearing magnificent green robes, the same ones he'd been wearing that fateful day in the woods when I first met him. "Give up! You're surrounded!"

"All we want is the children!" My voice was firm and clear. "Let them go now!"

"Why, hello, dear Pinki!" said the Prince of Serpents, narrowing his eyes. "And Pinki. And Pinki." He nodded mockingly to all my copies. "Didn't you bring your traitorous friend, the moon girl Chandni, the one who warned us you'd be coming?"

"What?" breathed Kumi.

"It's not true!" shouted Aakash.

But I didn't even rise to the bait. "She didn't tell you. She wouldn't. It must have been her weak-willed Moon Mother, wasn't it?"

"Oh, tomato, tomahto!" Sesha snarled. "Yes, I suppose it wasn't Chandni, but her mommy dearest who warned us of your imminent arrival. Regardless, if Chandni hadn't gone to see her, we wouldn't have known you were on your way."

"It was a risk I knew we were taking," I said. I hadn't known this, of course, but I didn't need to tell Sesha that.

"Suddenly so confident, aren't you? Think you're so smart?" Green lightning bounced from one of Sesha's tented fingers to the other. He really was looking and acting more and more like a storybook villain—like, I guess, his dad. "Too bad you didn't tell your rakkhosh friends how you made a deal with me to learn how to control your powers."

"We know," said Kumi impatiently. "Remember, we went through this all in the marketplace?"

"You really need to get some new material, my dude." Aakash flexed his chest muscles in a weird, bouncy way.

"What kind of a monster are you?" I shouted. "What happened to honor among villains? Are you proud of yourself for terrorizing little children? Like your dad terrorized you?"

"Silence!" In his agitation, Sesha shot out a lightning

bolt, destroying some brick on a wall opposite his balcony. It crumbled noisily to the ground, startling us all.

At this, some of the kids in the cages began to cry. They were wordless wails of sorrow and pain. Their cries were of fear, and homesickness, and powerlessness. But worse still was that so many of the children just stared at us blank-eyed out of their cages, their thin fingers wrapped around the bars. It was as if they had forgotten even how to cry. As if they had cried so much they were beyond sorrow now and had no more tears left to shed. Or maybe it was that the snakes had taken not just their voices but their feelings, their very souls.

"Sesha!" I bellowed. "This is no retraining school! This is a prison camp! Even you must see that this is horrific! They're just kids!"

"This is no prison!" said Sesha so forcefully, I wondered if he was trying to convince himself. "This is a chance for these brats to become something more than their parents! A chance for them to forget their dirty ways and learn what it means to be good snake citizens!"

"You're delusional!" I yelled, spitting embers. "If you don't let these kids out, we're going to break them out!"

"Snake flesh, snake flesh, toasty, crisp, and sweet!"

yelled Aakash, adapting an old rakkhosh war cry. All the Aakashes roared in unison, raising their clawed fists, batting their insect wings so that they floated feet off the ground.

The real Kumi finished the famous lines: "We'll break their bones, suck their marrow, and curry up their feet!" She and ghostly clones spat water, flexing and snarling, all ready for the coming fight.

"Keep away from the cages, you dirty demons!" yelled one of the snake soldiers.

"Not until you open them and free every one of these children!" I spit out, spitting fire too. My clones threw some flames right along with me. I had to say, we were an awe-inspiring and fear-inducing sight, dozens of air rakkhosh who looked like Aakash, water rakkhosh who looked like Kumi, and fire rakkhosh who looked like me. We were fierce, and strong, and powerful.

"I don't think so, you scum!" Sesha gave a signal, and even more serpent soldiers emerged from the buildings, these ones not holding weapons. On a barked command, they held up their hands, shooting out green bolts of lightning out in our direction. The bolts pelted right through some of the ghost rakkhosh, and I saw Sesha notice this, a befuddled look on his face.

"Tell the bhoot to duck out of the way of the bolts, like they're real rakkhosh!" I hissed to Toto. "Otherwise these snakes are going to realize they're ghosts, and this jig is up!"

"Emote like a rakkhosh! Fear like a rakkhosh!" Toto spread the word among the bhoot, flying first to one group and then another. But even as the ghosts pretended to duck from the green bolts of serpent magic, shrieking in mock terror, I knew we had to act quickly. Sooner or later, Sesha would figure out that most of the frightening rakkhosh attacking their stronghold were actually not-so-scary bhoot. Time for the next part of the plan.

"You're up, flyboy!" I hissed to Aakash.

The air rakkhosh gave his ghostly copycats a signal and en masse they began creating a storm so fierce and strong it blackened the air, whipping up biting winds so fast and howling they soon became a dozen whirling tornados, spinning around the buildings. The children's cages rattled and banged. The storms picked up several of the unsuspecting serpent soldiers into their twisting forms. Their screams were terrible as they were carried away.

Before their screams even faded, Kumi gave a signal to her clones, and they began vomiting up a typhoon's worth of waves, which rumbled at the walls of the retraining school, hitting them again and again, drowning a few serpent soldiers in the process. She couldn't aim her waters too high, because there were the children to consider. Still, the buildings started to sway and buckle in the onslaught of all the Aakashes' and Kumis' joint powers, and for a moment, it looked like I wouldn't even have to risk my own uncontrollable fire harming all these caged children. I would be lying if I said I didn't feel relieved.

But then Sesha, who had been watching this whole time from his high balcony, got in on the act. He ignored the wind, was unbothered by the waves, and was staring straight at me.

"You're going to have to do it, demoness!" He put up his right hand, creating a green, force field–like wall that bounced out from his palm to hit Aakash and every one of the air-rakkhosh ghosts. The serpent magic encased them each in a ball-like prison. They screamed and howled, pounding to get out. Then Sesha twisted his hands, uttering a fierce spell, and all those trapped fell to their knees, shrieking. Aakash writhed about on the bottom of his magic sphere, obviously in agony.

Sesha put up his left hand and sent out the same diabolical magic at Kumi and every one of the water-rakkhosh ghosts. And that's when Kumi, my irritating roommate, that thorn in my side, that fierce warrior, screamed in such distress, it curdled my very soul.

"Stop! Sesha, Stop!" I shouted desperately across our now two-thirds-felled army. My heart was beating wildly, and I was breathing out plumes of smoke. But even though I felt flames rising inside, I didn't dare conjure them with all these hanging cages full of children around.

Sesha's green eyes bore across the writhing bodies and into my soul. "Make me!" he growled, his voice echoing across the crowd. "Oh, but you can't, can you? Too bad you can't use your flames without risking burning everyone here to a crisp!"

Sesha twisted the green lightning emanating from his hand. In their magic orbs, the Kumis gave earsplitting shrieks, the real demoness arching her back almost in half. He did it again, and the Aakashes bellowed, clawing at their skin as if their bodies were on fire.

"Let them go, Sesha!" With my words, I spit sparks and flame.

"Why should I?" Sesha's face was twisted with fury, and although his cheek still bore the scars of his father's violence, he looked more like the Governor-General than ever. His eyes gleamed with the pleasure of causing others' pain. "You're the traitors rising against your rightful rulers. You're the ones who are breaking the law, you rebel scum. Do you know how little power you have, how nothing you do will actually change anything? Do you know how badly the Serpent Empire can crush you?"

Nothing we did would change anything? He had to be kidding. So much had changed already. We'd all found each other. We'd teamed up and gotten here. I'd learned there were more important things than being a loner. I'd started to learn how to not fear my own power. Nothing had changed? It couldn't have been further from the truth. Everything had changed.

"You're not a torturer, Sesha. You know how it feels to have someone treat you with violence. I know you don't want to do this!" I shouted.

"Burn him up, princess!" squawked Toto from my shoulder.

"Try it, and I'll tell my snakes to cut the chains holding all the cages!" Sesha snapped his white teeth. "Or maybe I'll just kill these prisoners my soldiers just found."

With dread, I realized that Sesha was not alone on the balcony. Because gagged and bound next to him were none other than Arko and Chandni. They were made powerless by green cords of magical rope crisscrossing around them. They stared at me with panicked, expressive eyes.

"Should I kill them now, Pinki? Throw them off the balcony?" drawled Sesha. With a flick of his hands, he moved Arko to dangle precariously over the edge of the parapet. "Or should I make you choose which set of friends I kill first?" Now he twisted his hands again, making Kumi, Aakash, and all their duplicates yell in pain.

My eyes shot from my friends captured on the balcony to my friends captured on the ground. If Sesha's soldiers caught Arko and Chandni, where was Deembo?

Then, suddenly, I saw her. Deembo, who had somehow snuck out of whatever hiding place Arko had left her while everything else was happening. She was crouching beside the real Aakash's orb of torture, her face soaked with tears. Aakash, like Kumi, was beyond recognizing her now, his eyes squeezed shut, howling in agony. She stared at our rakkhosh friends and then up at Chandni and Arko, next to Sesha.

"Deembo, it's too dangerous!" I whispered. "Get out of here!"

But there she was, in full view of everyone, unafraid. Only her tiny size had stopped Sesha from spotting her yet. And she used that time to her advantage. Whereas I was frozen with fear, unable to act, Deembo had no such issues. Placing her hands on the ground, her face tense with concentration, Deembo made the biggest land-quake she had ever created. First, there was a terrible screeching, rumbling sound. The ground beneath us cracked, and little spurts of water started shooting up through where she must have breached the protective undersea bubble.

The land buckled and swayed now, making the buildings rock. The guards struggled to get their balance, and even Sesha on his balcony began to lose his footing. When that happened, his magic spell over Aakash, Kumi, and all their ghostly duplicates broke, releasing our rakkhosh friends from their terrible prisons of pain. At a second roiling quake, Sesha almost fell, and this time, his magic ropes over Arko and Chandni seemed to vanish. She had done it! Deembo had freed our friends!

Unfortunately, right at that moment, Sesha spotted her. "Stop! You!" he snarled, sending a green bolt of lightning at Deembo's hearts.

"No!" I yelled, but it was too late.

The green bolt hit its mark, and little Deembo lay at my feet, as still as death. I screamed, my voice piercing from one world to another.

CHAPTER 22

Don't You Ever Let Anyone Lessen Your Fire—Not Ever. You Hear Me?

After the shock and before the sorrow came the anger. Anger so red-hot and dangerous it threatened to burn me from the inside out. Anger molten like lava. The anger that I had always been afraid of, anger that so often fueled my out-of-control spurts of fire rage. But this anger now came not from jealousy, or insecurity, or loneliness, but from love. The anger that rose up in me wasn't a selfish thing; it was like an avenging goddess armed with a flaming sword. It was the anger of the downtrodden protecting their own throughout the ages, throughout the galaxies. It was the anger that we are told makes us monstrous but, in fact, makes us divine.

I cradled Deembo's broken body in my arms, feeling

my fire erupt unchecked and unfettered. It spoke, it sang, it shouted, it made me who I was. My fire was as much a part of my voice as my words, and if I didn't claim it, I would be silenced forever.

"Now!" I screamed to Aakash and Kumi, who were using all their powers to make it storm and rage.

"Now!" I yelled to the ghost rakkhosh, who were all waiting for my command.

"Now!" I yelled to Arko and Chandni on the balcony.

"Now!" I yelled to Kawla and Mawla, petrified in shock at the sight of Deembo.

"Now!" I yelled to the skies, to the land, to the waters, to the fire, all of which were around but also within me.

"Now!" I yelled to my hearts, bleeding within me like a river of power and sorrow.

Not caring about controlling or limiting my power in any way, I let my fire flow. The ghosts who had taken my form also let streams of ferocious, unchecked flames shoot from their mouths and noses. Our collective fire streams swirled and danced, sometimes coming together to form inferno balls and at other times sheer walls of molten heat. Our power raged and pummeled the school that was a prison, avoiding Kumi's waves, lest we be extinguished, avoiding Aakash's gusts, lest we be thrown off course. Our flames shot out straight and true, wild and fierce, full not of embarrassment or insecurity but of fury and righteous ferocity. Our powers hit the buildings and the serpent soldiers but avoided the caged children, cocooning them in expert curves of flame. We avoided Arko, who leaned over the balcony, his hands wielding golden light. We avoided Chandni, next to him, who joined his golden light with her own silvery moonbeams.

The serpent stronghold shook from the powers of sun and moon, air, water, and flame. Then Kawla and Mawla, imitating Deembo's gesture, stuck their hands out of their cages, reaching out to the ground below. In this way, they continued the vibrations of the ground quake that their sister had started.

"Break their cages, Pinki!" yelled Chandni, and I didn't hesitate. I'd been afraid before, but losing Deembo had focused something in me, made me able to face and name exactly what lived inside my hearts. It was love. Love for my family, love for my friends, love for my freedom and myself.

I shot out fire to burn the bars of Kawla's and Mawla's prisons. Before my cousins could fall, Aakash caught them on a gust of wind, and Kumi cushioned them in a bubble of water. Then Arko and Chandni dived down on beams of their sun and moon magic, catching my cousins easily in their arms before floating down to the ground. They were free, my twin baby cousins were free. But I couldn't feel any happiness, because Deembo was forever imprisoned in the cage of her own death.

As Arko and Chandni came to land on the ground beside me, I wordlessly handed them Deembo's small body. They took her from me, gently, lovingly, but when Arko opened his mouth as if to say something, I shook my head, cutting him off before he even started. Then Chandni gripped at my arm, and I physically shook off her hand. I gave Kawla and Mawla quick hugs, squeezing them to me hard and tight before pushing them away again. But now was not the time for reunions. Now was the time for revenge.

Without even knowing that I could do such a thing until I did it, I breathed out a bridge of fire from the ground up to the balcony. Then, without so much as singeing a hair on my head, I climbed that magical bridge of my own power up to where Sesha stood, now alone.

"Look what you have done!" I said in a controlled voice that was both hot and low. I may not have screamed, but he heard me all right. The anger coming off me in waves was so unyielding that Sesha began to sweat from the heat of it.

"I didn't mean . . ." Sesha exclaimed, but I threw a

fireball at him, and he slammed sideways to his knees to avoid its deadly force.

"You've killed her!" I spat, no longer quiet and controlled. I pointed down to Deembo's tiny body. Now my voice was so loud it shook the foundation of the balcony itself.

Sesha was cowering before me, but I was too far gone for mercy. I had not only learned how to control my fire, I had discovered that I *was* my fire. And my fire was me. It burned as it raced along my skin, flowing from my hair and blazing from my eyes. Sesha had tried to tell me that I needed to limit my power to control it. He'd just about convinced me that I needed someone like him to hem in my fire, to quiet and control my voice. He had been so, so wrong. I needed to become my power—not to control it but to wield it, embrace it, own it.

I looked down at his hateful face, now so afraid. This coward, this murderer, this pathetic boy who dared to still breathe while Deembo could not. Like an arm, a noose, a fist, a blaze of flames shot out of me and grabbed Sesha by the neck.

"What are you doing? Let go!" he sputtered. But the fire arm gripped on harder, burning him, strangling him, until he was turning purple and barely able to get out a word.

I felt a strange surge of happiness at his suffering, and it scared me. But not enough to stop. Never enough to stop.

With a fierce jolt of pleasure, I dangled him over the balcony parapet as he had dangled Arko. My words rang out across the courtyard, my voice so fierce and loud I could barely recognize myself. "Look what destruction your weakness has caused! You could have stood up to your father! You could have done what you knew was right!"

Sesha mewled, begging for his life. "Pinki, please! Don't do this! We were once friends! Or at least, almost friends!"

"Pinki, no!" Arko cried from the ground below. Kawla and Mawla were gripping his legs, looking up at me with their huge, round eyes.

"This isn't you either!" Chandni yelled. She cradled Deembo's still form in her arms, and the sight cracked me open all over again.

"What do you know about who I am?" I yelled. I could hardly think anymore, the roaring in my ears was so loud. Whereas once I had been afraid of it, now I was nothing outside my anger; I was nothing beyond my fire.

He barely had any voice left, but I could read Sesha's lips as he spluttered, "Please, mercy! Mercy!"

"Leave him and look forward. Break the children's cages, Pinki!" Chandni yelled.

"That snake scum isn't worth it!" shouted Kumi.

"Free all those other kids instead!" added Arko.

"I don't know, I think it's pretty dang awesome how she's controlling her power finally," said Aakash. "Yo, I totally think she should kill that snake dude."

Kumi, Arko, and Chandni whirled on him. "Aakash!"

I would have laughed if I had the energy. As it was, all I could manage was a twist of my lips, a gesture more full of cruelty than humor.

"Please!" Sesha whimpered again as I held him even farther over the balcony's edge. He sounded broken and scared. "I can change! I can learn!"

I didn't know if Sesha was lying, but it didn't matter. I never had to face what I was fully capable of, because, just then, out of nowhere, there was a trumpet call.

"You should have killed me when you had the chance!" snarled Sesha. He was still dangling from my fire limb like a rag doll, but suddenly, there was a new confidence to him.

I lifted my head to see what was happening. It was the absolute worst thing possible. It was the Serpentine Governor-General, Sesha's father, attacking the courtyard with a fresh troop of soldiers.

"No!" I shouted. "Not now!"

"You're doomed, rakkhoshi!" spat Sesha.

"You're remarkably confident about that for someone dangling from a balcony!" I snapped, shaking Sesha's body until he cried again for mercy.

Below us, the Governor-General was spitting green poison bolts from his mouth and shooting green lightning from his hands. And somehow, he knew already about the ghosts. His soldiers were armed with iron weapons that cut through my army of bhoot like they were made of tissue.

"They aren't rakkhosh! Most of these rebels aren't rakkhosh at all, but ghosts!" he bellowed. "Soldiers, use your iron weapons!"

And they did. My ghost army had been found out and was getting decimated while I watched from my balcony viewpoint. There were serpent soldiers with iron bayonets, guns that shot iron bullets. There were iron swords that sliced through the bhoot, reducing them to ash. There were iron rods that impaled them, making them vanish into the ether.

"My father's killing your ghost army!" Sesha wheezed. And of course he was right. Even in the few minutes since the snake reinforcements arrived, my army had been slaughtered down to half its original size. "Your friends aren't going to win without you to help them!"

I looked down to see Aakash and Kumi back-to-back,

launching wind and water at our enemies. I saw Arko fight-ing off a dozen soldiers with a beam of sun magic and Chandni flying above a dozen more with her twirling moon staff. Between them were Kawla and Mawla, their hands on the ground, their faces screwed up in concentration as they made the ground quake and sway. I couldn't see where they had put Deembo's body, and suddenly, I was desperate to know where it was. Because despite all my friends' efforts, despite their collective power, they were already outnumbered. As each minute saw more of our ghostly army disappearing, it was clear they were going to lose. I looked at Sesha's twisted and bruised face and knew then what I had to do.

Abruptly, I dragged Sesha back over the balcony's edge and threw him unceremoniously to the floor of the balcony. He gasped and choked, desperate to catch a full breath. Then he looked up at me, confused. "I was sure you were going to let me fall," he breathed, rubbing at his burned and bruised throat.

"I was sure I was going to let you fall too," I admitted.

I eyed the fighting below, gauging the lay of the land. Before I jumped off the balcony, I looked back at Sesha. "But watch it, because next time, you might not be so lucky," I said. "Next time I see you, I'm going to kill you."

Then I left the snake prince wheezing and coughing. I had more important things to do than get pulled down by my enemies. I had to go and lift up my friends.

I don't know how I did it, but when I jumped off that balcony, I twirled in the air on fiery shots of my own power. I skated on spark and flame, flying and no longer afraid.

"It took you long enough, yaar!" Aakash yelled, when I landed on the ground next to him. He was blowing out storms from his lips.

"Did you kill that snake kid?" cackled Kumi, still making waves, still causing havoc.

I shook my head even as I launched a volley of fire-bombs at the approaching serpent soldiers. "You were right. He wasn't worth it."

"It's no wonder you couldn't control it before. You have more power than any fire rakkhosh I've ever seen," Kumi said. "Maybe any rakkhosh I've seen of any clan."

"Yo, Pinks, maybe you should run for Demon Queen after all," added Aakash.

I almost couldn't see them through the force of my flames, but I felt their friendship, their approval. I had finally found how to use my voice—not my jealousy, not my pettiness or insecurity but my true righteous voice—and claim its power.

"Where are the others?" I asked, and Kumi pointed toward where Chandni was fighting a hoard of snakes, with Kawla and Mawla's help. Chandni was swinging her staff wide and hard, keeping the soldiers at bay while my baby cousins shook the ground under their feet. Behind them all, Arko kneeled over Deembo, his golden magic weaving all around and through her.

"What are you doing, Prince?" I yelled even as I expelled a fierce universe of fire from within myself. "Leave her alone!"

Arko didn't answer, and in fact, I saw Chandni turn during a pause in the fighting and add her silvery moon powers to Arko's. I saw their celestial light pouring into my little cousin. Deembo—that silly, tiny land-clan rakkhoshi to whom the height of culinary pleasure was a pocketful of stolen eggs. Deembo, who loved head scratches, and belly rubs, and adventures, and her family. Deembo, who had freed all our friends with her small magic, only to pay the ultimate price. Deembo, who was of the land and felt her connection to all that was below her feet. And here were the powers of the sky washing over her, bathing her with their energy and healing light. It was as if the universe was saying, loud and clear, there is no creature so base that the sun and moon cannot wash its broken body. There is no being so high that it cannot lend its light to those who need it. Tiny as they were, Kawla and Mawla guarded their sister's body like fierce warriors. Their eyes streamed tears, but their backs did not bend.

There was nothing I could do for them now, nothing except defeat the Governor-General and his soldiers. Nothing except free the rest of the children. But I had no army anymore, hardly any warriors except Aakash and Kumi. Arko, Chandni, and my cousins were all with Deembo, and Toto was too small to be of much help. Except, to his credit, he did serve as a watchdog of sorts for us all, yelling out, "Watch it, Aakash! Incoming to your right! Kumi, protect Pinki's left!"

The serpents were closing in on us. The Governor-General's troops were swarming all around like a force of nature themselves. The tide had turned in the battle. There were too many enemies and too few friends. We were surely done for.

"Give up, you idiots!" shrieked Sesha from his balcony. "Give up before my father's soldiers slaughter you all!"

But I knew the Governor-General, and even if I hadn't known him, I could see what kind of a soldier he was. He wouldn't let us go, and if we gave up, he would kill us anyway. He had shown the ghosts no mercy, laughing with bloodthirsty glory as his soldiers had cut them down.

The soldiers and their lightning bolts were closing in on us from the front, the Governor-General himself from the side. Aakash, Kumi, and I were standing back-to-back-to-back now, each shooting out torrents of our power. We'd rotate and turn, following Toto's bird's-eye-view instructions. But even we knew we couldn't hold out much longer. While there had once been a path before us, any possibility of victory was crumbling fast. In front of our eyes, our future was disappearing.

"It was good fighting with you," Kumi said to me, grasping my hand with vicious glee. "And alongside you, fire wench!"

"I guess none of us will get the crown." Aakash laughed. "But who cares? At least we went down in an epic way. Yo, nobody's going to forget us now." He grabbed my other hand.

I squeezed both of their hands in turn. "We may not be kings or queens, but we're going to be legends!" I shouted over a mouthful of fire vomit. I hadn't thought I could achieve more oneness with my power than I had felt when facing down Sesha. But I was wrong. There was something purer, more powerful, truer about how I was using my fire now, alongside and for my friends.

"All right, ding-dongs! Let's go down in a blaze of glory!" I cried, exploding with molten fierceness. I raged, my fire something that defied the bounds of my body and consciousness. I was my power and my power was me, and I was no longer afraid of anything.

Then it happened, right when I thought all was lost. It came as a surprise, as so many revelations do. It was a voice, tiny as a spark but strong as the multiverse. Singing. Singing in a voice I hadn't heard in far too long. Singing Arko's song from the woods about believing in yourself. "Jodi alo na bhore . . . apon buker pajor jalie nie ekla jolo re."

"If there is no light, if the path before you rages with dark, then light your own heart on fire. Be the beacon. Be the spark."

It was Deembo. It was Deembo, alive and full of moon and sun magic. It was Deembo, who was of the land but also my heart's brightest star. She was the spark of my fire, and she was singing, having found her voice, just as I had, in the magic of our friends. Or perhaps she had possessed it all along, only we hadn't been able to hear. Through the cloudy field of battle, she ran to me, her hearts lighting her way.

"Deembo! You're alive!" I picked her up and held her tight, but she did not stop her song. I lifted her onto my shoulders, feeling like I could win any war. If Deembo was alive, I could do anything. Anything at all was possible. Even victory. Even freedom.

"Listen to her sing!" said Chandni as she rose up and began fighting the Governor-General with a power I had never seen. It was humbling, and terrifying, and utterly beautiful. With her hair flying, her eyes silver and wild, and her moon staff in her hand, she was like a painting of a warrior queen of old.

"Sing with her!" cried Arko as he rose up too and began fighting the snake soldiers, his sun magic a reflection of my own fire.

Arko, Chandni, and I began to sing as we fought. We sang of the fire in our own hearts, the fire that could light up any night. As we did, the young prisoners in the cages raised their heads, as if remembering who they had been before they'd been stolen, as if they were filled again with their identities, their mother tongues, their senses of home, their pride.

Aakash and Kumi then joined in, and something about all our voices united like that was stronger than any storm, fiercer than any thunder, more powerful than any fire. It echoed from beneath the sea to the skies, it shook the waters and the lands, it burned with the light of our passions and our collective strengths.

If there is no light, if the path before you rages with dark, then light your own heart on fire. Be the beacon. Be the spark.

As we sang, some of the children's eyes became clearer, and they began smiling. "Keep singing," I shouted. "Look at how they remember their language! Look at how it makes them strong!"

"Stop that!" Sesha snarled from the balcony. He had obviously regained his strength, because he raised his hands in the air, shooting green lightning between them. "Stop that infernal singing!"

But we didn't. Even when the song was done, Toto raised his wings, like he was a conductor, and we started in once again.

"Sing!" I called to the children still trapped in their cages. "Even if you are afraid, and your voice makes no noise, sing! You're not alone; we are here with you! Don't be afraid to find your voice! Sing!"

As we did, something unexplainable happened. Maybe it was the power of the air and the water, the fire and the land, the sun and the moon. Or maybe it was the sparkling starlight of the children themselves. But somehow, someway, the children's voices came back to their bodies, and they began to sing. Like a torrent of magic released from its bonds, our singing, our belief, our togetherness somehow broke whatever hold the serpents had over them.

"No!" yelled the Governor-General. "That magic is ours! Those voices are ours! No one speaks without our permission! No one sings anything but what we let them!"

"Their voices belong to them!" I yelled, exploding the children's cages with the force of my fire. "You cannot take them!"

"We will rip your land apart!" yelled Sesha. "We will make sure the Kingdom Beyond is scattered to the winds!"

"We humans and rakkhosh won't be afraid of your

decrees!" yelled Aakash, catching the falling prisoners on cushions of wind and cloud. "Or, like, each other!"

"We won't be afraid of our own powers!" yelled Kumi, scooping up the freed children in the arms of a storm.

"We won't be afraid of our own anger!" said Chandni, bringing the children down on the wings of a moonbeam.

"We won't hide, but rise up, together, and stop you!" said Arko, protecting them all with an arc of sun.

"We will speak! We will sing! We will fight!" The words escaped my lips like light and fire as the battle raged on. But I wasn't afraid. We had freed the children, and I knew we would free ourselves. Because I had my friends around me, my friends who had become my family. Because I had my three hearts back—Kawla, Mawla, and Deembo—my fire, my beacons, my stars.

And so it was. Not that day. And not the day after. But like the spark that ignites a giant bonfire, that battle was the beginning of something new. As Arko and Chandni had healed Deembo, we had breathed life into the seemingly dead revolution of our parents' time. We had joined together to battle what was wrong in our world and to search together for something better. Like seekers looking for stars in the night, we were looking for a truer tomorrow. That magical day was a taste of what was to come.

We had felt freedom. Freedom from our own fears, freedom from society's dictates, freedom from old habits and old ideas. We had tasted freedom and we wouldn't stop until it spread across the land, flowing like air and water, burning like fire, shining like the sun, moon, and stars.

Author's Note

Force of Fire is an original story that, like the three Kiranmala and the Kingdom Beyond books (*The Serpent's Secret*, *Game of Stars*, and *The Chaos Curse*), draws from many traditional Bengali folktales and children's stories. These are stories beloved in West Bengal (India), Bangladesh, and throughout the Bengali-speaking diaspora.

Thakumar Jhuli and Rakkhosh Stories

Folktales involving rakkhosh are very popular throughout South Asia. The word is sometimes spelled *rakshasa* in other parts of the region, but in this book, it is spelled like the word sounds in Bengali. Folktales are an oral tradition, passed on from one generation to the next, with each teller adding nuance to their own version. In

1907, Dakshinaranjan Mitra Majumdar published some classic Bengali folktales in a book called *Thakumar Jhuli* (*Grandmother's Satchel*). This collection is full of tales about princes and princesses from the Kingdom Beyond Seven Oceans and Thirteen Rivers, as well as stories about evil serpent kings, soul-stealing bhoot, and rhyming, carnivorous rakkhosh—who are the monsters everyone loves to hate.

Force of Fire is my imagined origin story for the same demon queen who appears in the original Neelkamal and Lalkamal tale, as well as my own Kiranmala trilogy. Her mother, Ai-Ma, also appears in both the original Neelkamal and Lalkamal story as well as my own previous books. Prince Sesha, who eventually becomes the serpent king, is a character of my own making in the Kingdom Beyond novels, but he is based on all the evil serpent kings of the original *Thakurmar Jhuli* tales. Chandni, the moon girl, is the younger version of Kiranmala's own moon mother (the word *Chandni* means "moonlight" just as *Kiranmala* means "garland of moonbeams"). The Seven Brothers Champak come from the *Thakurmar Jhuli* story of shat bhai chompa—seven princes who were turned into champak flowers by their evil stepmothers.

The rakkhosh figures Ravan, Surpanakha, and

Ghatatakach in *Force of Fire* are not from *Thakurmar Jhuli*, but from Hindu epics. Surpanakha is the sister of Ravan, the main antagonist of *The Ramayana*. She's attracted to the hero Ram, but when she approaches him, he rejects her. When she then tries the same tactics with his younger brother Laxshman, she is again rejected. Humiliated by the two brothers, the demoness goes to attack Ram's wife, Sita, but has her nose cut off by Laxshman instead. She tells her brother Ravan about this shameful event, and sets off the events of the epic, including Ravan's kidnapping of Sita. I always thought that *The Ramayana* treated Surpanakha pretty unfairly, so I made her the headmistress of the rakkhosh academy in this book and *The Chaos Curse*. Ghatatkach (after whom the made-up demon Academy of Murder and Mayhem is named) is a rakkhosh from another epic, *The Mahabharata*. The son of the second heroic Pandav brother Bhim and the rakkhoshi Hidimbi, enormously strong Ghatatkach fought alongside his father and Pandav uncles in the great war upon which the epic is based. Even though he was raised by his rakkhoshi mother, he was enormously loyal to his father and family and was an almost undefeatable warrior, so it made sense to me that he would have a rakkhosh school named after him!

Thakumar Jhuli stories are still very popular in West Bengal and Bangladesh, and have inspired translations, films, television cartoons, comic books, and more. Rakkhosh are very popular as well and appear not just in folk stories but also in Hindu mythology. Images of bloodthirsty, long-fanged rakkhosh can be seen everywhere—even on the back of colorful Indian trucks and auto rikshaws, as a warning to other drivers not to tailgate or drive too fast!

Stories of Bhoot, Petni, Shakchunni, and Daini

Stories about bhoot, or ghosts, are very popular in Bengal. Bhoot are not exactly like the white-sheeted, chain-rattling notion of ghosts in the West but are their own kind of horrible monster creature. Different types of bhoot also have different personalities and traits—petni are female ghosts (women who usually died unmarried), and shakchunni are the married version. They, like many other types of ghosts, want nothing more than to capture a human being and put them in a coconut or other tree trunk for safekeeping while taking over their physical form and then trying to inhabit the human being's life. If you're ever walking by a haunted coconut grove or lake, particularly at dusk, never turn around when you hear your name being called—or your soul is up for grabs! Petni and shakchunni can also be identified by their backward facing feet (a dead giveaway!) or when they use their supernatural powers to do housework—like when they reach their extendable arms out a window to pluck lemons, or stick their own feet into the fire because they're too lazy to go get firewood. Other kinds of bhoot mentioned in this story include mechho bhoot (fish-eating ghosts) and skondokata (headless ghosts).

The Indian Revolution

The other backdrop to *Force of Fire* is the Indian freedom struggle against the British. Although Britain ruled mercilessly over South Asia for over two hundred years, Indian revolutionary fighters of multiple generations fought valiantly against imperialist rule. Freedom for the region was finally achieved in 1947 due to the activities of both nonviolent revolutionaries like Mahatma Gandhi and revolutionaries who believed in meeting force with force like Bengali revolutionary leader Netaji Subash Chandra Bose. It was Netaji who actually said the famous quote "Give me blood and I will give you freedom" that Headmistress Surpanakha says early in the book. The undersea battle scene at the end of *Force of Fire* is a reimagining of the massacre of Jallianwala Bagh in 1919 when British forces, under the command of Brigadier General Reginald Dyer, slaughtered possibly upward of a thousand men, women, and children who had been trapped in the enclosed area. Nobel Laureate Rabindranath Tagore formally repudiated his British knighthood over this brutal killing.

Like Pinki's parents, many members of my own family were imprisoned for their revolutionary activities against the British. My entire life, I heard stories about and from these heroic family members, wondering at how much they had sacrificed for an idea called freedom. Like Pinki, I had to figure out my own place in this revolutionary family history. My father's aunt, Banalata DasGupta, was imprisoned by the British in her early twenties, when she was still a college student. Far too young, she died in captivity from a lack of treatment for her (curable) thyroid goiter. My maternal grandfather, Sunil Kumar Das, was only fifteen when he was jailed by the British for his involvement in the Chittagong Armory Raid (a raid which I loosely refer to in *Force of Fire*, when Chandni comments that Pinki's parents were involved in a raid against the snakes). My grandfather survived years of imprisonment but suffered many ailments his entire life due to the poor treatment he received at the hands of the British. When he died in his nineties, he was one of the oldest recognized Indian freedom fighters. I wish now that I had recorded more of his wonderful stories, that I had him on video telling me about all that he had done. I can only hope that this story, combining the folktales I heard from my grandmother with the real-life revolutionary tales I heard from my grandfather, is some sort of small tribute to all I have inherited from them.

The Stealing of Language

In *Force of Fire*, one of the main horrors the Serpent Empire is committing is stealing children away from their families and forcing them to abandon their language. Early in the story, Arko (disguised as the schoolteacher Shurjo) says, "Destroying a people's language, not letting children learn the ways of those who came before them, is the surest way to kill a culture." The caged children whom Pinki and her friends rescue at the end of the story have literally had their voices ripped from their throats by the snakes; they cannot speak. This kind of linguistic violence is sadly not something I made up. (I only made up the magical ability to steal voices.) There are unfortunately many examples throughout the world of languages being stamped out like this. Sometimes it is a result of neglect and colonization, and sometimes it is a purposeful act by those who want to see the future of a community wither away.

Not only did the British Empire impose English as the language of commerce, political power, and higher education in South Asia, but they impacted regional languages in other ways. For instance, when the British finally quit South Asia in 1947, they left behind violent turmoil in the form of "the partition"—and the separation of the area into majority Muslim Pakistan from majority Hindu (although secular) India. When Urdu was declared the national language of newly independent Pakistan, the majority Bengali speakers of East Pakistan (a region that would eventually gain its own independence in 1972 to become Bangladesh) rose up to protect their rich linguistic history. In 1952, students at Dhaka University marched in protest to protect Bengali heritage, but many were killed by the police. The date of this occurrence, February 21, was later declared by the independent government of Bangladesh as Language Martyrs' Day, and UNESCO eventually decided to observe it as International Mother Language Day. The Language Movement (Bhasha

Andolon) was a critical part of Bangladesh's eventual liberation war from Pakistan and creation of their independent, Bengali-speaking country. During this war, however, one group targeted and executed were Bengali intellectuals, including professors and journalists—those who teach and share culture and language. The thriving existence of Bengali today is in large part due to the hard work of Bangladeshi language liberation activists and the way they connected political and economic independence with freedom of mother language.

I was not only inspired by the Bhasha Andolon of Bangladesh, but by a violent history even closer to my current home: the Native American residential boarding schools of North America. These government-run schools of the US and Canada (as well as places like Australia), some of which operated until the 1980s, were violent and frightening places where Indigenous children were taken from their families and communities, forced to convert to Christianity, speak only English, and assimilate to non-Native, white life. There are many stories of abuse at these schools, as well as stories of linguistic erasure—for instance, children who were severely punished for speaking their own language, even with friends and siblings. Movements among various Native communities to preserve, protect, and pass on their Indigenous languages is a response and resistance to these violent histories of attempted erasure.

As someone who lives in the US, I wanted to connect the way that colonialism and imperialism work through the world and through history. The numbers attached to the various snake decrees in *Force of Fire* actually gesture to global colonial events: 1830 is the date of the Indian Removal Act in the US, signed into law by President Andrew Jackson to legislate the settlement of Native American ancestral lands west of the Mississippi by white settlers. 1858 is the date of the Government of India Act, which marked the beginning of the British Raj, while 1947 is the year that India and Pakistan became independent nations, free from British rule. 1492 is of course the year Christopher Columbus happened upon North America, thinking it India, and began a terrible and too often overlooked history of murder and violence against the Native peoples of this land. Finally, 1619 is the year that the first enslaved African people were brought to Jamestown, Virginia.

Erasing children's voices—their ability to speak, think, and sing in their own languages—is a way of destroying culture. Language, story, and voice are the beating heart of any thriving cultural community.

Rabindranath Tagore and Other Bengali Songs

As are many Bengalis, growing up in South Asia or throughout the diaspora, I was raised on the poetry, prose, and songs of Nobel Laureate Rabindranath Tagore. Many of his poems and songs were, in fact, written about Indian independence. The song that appears several times in *Force of Fire*, "Ekla Chalo Re," was written in 1905 by Tagore and is a revolutionary song that Mahatma Gandhi often referred to as one of his favorites. One line in the song becomes the heart of Pinki's story and is loosely translated by me as "If there is no light, if the path before you rages with dark, then light your own heart on fire. Be the beacon. Be the spark."

The names of Kanchkawla, Kaanmawla, and Deembo are all borrowed from a well-known absurd Bengali song called "Shing Nei Tobu Nam Tar Shingho" that was sung by Kishore Kumar in the 1958 Bengali film *Lukochuri*. The original lyrics were by Gauriprasanna Mazumder and the music by Hemanta Mukherjee. While *Kanchkawla* are underripe bananas, *Kaanmawla* means "boxing someone's ears." While *Deem* are eggs, *Deembo* implies a nothing sandwich—a whole lotta nothing. (But of course our dear Deembo in the story is quite the oppo-site, a whole lot of heart, spirit, and love!)

The image of the bird trapped in a cage is borrowed from a well-known Baul folk song *Khanchar Bhitor Ochin Pakhi*, in which the bird symbolizes the human soul trapped in the cage of worldly illusion. I used this image and combined it with my own distress at the many chil-dren at the US border (even now at the time of writing this book) who are caged, away from their parents, by immi-gration authorities.

Toto/Tuntuni

Toto is a character of my own making, but I imagine that he is the father of the wisecracking bird Tuntuni who appears in the Kiranmala books. Tuntuni is a favorite, and recurrent, character of Bengali children's folktales. Upendrakishore Ray Chowdhury (also known as Upendrakishore Ray) collected a number of these sto-ries starring the clever tailor bird Tuntuni in a 1910 book called *Tuntunir Boi (The Tailor Bird's Book)*.

Astronomy

While *The Serpent's Secret*, *Game of Stars*, and *The Chaos Curse* have quite a few references to astronomy, there are fewer in *Force of Fire*. Yet, Pinki does refer to the multiverse while Chandni and Arko are undertaking a rescue operation where they smuggle out endangered children and families to another dimension. These ideas stem from string, or multiverse, theory, the notion that many universes may exist in parallel to one another, which are simply not aware of the other universes' existences. String/multiverse theory appears in all the Kingdom Beyond books because it feels in keeping with the immigrant experience—the idea that immigrant communities are space explorers and universe straddlers.

Like in the Kiranmala books, rakkhosh in *Force of Fire* are the manifestation of black holes. Even though this pairing of folktales and cosmology may seem strange, I did so to tear down the stereotype that cultural stories are somehow unconnected to science. In fact, like in every culture, traditional Bengali stories are often infused with stories about the stars and planets. That said, please don't take anything in this book as scientific fact, but rather use the story to inspire some more research about astronomy, astronomers and physicists, black holes, and string theory!

Acknowledgments

The Rabindranath Tagore song that threads this novel together, "Ekla Cholo Re," is about walking your path alone even if no one answers your call. I have luckily never had to do that, because so many have helped light this path of my writing career. Thank you to my agent team of Brent Taylor and Uwe Stender at Triada US for believing in me and walking this path with me. So many thank-yous for the love and light given by the generous (and hilarious) editorial collaboration of Abigail McAden and Talia Seidenfeld. With them, I would journey anywhere.

Thank you to Vivienne To and Elizabeth Parisi for the beauty of this cover and the book's illustrations. Gratitude to Melissa Schirmer, my production editor; Josh Berlowitz, my copy editor; and to the rest of my Scholastic family including Ellie Berger, David Levithan, Rachel Feld, Julia Eisler, Lizette Serrano, Emily Heddleson, Danielle Yadao, Lauren Donovan, and Elisabeth Ferrari! Thank you to the team from Scholastic Book Clubs as well as the wonderful Robin Hoffman, and the team from Scholastic Book Fairs, for getting this series into the hands of so many readers. Thank you to Donalyn Miller, John Schumacher, and all the other wonderful reading champions around the country who are out there doing the good work!

Thank you to all those author friends I've made on this wonderful journey, including my We Need Diverse Books, Kidlit Writers of Color, and Desi Writers families. Thank you to my narrative medicine/health humanities colleagues and students at Columbia and around the country. Thank you to my extended family, as well as my wonderful Bengali immigrant community of aunties, uncles, and friends.

To my beloved parents, Sujan and Shamita; my husband, Boris; and my darlings Kirin, Sunaya, and Khushi—it is for you, I light my heart on fire. You are my beacons, you are my spark.

From *Crown of Flames*
THE FIRE QUEEN: BOOK TWO

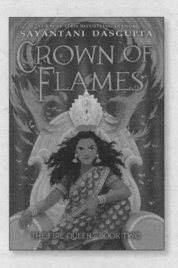

It all began with me being forced to wear a crown of flames. Which, as you can imagine, was a bummer. A serious bummer.

Since I'd officially/unofficially joined the rebellion against the Serpentine Empire, and rescued all those human and rakkhosh kids from an undersea retraining center a few weeks before, I'd been having trouble sleeping. It wasn't just the bounty I was sure that Sesha, the two-faced slimeball son of the Serpentine Governor General, had on my head. Which was a thing, sure. But it was more the fact that a lot of my fellow rakkhosh students at Ghatatkach Academy of Murder and Mayhem doubted that the undersea raid ever happened.

So I'd done what I always did when I couldn't sleep. I'd snuck out a bunch of old, dusty books from the school library and started reading. That's when it happened. I was lying in bed, in the middle of looking through a crumbling, silver-covered volume called *Thakumar Jhuli*. Like I had since I was a lonely kid, I was reading the words aloud to myself, only softly, so as not to wake my roommate Kumi. That was when I felt the strange, sucking sensation of being pulled out of my reality. One moment, I was reading in my dorm in the middle of the night, and the next moment, I whirled, as if through a wormhole, right out of my own body, my own place, and most importantly, my own time.

Now, if you've never traveled unexpectedly through a time vortex magically created by an old book you stole from the library, I don't recommend it. At least without a helmet and some serious anti-nausea medication.

When my swirling vision cleared, and stomach somewhat settled, I found myself in a royal court lined with high columns and majestic silk banners. Snoring Kumi was no longer there, nor anything from my familiar dorm room. I was still feeling queasy, but had to stifle the urge to yuke, because before me upon the high throne, was a regal rakkhoshi queen. Her long, black hair flowed over her sharp horns and broad shoulders like a mighty river from a mountain. Her dark all-seeing eyes swirled like two galaxies upon her face, and the longest, sharpest, tusklike fangs I'd ever seen curved like small daggers over her unsmiling lips. I was, to be honest, in awe. Especially since I recognized her right away.

"Hidimbi!" I breathed, trying not to burp. I wasn't sure burping was considered appropriate behavior when meeting a legendary queen of old.

The rakkhoshi looked unsurprised. "I've been waiting for you, young fire rakkhoshi."